BURIED AT THE LAKE

A LUCA MYSTERY
BOOK 13

DAN PETROSINI

Print ISBN: 978-1-960286-13-0
Naples, FL
Library of Congress Control Number: 2023903979

OTHER BOOKS BY DAN

Complicit Witness

Push Back

Ambition Cliff

1

_____

LUCA

It wasn't like me to be late. Mary Ann had a neurologist appointment. Normally, being back on the force for just a week, I wouldn't have gone.

But nothing was normal the last two months. We'd gotten too comfortable with Mary Ann's MS. The occasional flare-up, fading in a couple of days.

I didn't want to alarm Mary Ann, but things shifted with an attack lasting ten days. Followed by a second flare-up five days later. Things were wrong; the question was how badly they were going to go.

If there was a God—and in my business, I had doubts—he or she provided an opening. In the midst of the second, extended bout, Sheriff Chester left the department. He took the high-profile job in Tallahassee he'd told me about. Chester tried to get me back before leaving but I was on the fence and, childishly, didn't want to give him a win.

After almost a year on my own, I was doing okay. Derrick had taken Chester's bait and was pressuring me to return.

Though I loved Derrick, it wasn't the friendship or the need to catch killers that brought me back.

Maybe it was a combination, but the health insurance the department provided was good. Our Cobra coverage had six months to run, and Mary Ann's medical bills were off the charts.

I also needed time off and, as a private investigator, I was only paid when I actually worked. Employed by the Collier County sheriff, I was entitled to paid time off and family leave, if needed. Plus, Derrick could cover short bursts of time when necessary.

When the new Sheriff, Bill Remin, called, it was an opening I couldn't pass up. He'd been a homicide detective before moving up the chain. I'd met him twice. Remin seemed like a decent man and good cop but was prone to interfering. He wanted me back. I gave him the bs about missing the guys and job and here I was.

Nobody knew the true bag of motivation. Not Mary Ann, not Derrick, not Bilotti. Nobody. They all bought my line about hunting down killers. Most figured I missed the job. Some thought it was Chester leaving. I can't say more than, it was complicated.

The office was empty. I wriggled out of my jacket, wondering where my partner was. Sliding behind my desk, Derrick came in.

"Hey Frank, we got a body..."

It was a phrase that shot adrenaline through me better than a case of Red Bull.

"Uh, should've said a skeleton."

"Where?"

"Pine Ridge Estates. Property is owned by a William Miller."

"Who discovered it?"

"A landscaper. They were working in the area and one of their guys dug it up."

"Male or female?"

"Didn't say. Guy who discovered it took off when he found it, and the owner's wife called it in."

"Any age range?"

"Nope."

I reached for the phone. "I'll call Bilotti."

"Already did. He's going to meet us down there."

"Let's get on the move."

2
———

BILL MILLER

Tee time was 4:00 pm. I was looking forward to using my new Honma driver. If it was anything like their putter, it was worth the money. There was enough time to hit some balls and get used to the new club.

Why couldn't we make clubs like that in America?

My handicap had been stuck at ten for two years. Wondering how much the high-end Japanese club would lower it, my cell rang. It was my wife. I hesitated before answering. It'd been a week since I played. About to blow her off, I worried it might be about Mark. Again.

"Hey, Cathy, what's up?"

"They found a body on the property. Our property—"

I froze. "A body? Was it a man or woman?"

"I don't know. Why?"

I stopped for a red light at the intersection of Collier Boulevard and Davis Boulevard, "Just asking. Who found it?"

"A guy who works for Jimenez."

She had to build that frigging wall. I swallowed, "Was it

there long?"

"I don't know. Who do you think it is?"

I couldn't tell her I thought it was Kate Swift. "I don't know. It's probably been there for ages."

"You think so?"

"Sure."

"The police are here. They got everything roped off down there."

"The police?"

"Yeah, what did you expect?"

A chorus of beeping horns made me realize the light had turned green. "I don't know, this caught me off guard."

"You've got to come home."

"Okay, I'll cancel my game. Let me call the guys and tell them. I'll see you later."

This could be another turning point if it wasn't managed. It would spell the end of our family, the business, our standing. The embarrassment and shame would be too much. I had to manage this.

I pulled into a Walmart lot, parking in a corner at the end of the building. As if I needed the reminder, a June's Diary truck chugged by. It had been nine years; June 1, 2013. It never faded, but the last couple of years, I was sleeping much better.

Everyone considered Katie a typical Florida teenager: blonde hair, athletic and a thousand-watt smile. But she was much more. What separated her was the genuine compassion and wholesome goodness she exuded. With Katie around, life was sweeter.

After it happened, the community was never the same. Tension replaced the laid-back, relaxed way of life. Suddenly, the fear lying beneath the surface of every major city had poked it's head up in Naples.

We all changed. But no one as much as me. My mind drifted back, to that day.

My alarm went off at six-thirty-five. I hopped out of bed, the sun rising in a cloudless sky. I poked my head out the sliders. The crisp air was infused with a honeysuckle smell. The weather was playing along with my plans for a perfect Sunday; Mass at 9:00 a.m., followed by a round of golf. Then, it was cocktails with the boys before heading home.

Cathy was in Miami visiting her sister, so I bought a Wagyu steak at Seed to Table on the way home last night. I'd started drinking as I grilled and was feeling good. A little too good. I enjoyed my steak on the lanai and was watching the game.

As soon as I'd come home, I tried keeping an eye on Mark. My brother was in a bad mood since yesterday when I told him my foursome was already set. It wasn't and I had the feeling he knew. But Mark was easily distracted, and I hated playing a four-hour round of golf.

Katie had stopped over, returning a tennis racket my wife lent her to try. She mentioned she was in a rush, but Mark insisted on taking her for a ride in his boat. She happily agreed, surprising me. I wished she would've told him no.

Mark ran down to the dock. As he raised the Bimini top, I walked to the lake with Katie. She was maturing into a woman but maintained an infectious playfulness. The way she laughed filled me with joy.

I helped her climb onto the boat, her hand soft and warm. After warning Mark to take it easy, I untied the boat. Standing at the dock for a couple of minutes, I watched them buzz around the lake.

The horn of a tractor trailer blew twice. I looked up. It was a Walmart truck. The driver was pointing at a sign. I was parked blocking the way to the loading docks.

3

_____

LUCA

Derrick turned off Pine Ridge onto East Road. The homes and lots they were on expanded as we drove farther into Pine Ridge Estates.

He said, "Geez, look at that house. The gates are worth more than my entire home."

A pair of black wrought-iron gates hung from stone pillars the size of a small building.

I said, "You don't have gates with your initials on them?"

"Must be nice to have this kind of money."

"Yeah, but that don't mean they don't have problems."

"It's tougher to teach your kids values when you have money."

"Funny you say that; I just saw something on TV with this guy. Some New York hedge-fund guy worth billions. He's involved with the Naples wine auction. Anyway, he said it's easier raising kids in a middle-class household than when you're rich."

"Really?"

"I'd like to try. With everything going on with Mary Ann, I'd like to do as much for her as I can before the MS gets any worse."

"She'll be okay."

"I don't know, Derrick. I'm getting worried."

"Anything we can do to help out?"

"Nothing, but thanks. I'll let you know. That's the Miller house on the left."

A squad car was parked at the bottom of a long driveway.

"Nice spread. Wonder what this guy Miller does."

Another chemo brain clog slowed my thinking, but it hit me which Miller this was. "The family is in the building-supply business. They have places in Industrial Way and on Santa Barbara Boulevard."

"Oh yeah. They even have a store in Estero."

"They've been around a long time."

"Can't be easy competing against Home Depot."

We walked up the paver drive, where a white Maserati, roof down, was parked. As the medical examiner pulled up, I said, "Bilotti's here."

"The doc has good timing."

A uniformed officer was standing guard at the top of the driveway. He'd strung police tape from the handle of one of the six garage doors to a palm tree thirty yards away. Derrick said, "This Miller guy must collect cars."

We flashed our badges and signed in. "The guy who found it is inside with his boss and Mrs. Miller. You going to talk to him?"

"Not yet. I want to see the scene."

He pointed toward the back of the property. "There's a stand of mango trees before the property slopes down to the lake. Me and McQuire roped it off. He's back there."

We put gloves and booties on and snuck under the tape. Derrick said, "You're not waiting for Bilotti?"

"I'd like to see it on our own."

I surveyed the area as we walked. The view from the back of the house was impressive. Though there was a nice pool area and a tennis court on the left side, it was the glistening lake that drew your eye.

It was so large you couldn't see the entire body of water. Looking across the lake, I said, "Looks like there's no houses with a view to this place."

"They've got a ton of privacy."

"Making it a good place to bury a body."

"It's got to be a homicide."

"No doubt."

Maybe it was the shining sun or the fact it was a skeleton, but McQuire was grinning like he'd won the lottery.

"Hey, Frank, what they have on you guys to get the both of you back on the job?"

I wanted to tell him I still hadn't figured it out, but said, "How you been, Mac?"

He held up the tape, and we headed to the gravesite as the officer said, "Good. What about the new sheriff? You like him?"

I didn't answer. As we walked away, Derrick whispered, "What a clown. Remember when he got bombed at the Christmas party? Made a fool of himself."

"Yeah, we all do that from time to time."

"Nah, he's a Muppet."

"What?"

"Most Useless Police Officer Ever Trained."

"That wasn't funny."

A tractor that looked like a toy version blocked the way.

Circling around, I saw the skull. There wasn't a trace of skin or hair. The body had been buried a long time. We crept closer.

"Looks like an adult. Can't tell if it's male or female."

"Lucky this guy didn't crush it."

"It wasn't buried too deep. You can see where the shovel hit. About ten inches away. It looks intact."

"It seems weird it's buried pointing to the lake rather than horizontally."

I nodded. "True, but it could be nothing."

"You think the lake could've come up this high?"

I looked around. "Don't see any water markings, but as soon as we find out how long it's been here, we'll check the hurricane flood records."

"Right."

"But why not weigh it down in the middle of the lake?"

"Maybe they didn't have a boat."

"The soil doesn't seem like the kind in a lake, but we can have forensics test it."

"Maybe—"

I put up a hand. "I need a few."

"Sorry."

A part of my MO was envisioning how the crime scene came to be. The first question I wanted answered was whether the body had been moved here. The lake provided an easy way to travel from a distant shore, sight unseen. The body could also have been driven here. That would mean someone in the family may have been involved.

It was also possible someone knew they were away and slipped onto the property. That would make it premeditated murder. It was impossible to determine what percentage of homicides were planned. Killers knew sentences were longer and framed their crime as an argument gone wrong.

I was hoping Bilotti could quickly clear up whether this skeleton was evidence of an impulsive killing. I crouched by the skull. Who was this person?

"Frank, Bilotti and his crew are here."

4

MILLER

I called my other brother. "Greg, they found a body on my property."

"Oh no."

"Take it easy. I'm feeling good about this."

"What do you mean?"

"I'll tell you when I see you."

"Tell me what the hell you're talking about."

"What are you doing right now?"

"Working, what do you think?"

"Meet me in the parking lot of the Chick-fil-A on Airport and Pine Ridge," Bill said.

"Now?"

"Yeah, now. You'll want to know this."

Both drive-through lanes were full. I pulled into a spot next to Greg's Corvette. He got out and climbed into my Tahoe.

"What are we, spies now?"

"Can't take a chance, but I think we're in the clear."

"I have no idea what the hell you're talking about."

"The body on my property. If it's you-know-who, then Mark didn't do it."

"How can you be sure he didn't?"

"He put Katie in the lake."

"I'm not so sure about that."

"He weighed her down with the anchor. You forget, the anchor on his boat was missing? They found the skeleton by the mango trees."

"But—"

"That's why I'm relieved—"

"Mark had mud on his shoes."

"So what?"

"When I came over the next day, he had a couple of mangoes in his room. He shrugged when I asked where they came from."

"So?"

I asked Cathy if she bought or picked them, and she said neither."

"Mark could have picked them and just wasn't talking. You know how he gets."

"Yeah, and Katie could've been abducted by an alien."

"You really think Mark did it?" Bill said.

"Me? You're the one who orchestrated the cover-up."

"Cover-up? That's nonsense. I was trying to protect him, the family, protect the business."

"You made me lie to the police. I told you we should have told them what we knew. We've been carrying this goddamn secret for nearly ten frigging years, and now it's going to bite us in the ass."

"Hold on a minute. Don't panic. At this point, we don't know if it's Katie."

"Oh, come on, man. You're living in denial. Who else could it be?"

I shrugged. "We'll find out soon enough."

"And then what? What's your amazing plan this time?"

"Don't worry, I'll handle it. I always do."

"What the hell does that mean?"

"What does it mean? I'll tell you; who does everybody come to when there's a problem? Who's taking care of Mark? I didn't see you stepping up."

"You're a control freak."

"Don't give me back talk. If it weren't for me, when Dad died, the business would have collapsed."

"Oh, so you're a savior now?"

"That's right. I stepped in and held it together when you didn't know which way was up."

"Yeah? And who built the business? It looks nothing like what Dad started. He was mom and pop, and I got us into the big leagues," Greg stated.

"When Dad blew his head off, the business almost collapsed. I didn't want to, but I had to go from running the lumberyard to trying to keep the place running."

"Don't be so dramatic. I did more than my share."

"You couldn't have done anything without me. I saved your ass so many times, I stopped counting."

"Yeah, and you got me into this goddamn mess. I could go to jail."

"Typically selfish. You're only worried about yourself."

"Oh, you know what? Forget it." He opened the truck door, got out, and climbed into the Corvette.

I watched him drive off. He was a hothead. I wouldn't have gotten him involved, but I had no choice. Everybody only cared about themselves. It was up to me to look at the big picture.

Though Greg was thirty-two, he was immature and selfish. The nerve of him believing he built the business. I gave him credit for building the business up and expanding to Bonita, but he ignored the fact that without me, there would *be* no business.

It wasn't easy. Word got out that Dad's will had given control of the company to Mark as a way to make sure he was provided for.

We had competitors looking to eat our lunch, and some employees were threatening to leave. It was a big mess. I didn't know what the hell I was doing, but I kept it together.

Now this was another situation in need of saving. But the stakes were as high as they got.

5

THE MEDICAL EXAMINER AND THREE OF HIS STAFF approached. "Hey, Doc."

"Hello, Frank. Body aside, it's good to see you."

"Ditto. I'm hoping you can give us a head start with this one."

Bilotti opened a bag, pulling out a handful of small, red flags. "We'll see." The doctor walked around the gravesite, encircling the remains with the markers. He said, "I want the entire area excavated." He probed the earth near the skull. "This is shallow. Let's go to a depth of four feet to be sure."

Derrick said, "Who'd bury a body under so little dirt?"

I said, "Someone without time or someone nervous. Could've been an impulse killing."

"I'm surprised the body wasn't found earlier."

I took a step toward Bilotti, thinking it could mean someone on the property kept an eye on it. The doctor was using a brush to clear dirt from the skull. "Anything telling?"

"Skull appears intact."

That ruled out a bullet to the head. "Any evidence of a blow to the head?"

"Nothing apparent, but I'll go over the remains at the office."

His idea of an office was a lot different than mine. "Thanks. What's the expected time line? I'd really like—"

"After six or seven years of working together, or should I say, you pushing me, you're anxious for clues."

"Come on, Doc. I'm not that bad."

Bilotti chuckled. "You certainly are. But if something ever happened to me, I'd want you heading the investigation."

"That's a weird compliment, but I'll take it."

Bilotti stood and issued instructions to dig out the skeleton. He turned to me. "How's Mary Ann doing?"

"About the same. Like you said, it's taking longer and longer each time she has a flare-up."

"How much time elapses between episodes?"

"Used to be months, now it's closer to ten days."

"Keep a journal; the neurologist may find it useful."

"Will do. Hey, sorry I missed that Brunello tasting. How was it?"

"The 2016s are going to be special. That makes two in a row, but you need to wait to drink them."

"How much are they going for?"

"Well-known producers aren't cheap, but that's what makes years like 2015 and 2016 interesting; almost every winery made great juice."

"I have to check them out."

"If you're free sometime next week, we can do a tasting at my house."

"Sounds great. Let me see how Mary Ann is feeling."

"Of course."

"Look, we have to talk to the guy who unearthed this."

Mrs. Miller and Hector Lopez, the landscaper, met us on the rear patio. It was a multitiered deck that could comfortably hold a party of a hundred lucky souls. The lake looked inviting from here.

Derrick introduced us, and Mrs. Miller said, "I can't believe this. It's surreal."

"We have a couple of questions for both of you."

"Sure. Do you know who it is? Hector said it's a skeleton. How horrifying to think it's been here all the time."

"How long have you lived here?"

"About ten years. Bill's dad lived here for ages. And when he, uh, died, we moved in. I wasn't so keen to come here, but Bill insisted, and we moved in. It's been good, and it's a pretty setting."

"And your father-in-law, how long did he live here?"

"Oh. He was living here when I met Bill." She smiled. "That's close to forever."

She had porcelain veneers but seemed down to earth. I pinned her as mid-to-late thirties. Her body was taut, and I wondered whether she'd given birth.

"He lived here more than twenty years before you moved in?"

"Certainly. All the boys were born here."

"Boys?"

"Bill and his brothers, Greg and Mark."

"It appears the body has been there a long time, but I have to ask if you can recall any activity down in the area, or any person with a particular interest, or anything unusual since you moved in."

"Well, that's a long time span to consider. Nothing comes to mind immediately, but I'll think it over."

"We'd appreciate that. Anything you might remember, no matter how small or crazy it may seem."

"I'll let you know. Say, how long until this is all over?

We're having a little get-together next Saturday, and I'd hope this would all be gone by then."

"We'll do our best to limit our footprint, but it will depend on what the autopsy and initial investigation reveals."

She frowned. "Okay, I understand. But you'll keep us informed?"

Hector Lopez kept his eyes down and shifted from foot to foot as she spoke.

"As best we can."

"Mr. Lopez, you found the remains?"

"Yes. I was preparing the area."

"What were you doing?"

"Mrs. Miller, she wanted to have a wall with a step—"

"I never liked the way the ground just sloped off. It didn't fit with the rest of the grounds. My idea was to put two low retaining walls in with a step or two in." She swept her hand toward the back of the house. "It would mirror what we did with the deck."

Derrick said, "Sounds like it'd look nice."

"It sure would, but Bill, my husband, never wanted me to do it."

"Why he'd change his mind?"

She smiled. "To be honest, I think I just wore him down."

Was that really it, or did Bill think enough time had passed to safely work in the area? I said, "Yeah, it sure sounds like a good idea. What didn't he like?"

"He just didn't want to do it. Said it looked fine the way it was."

"He a naturalist or something?"

"Bill? Did you forget he's in the building-supply business? He makes his money when things are built."

"How's business these days?"

"It's busy. They're building everywhere. I don't know how many more people the area can handle."

I had the same concerns. "I guess business must have steadily increased the last twenty-five years."

"Pretty much, but it got a little rocky when Bill's dad died. He ran everything, and you know, with him gone and the boys taking over, it took a little time for them to get a handle on things."

"I'm sure it was hard. They were, what, mid-twenties?"

"Yeah, Bill was twenty-five and he's the oldest."

"Did you hire the landscapers for the job?"

"We've been working with them forever. My father-in-law used them."

Lopez shook his head in agreement.

I said, "Thanks for your time today. We may have further questions."

Lopez frowned. We turned to walked away, and I hiked my head at the landscaper. He pointed at his chest and mouthed, *Me?* I nodded.

He took a step, and I lowered my voice. "Look, I don't think you had anything to do with this, so unless that changes, you have nothing to worry about. Nobody is going be calling immigration or any agency."

"I didn't. I didn't know—"

"Have a good afternoon."

Derrick said, "Guy was scared out of his mind."

"Digging up a skeleton would spook anybody."

Derrick smiled. "Yeah, right."

"I want to talk to Bill Miller, but I'm wondering if we should wait until we see what Bilotti can tell us."

6

LUCA

I peeled my jacket off. "First thing we need to do is check the missing person list. Until Bilotti narrows it down, we're looking at an older case."

Derrick said, "We should be looking at Lee County's as well."

"No doubt. Let me call Bilotti before we start."

"But it's only been two hours since he said there was no obvious cause of death."

I grabbed the phone. "I know, but by now he'll know if it's a male or female, and maybe an age range."

Bilotti was in the autopsy suite. I told the secretary it was important. Two minutes went by before he got on the line.

"You're lucky I like you. What's urgent?"

"Sorry, Doc, but I need something to work with on the remains."

He sighed. "I'm as anxious as you are, but whoever it is, they've been in the ground for years. Another day or two isn't going to matter."

"I get it, but I want to know if it's male or female. And an idea how old they might be."

"It's a female."

"How sure are you?"

"The pelvis has distinct features adapted for childbearing."

"You're the best, Doc. How about an age?"

"Microscopic examination of the cranium puts the age range sixteen to twenty years of age, but based upon the early stages of wisdom-tooth formation, I'd place her about eighteen at the time of death. What we have is likely an eighteen-year-old female."

"Too close to home, Doc."

"Don't dwell on it, Frank. Worrying is practicing for failure."

"I'm graduating at the top of the class."

"You have to work on shifting your thoughts when you find yourself agonizing over something."

Good advice to give but harder to put into play. "You're right. I'll let you get back to it. If you find something, call me."

"Will do."

"Thanks again, Doc."

I hung up. "All right. Bilotti said it's an eighteen-year-old girl."

"Geez. Poor parents."

"Makes you think, don't it? Being on this side of things is bad enough. I can't imagine what a disaster it'd be as a father."

"I saw something on TV the other day. They said the divorce rate for couples who lose a child is off the charts."

"Makes sense. You're angry and need somebody to blame. You end up beating each other up."

"Damn shame. I'll call Lee County and then pull what we have in missing persons."

"Go back fifteen years."

While Derrick was on the phone, I plugged 11747 Myrtle Road into Google Earth. I wasn't interested in the street view of the Miller house. What I wanted was a sense of the area. I went to the aerial view.

The lake was so big, I had to zoom out. The first thing that popped into my head was it was shaped like a hammer-head shark. The Miller house sat at the bottom, where the tail would be.

It was an interesting body of water, but what troubled me was all the blind spots. The Millers had one of the longest lake views I'd seen, but you could only see about half the lake from their property.

A boat could have hugged the coastline, traveling more than two thirds the way to the Millers without being seen. I zoomed along the shoreline. There were more than twenty houses with direct access to the water. Seven docks protruded into the lake.

There also appeared to be a path or walkway around parts of the lake. It may be how some of the houses, behind those on the water, had access. My eyes zeroed in on what appeared to be a boat ramp. Zooming in, I shook my head. It was a public place to launch a boat.

The possibilities were multiplying, and I closed the tab. We didn't have anything to go on. I liked to get ahead of things, but at this point, the only thing I was doing was keeping my productivity shame at bay.

I picked up the phone. "Hey, how you feeling?"

Mary Ann said, "Pretty good."

"You sure?"

"Yes. Don't worry. The pain in my face is hardly there. The meds are working."

"Good. Don't do too much."

"You know the doctors all say I have to keep moving."

"Why don't you get in the pool. It always helps."

"I was planning on it."

"Great, just don't overdo it."

"I won't. What's going on with you?"

"Working the Pine Ridge remains case. Turns out it was an eighteen-year-old girl."

"Oh my God. How terrible."

I exhaled. "Yeah, it certainly is."

Derrick was waving a sheet of paper. "Look, I gotta run. I'll see you around six." I hung up.

"What have you got?"

"Sixteen in Collier that could be her."

"Let me see."

He handed me the sheet, saying, "The range is fourteen to twenty-two-year-old females. Remember the O'Brien girl. It was right before I got shot."

All the names were vaguely familiar. "Yeah, but unless they used an accelerating agent, the body wouldn't have decomposed to that level in a year or so."

"Bilotti can tell us if they did."

Two other names whispered to me: Janet Clower and Pamela Kelsy. I pointed to the page. "These two went missing before you got here. About eight years ago. I remember the names but can't place the faces or circumstances."

Derrick went to his desk and, standing, tapped on his keyboard. "Here's the Clower kid."

A smiling seventeen-year-old, with a black pixie haircut, filled the screen. My heart sank. "Yeah, she was the one the mother suspected her ex-boyfriend of abusing. He was scum of the earth, but we couldn't find anything linking him to her disappearance."

"They never heard from her again?"

"Nope. I always felt she was dead."

"It could be her."

"Sure could."

"Who would've killed her?"

"I always figured someone got her confidence, took her away somewhere far from here and killed her. It looks like I might be wrong."

"Be the first time, no?"

"Don't be a wiseass. Bring up the Kelsy kid."

Hair parted to the side, the brunette was wearing red-framed glasses. Her mother's face popped into my mind. I shook my head. "Her parents were so devastated they could hardly function. I remember the kid got accepted into Princeton the day before she went missing."

"Talk about from high to low."

"Nothing about that case made sense."

"Maybe it's her."

"Could be. See if we have dental records on both of them. In fact, round up dentals on everyone on the list. We'll save time."

"Most of these are too old to be in the system. I'll run down to records and send whatever we have to Bilotti."

"If there's no match, you'll have to get Lee County moving on it."

"Got it."

Derrick left, and I collapsed into my chair. Whoever it was had been dead for a decade. What was I afraid of? Selfishly, I didn't want it to be the Kelsy kid. Sure, I wanted the kid to be alive, but deep down, I couldn't face the parents.

7

LUCA

I got back from shopping at Publix, and I was helping Mary Ann put things away when my cell rang. It was Bilotti. The clock said 8:15 p.m. "I gotta take this."

"Hey, Doc. What's up?"

"We got what looks like a match on the dental records."

"It's the Kelsy kid, right?"

"No. We need to run DNA testing but believe the victim is Kate Swift."

"Kate Swift." My mental filing cabinet began sorting. The name rang a distant bell. She went missing before I moved to Naples. I braced myself. "How old?"

"Seventeen."

I sighed. "What a screwed-up world we live in."

"Been that way since Adam and Eve. It's why I drink wine. It shakes the dust of life off your shoes."

"Doc, if I did what you did, I'd have a vodka IV hooked up to me."

"It's all about compartmentalizing. You should know that by now."

Oh, I knew it. I just couldn't do it. "I'm trying. Anything else you can tell me about the remains?"

"Not yet, Frank. I've requested a toxicology screening be performed on a thigh bone."

"Thanks, I'll talk to you later."

I was all for getting as much information as possible, but if they found something, it's use was limited in a homicide. Whatever was found in the bones would get ripped to shreds by a defense lawyer because there was no way to determine when the toxins were deposited.

We could find the kid's bones riddled with a toxin but not know when it entered the body nor if it had accumulated over a period of time. It was one of those maddening caveats about the law. You couldn't make the assumption leap; you had to irrefutably prove it. And that was tough.

I stood in the den, rolling the name Kate Swift around. Every time a victim's name was learned, it made the horror real. We now had a real person, someone with a family, friends, a place in the community. It was the depressing part but also the starting place.

I trudged back into the kitchen. "Bad news?"

Mary Ann saw right through me. "Nah. Just a case. You all right?"

"I'm good. Go ahead. Do what you have to."

"No, I don't have anything to do."

She tilted her head, smiling the smile that hooked me a decade ago. "What case?"

"The remains of that kid. Damn near Jessie's age."

"Don't start projecting, Frank. Wasn't it you who told me that?"

She was right, but that was before we had a daughter. "I know. It's just I can't help feeling for the parents."

"It's terrible, but all you can do is bring them a measure of justice."

Right again, but maybe she'd like to tell the parents we'd found their little girl's remains in a ditch. "I know." I exhaled. "Not looking forward to notifying them."

She put her hands on the table to get up. I walked over, saying, "Sit. If it's consolation you're offering, I'll take a rain check till, say, ten thirty tonight?"

As I kissed her cheek, she said, "You've got a date. Now, go get whoever did this."

I massaged her shoulders. "Oh, that feels good."

"You like that? Just wait till later, there's much more coming."

"Get going, will ya?"

I closed the door to the den and logged on to my office desktop. As soon as I pulled up the file on Kate Swift, I winced. My stomach lurched when I read through the summary; the second-to-last place the kid was seen was the Miller property.

That wasn't surprising since her body was found there, but it strengthened the possibility she was killed there. I wanted to read through the entire file, but it was a decade old, and the details weren't uploaded back then.

When she went missing, her address was 1099 Satin Leaf Road. I plugged it into the search bar. It was in a community known as Calusa Bay. A neighborhood in a great location but starting to show its age.

Zooming out, I shook my head. She lived within walking distance of the Pine Ridge Estate home where her body was found. All she had to do was cross Goodlette-Frank Road, and within five minutes she'd be there.

I picked up the phone. "Derrick. We got a name. The remains belong to a Kate Swift. She went missing just over nine years ago. About a year before I moved down."

"How old?"

"Seventeen."

"Terrible. I'll go with you to notify the family."

"Let me see if they're still living in Calusa Bay."

I typed James and Sally Swift into the search bar.

"They're not there anymore. I can't find any records with both parents."

"Maybe they split up."

I sighed. "It's possible."

"It's getting late. Why don't we do it in the morning?"

"I don't know..."

"She's been gone for a long time, Frank. And we need to track them down."

"I guess so. I'll see if I can nail down their whereabouts, and we'll take the ride in the morning."

"Sounds good. See you tomorrow."

It took me six attempts, but I found the right James Swift. He was living on Estey Avenue. I couldn't find Sally Swift. Mary Ann stuck her head in. "You going to make our date?"

"Uh, yeah. I'm done here." I closed the laptop and followed Mary Ann. She was walking slowly, and I wondered what the future held for us.

She closed the bedroom door behind me and brought me back to reality by slipping her robe off her shoulders. Little Luca perked up. I pulled off my T-shirt, dropped my drawers, and slid into bed. The cool sheets were a nice contrast to the heat running through me.

Mary Ann may have had something physical going on with her, but her skin felt as silky as it always did, maybe more so. I threw my leg over hers, and the fuse was lit.

It was as good a release as I'd had, but when Mary Ann drifted off to sleep, my mind went to Kate Swift. Tomorrow, I had to let the parents know we'd found her.

8

LUCA

Riding north on Route 41, I made a right at Mr. Tequila's and slowed down. The lawn of the Ridge Street home was a week overdue for a cutting. The home was a small, concrete affair painted light blue. I never liked to pull into someone's driveway, but I was afraid I'd get clipped parking on the narrow street.

The smell of cigarette smoke hit me as soon as we stepped out of the car. "Ugh, cigarettes."

"No doubt."

I stood there.

"You all right?"

It was my nerves. "My stomach's acting up."

"Stay here, I'll do it."

It was the best offer I had since John Jay College, when a girl invited me into her dorm room. "I'm okay."

The door swung open, and a man with a slight hunch looked at me. His Adam's apple bobbed as his eyes bounced between my partner and I.

Derrick said, "James Swift?"

"Yeah. You are?"

Swift reached for the doorframe when Derrick introduced us. "Can we come in?"

"Okay."

James Swift had more lines on his face than a map. Derrick asked, "Is your wife home?"

The way he nodded, it was clear he knew what was going on. I wanted to tell Derrick I'd take him up on his offer to handle this.

Swift led us to a kitchen that was state of the art when Formica first came out. He asked, "This about Katie?"

"I'm afraid so, sir."

He stuck his head in the hallway. "Sally! The police are here."

A thin woman, in a faded housecoat, appeared in the doorway. She stayed just outside the kitchen as Derrick introduced us. Neither of the parents looked anything like the photos in the file. It wasn't the past nine years that hollowed them out, giving them a gray tint. It was the loss of their only child.

Wearing no makeup, Mrs. Swift picked at a fingernail, saying, "You found Kate?"

"Yes, ma'am."

Her shoulder sagged. "Are you sure?"

"I'm sorry, but based on her dental record, we're confident it's your daughter. We'll need to confirm with a DNA match."

Her face crumpled, but she composed herself quickly. Her husband wobbled before sitting down. It was sad they didn't look at each other or try to console one another.

She pulled her shoulders back. "Where was she?"

"Pine Ridge Estates."

"It's her. I knew it."

I said, "You knew what, Mrs. Swift?"

"I told them it was that Miller kid."

"Which Miller are you referring to?"

"The younger one, Mark. He and Kate used to be close, but after the accident, well, he just wasn't right."

"Needless to say, but we're considering this a homicide. We'll review the case files and conduct a thorough investigation."

"They should have done that when she went missing."

"That was before both of our times. I know it's not going to bring your daughter back, but we're going to stay on this until we can deliver a measure of justice to you and your family."

James Swift said, "I want to see the bastard who did this hang for it."

"I understand, sir."

"I hope it's not going to take you another nine years."

"Given the time that's passed, it makes it harder, but we're going to start working this case as soon as we leave here."

He nodded and his wife said, "When can we see her?"

My stomach turned. "The medical examiner is still running tests to see what we can learn from her remains."

At the word remains, the poor woman lost it. She began sobbing, and I helped her into a chair.

"Are you going to be all right? Do you want us to call someone to stay with you?"

"No, we're okay."

"We're sorry to have to do this but... we'll be in touch in a day or so. I'm sure we'll have questions for the both of you, and we'll need the DNA sample."

I kept myself from running to the front door. Derrick closed the door behind us. "Man, that was weird."

"Losing their daughter sucked the life out of them. I've seen it too many times."

"What about the Miller kid?"

"Was just going to say the same thing. We have to dig the file out and read what's there."

I FLIPPED OPEN the missing person file. Kate Swift was reported missing by her mother in the early morning hours of June 2, 2013. An officer named Talis responded, showing up at their Calusa Bay home at eight in the morning.

Sally Swift told him that Kate had left the house when she and her husband had gone to brunch with friends. She had spoken to her daughter around noon. Talis had penciled in a time of 11:42 a.m.

It was the last time she heard her voice.

"Derrick, you see the kid left her phone home?"

"Yeah, I thought it was weird. Nobody goes anywhere without their phone, but this was back in 2013. I can't remember, but I don't think we were so glued to our phones back then."

I couldn't recall either. According to a Google search, almost a decade ago, about half the country had a smart phone. But people weren't obsessed with them. I couldn't help thinking the good old days were really better in this instance.

"It's something to keep in mind, but I don't think it means she rushed out of the house, forgetting it."

"We'll ask her friends, see how much they used them back then."

I scanned the list of people Talis spoke with. "The Millers own the building-supply company."

"Oh yeah, it's a good place. They had the best price on pull-down attic stairs."

"Bill Miller said Kate had come over to return a tennis racket."

"He the last person to see her alive?"

"Looks that way."

"And it went nowhere?"

"Yep. It's time to talk to him."

9

MILLER

I was in my office reviewing the number and type of building permits the county had issued. Dad used to say he had a handle on the housing market because he knew so many builders. But when I'd taken over, we almost drowned by being overstocked.

There had to be a better way to project how much inventory we needed, and after a couple of miscues, I stumbled upon permits as a way to estimate inventory levels. It was a leading indicator that I had to learn to interpret, but it worked.

Jotting down the number of new building permits issued, the intercom sounded. "Mr. Miller? There's a Detective Luca on line two. You want to take it?"

"Sure."

The call rang in, and I stared at the blinking light. What did this cop want? When it rang again, I told myself to play it cool.

"Bill Miller."

"Mr. Miller, this is Detective Frank Luca from the Collier County Sheriff's Office."

"Hello, Detective. What can I do for you?"

"I have questions to ask you."

"What's the nature of them?"

"Kate Swift. The remains we found on your property."

"Oh yeah. I'd almost forgotten about that."

It was a sloppy thing to say, and the detective's pause in responding confirmed it. I was recalibrating when he said, "Are you free now?"

I stuffed "no," back in my mouth, saying, "I'm busy, but I'll make the time."

"Good."

"Can we do this here?"

"I'll be there in an hour."

I disconnected the call and punched in another number.

"Hello?"

"Benny, it's Bill. Do me a favor; grab Mark and take him to Interstone Quarries. Look over the slabs they have."

"What kind?"

"Granite, uh, neutral colors. Check the quality. We may be adding another vendor."

"All right. We'll go tomorrow."

"No, it's got to be now."

"Right now?"

"Yeah. I want to know my options. I'm talking to Smith-field in an hour, so get moving."

"You got it."

I replayed the call with the detective. It was probably routine for the police to interview the owner of a property where a body was found. But we'd been through that years ago. How interested was this Luca in digging into a nine-year-old case?

Just when I'd started to believe it was behind me, it'd come roaring back. My eyes landed on a photo of my dad.

My mom took the picture the day the sign was being installed outside of this store. We were three days away from opening, and it was all hands on deck tying up loose ends.

The day flooded my thoughts I was hanging fixtures in the lighting department when I heard my father raise his voice. Setting down a ceiling fan, I hurried to the back of the store. He was talking to an inspector. I heard him say, "We can work this out. Just give me a minute."

He came down the aisle, and I said, "What's the matter, Dad?"

"Prick is going to fail us on the sprinkler system."

"Why?"

"Some bullshit about the type of heads. Even if I can get O'Brien down here tomorrow, this idiot said earliest reinspection appointment was ten days out."

"Oh no. What are we going to do?"

"I'll fix it."

"How?"

"Go back to what you were doing."

"But—"

"Let me handle it."

My dad bounded the stairs to this very office, reappearing a minute later. I tiptoed down the appliance aisle, peeking around a refrigerator. I saw my dad hand the official an envelope.

The inspector looked in the envelope, then around. He took out the contents, fanning the wad of cash. He stuffed the money in his cargo pants and left.

I waited until the inspector left before approaching my father. "What happened?"

"Everything's good."

"But you said he was failing us. What happened?"

"I convinced him."

"What did you say to him?"

"Sometimes you have to do what's necessary, or the world will smother you."

"What do you mean?"

He turned and poked his finger in my chest. "No one is going to look out for you except your family. Nobody else gives a damn. It's up to you to protect and control what's important to you."

Dad was right. People talk about the stars aligning when good fortune graces someone. In Dad's case, it wasn't luck. He willed himself to success, doing what was necessary, whether it was working twenty hours a day, borrowing money to expand, or paying a bribe when he had to.

He was responsible for it all. Good and bad. Everything he'd worked for, he achieved: status, wealth, and a close-knit family.

It was still hard for me to believe how everything had gone to shit. Dad had made a mistake and compounded it. I was forced into picking up the pieces, putting them together.

It wasn't easy or pretty, and like a teacup glued together, it's fragility was ever present.

10

LUCA

Hanging up, the tiniest of vibrations ran up the back of my neck. Something was off. When I called Miller, he made like he had no idea what the call was about. This guy was in the building-supply business. How many calls was he getting from law enforcement?

And I was bothered by the way he referred to the victim. From what I read, he and his family knew Kate Swift well. How could he refer to her remains as it? Most people get weird when talking to the police. I understood. Even when you didn't do anything wrong, you still worried.

I got it, but if you didn't commit a crime or were trying to protect someone, you had nothing to fear. I blamed movies and TV shows with bad cops planting evidence. It was total nonsense. In my entire career, I never knew an officer who framed someone.

Don't get me wrong; as in every profession, there are bad players, but they are a tiny fraction of the thousands of men and women putting their lives on the line to protect the public. I tried not to let it bother me, but if the public had no trust in us, why were we the first called when something went wrong?

Derrick came in. His shirt was dotted with water spots. He said, "It's about to start coming down."

"It'll be over in ten minutes. I'm going to take a ride to see Miller. You want to come along?"

"I'd like to, but I told you I needed the afternoon off. Lynn's parents are coming in, and after we pick them up at the airport, we're going to the Naples Zoo."

"No problem. I remember bringing Jessie there her first time. She went nuts. Wanted to take a penguin home and cried about it for hours."

Derrick laughed. "That's funny. I think she's too young, but Lynn wants to go."

"She'll love it."

"Keep me up to speed on Miller."

NAPLES BOULEVARD WAS PACKED with cars. Every big-box retailer seemed to have a presence. Mary Ann and I made monthly pilgrimages to Costco, and Miller Building Supply was in the next parking lot.

I like supporting the little guy, but for some reason, I always went to Home Depot. Maybe their bare-bones look worked, as I rarely went to Lowes and had never shopped at Miller's.

A steady stream of shoppers behind carts were clogging the entrance. The place had a split personality: half warehouse for contractors and the DIY set, and the rest, a place where all-thumbs people, like me, could shop for fixtures, appliances, housewares, and gardening goods.

The offices were on a second floor that spanned a quarter

of the store. I peered out a long window that overlooked the retail space. I counted twenty-six shoppers when my name was called.

A girl who couldn't have been much older than my daughter, bounced over. "Mr. Luca, Mr. Miller can see you now."

Bill Miller had a serious look on his face and a paper-strewn desk. Behind his desk was a credenza crowded with family pictures. We shook hands.

"Nice to meet you, Detective."

"Same here. Thanks for seeing me."

He spread his hands over his desk. "I'm extremely busy but want to help as much as I can."

"Appreciate the cooperation. Hey, before we get started, does your family also own Miller's Ale House?" I needed to soften him up, and I was curious anyway.

He laughed. "Wish I had a dollar for every time I've been asked that. No, it's a different family. But we get lunch at least once a week from them."

"You've been in business a long time."

"Our daddy started up, back in sixty-seven." He pointed to a picture on the wall. "That's him in front of the original store on Golden Gate."

"Wow. Great shot. He still around?"

"No. We lost him about a dozen years ago."

"Sorry."

"Thanks."

"Look, you're busy so I'll get right to it. Tell me what you know about Kate Swift. I understand she was at your home right before she went missing."

"Well, I wouldn't say right before because no one really knows what happened."

He was putting as much distance as he could between him

and the missing kid. "Fair enough. Tell me about that day and your relationship with Ms. Swift."

"She was a family friend. My wife was helping her learn tennis, and she hung around with my brother."

"Mark?"

"Yes. I mean, they were friends. The kid lived just across the way, and she'd hang out at the lake, like all the kids did."

"And that Sunday?"

"My wife was in Miami visiting her sister, so I played a round of golf and had an early dinner. Kate had come over to drop off a racket she borrowed from Cathy, and that was about it."

"Didn't she go for a boat ride with your brother?"

"Oh yeah. I forgot about that. They buzzed around the lake for a little while, and then she left."

"Where were you when she left?"

"I was on the lanai, watching the game."

"Remember who was playing?"

"Believe it or not, I do. I used to be a big Dolphins fan, but I don't watch sports anymore."

"And you saw her leave?"

"Yeah, she said goodbye and left."

"She drove here?"

"No, she lived in Calusa Bay, and as far as I know, she walked over like she did all the time."

I'd found it was the way you asked questions that generated useful information. "What did you notice that was unusual that day? Tell me what you saw while she was at your house and when she left."

"Believe me, I've thought a lot about that day. It was a pretty ordinary day, but there was a car I saw parked a ways down the street that I thought was unusual."

"When did you notice it?"

"I took out the trash cans. Monday is pick-up day."

"What time was this?"

"Maybe three or so. I think it was halftime."

Though I was anal about putting our cans out, I said, "Pretty early to take out the garbage, no?"

"I'd forgotten on Thursday, and my wife complains when they start smelling up the garage."

"I know what you mean. Tell me about this car. You know what kind it was?"

"I'm really not sure. I don't know too much about cars. To me they're just transportation."

The image of the six-car garage doors at his house flooded my head. There could be other reasons, but people with a lot of garage space were usually into cars.

"Feel the same way. Did you see the driver?"

"No. It was too far away, but I'm pretty sure it was a man."

"How do you know that?"

"I really can't say; it's what I thought at the time."

Miller was hiding something. I wanted to press him but needed more background, otherwise I'd alarm him, and he'd bury what he was hiding even deeper.

"How is your brother Mark?"

"He's good."

"You said he was on the boat with Kate that afternoon."

"He was, but they came in and she left. He doesn't know any more than I do."

"I'd like to talk to him."

"That's not a good idea right now. He's having health issues."

"Sorry to hear."

11

MILLER

I walked the detective into the hallway. We shook, and he headed down the stairs. Each step he took toward the exit, lowered my heart rate. He disappeared outside.

This went better than I hoped. It looked like the cops were covering their asses and would shelve it as a cold case. I knocked on Greg's door, asking him to meet me in my office.

"What happened with the detective?"

"I have it under control. They're just following procedures."

"You think they're going to want to talk to me? Or Mark?"

"Don't worry. If they do, just play it like we've been, and it'll be all right."

"I don't like this. What if they find out I lied?"

"Let me worry about it if they do, okay?"

"It's my ass. I asked Seymour, and he said it'd be an obstruction of justice."

I jumped out of my chair. "What, are you crazy? Talking to Seymour about this."

"What do you think, I'm a frigging moron? I gave him a hypothetical."

"Still not a good idea. Don't talk to anybody: not your wife, not Benny, nobody but me about this."

"All right already. Stop treating me like a kid. I gotta go. Benny didn't come in yesterday and missed an appointment with Seagate. They don't want to deal with him, and I have to cover it tomorrow."

"He was out again? What the hell is going on with him?"

"Some bullshit about his legs and circulation."

"I don't know how Dad put up with him all those years; he's always been a slacker."

"We should let him go. Give him a package and be done with it."

"I don't know. He stepped up for Dad, and I wouldn't want it to get out."

"It's more than ten frigging years ago."

"I'll think it over."

He pulled his phone out as he said, "Dump him. They need me in the nursery. Fiorelli's making a big buy for that new community they're putting up on Collier Boulevard. I have to run."

Greg left. I'd never get rid of Benny. Besides knowing the other family secret, he saved Dad's ass from going to jail. He'd taken advantage of us ever since, but things would have been worse if Dad was arrested for being under the influence.

Dad was bombed but had the foresight to call Benny when he smashed into the tree. Benny called 911 when he got there, claiming to be the driver. He even banged his head, cutting himself to make it look real. The ruse prevented Dad from being a murderer. Instead, he was a victim, a grieving widow and father of an impaired son.

Dad said Benny was only two blocks away, but I always

wondered if a delay in getting Mark to a hospital had contributed to his injury. I never bought the story but stood by Dad. It was a mistake, a tragic one, but it wasn't intentional. Dad was taking a muscle relaxant for a slipped disc, and two drinks had been too much.

That damn accident had changed everything. Mom was gone. Forever. It felt like a weird combination of being ripped off and raped at the same time. Warm and emotional, Mom was the counterweight to Dad's sledgehammer approach to realizing his ambitions.

Except it was Dad who crumbled. He never talked about it. I didn't know what to do or how long to give him to recover. I was suffering, too, but after six weeks of never setting foot in the store and mounting pleas from employees for help, I went to see him.

The shades were drawn. Dad was sitting in his recliner. The cocktail table was covered in plates full of half-eaten food. I made a mental note to call Clara. He'd banned the cleaning woman, but the place was worse than a college dorm.

"Hey, Dad. How are you doing today?"

He shrugged. "The same, Bill."

I squeezed his shoulder on the way to raising the blinds. "It's a beautiful day. Why don't we go onto the lanai?"

"I don't want to."

"You can't sit in that chair the rest of your life."

"It doesn't matter."

"You look tired, Dad. There's no way you can get a good sleep in a recliner. Do me a favor and sleep in your bed, then, okay?"

He shook his head. "I can't sleep in that bed anymore. Too many memories, Bill. I can't even go in that room."

57

"It'll take time, Dad, but slowly, it'll get better. You'll see, but you got to try. Sitting in the dark all day isn't helping."

He shrugged.

"Why don't you come to the store for a couple of hours. It'll be good for you."

"It isn't going to help."

"We need you. Everyone is asking for you: the employees, the customers, the suppliers."

"It isn't going to change anything."

"I think it would, and I'll tell you, it's not going to get better if we lose the business."

"I can't. You didn't see what I did."

"You've got to forget about it, Dad. You have to move on."

"I can't unsee what I saw, and it was all my fault."

"No, it wasn't. It was the medicine."

"No, it was me. All me."

"Beating yourself up isn't helping. Come on, Dad. You've got to rally."

"I can't. I'm sorry, Billy, but I just can't."

"And what about us? What about Greg and Mark?"

He winced when I said Mark's name.

"Huh? What about us?"

A tear rolled down his cheek. "You'll figure it out."

"Yeah, great advice, Dad. And what about the business? You're going to let it go down the drain?"

"I'm sorry."

He sniffled and closed his eyes. I left, bewildered at how quickly the fight had gone out of him. On the way to the store, I figured it would take him another month to crawl out of the darkness. I was never so wrong.

12
___

LUCA

I'd waited until we were in front of the Swift house. Derrick said, "I hope we get something from them. You ready?"

"Don't take this the wrong way; you're a great detective, but I think you can be better."

"Is that a compliment?"

"Absolutely. I've worked with six partners. I never thought I'd find anyone as good as JJ was. But you are, and I mean it."

"Thanks. So, what did you want to say?"

"You get better responses with the way you ask a question."

"You mean like Columbo?"

"No. I'm talking about phrasing. Here, let's say you're asking a witness or bystander if they saw something out of the ordinary. Most would ask, 'Did you see anything unusual?'"

"Yeah, that's right. But I don't get what you're saying."

"Instead of 'Did you see anything unusual,' try 'What did you see that was unusual?' You see the difference?"

Derrick nodded slowly. "You're basically assuming they saw something, and they'd feel compelled to say something."

"Yes, but on a deeper, psychological level, it triggers a need to respond."

"Yeah, but they could be making it up."

"Sure, but on follow-up, you'd flesh it out."

Nodding, he said, "I like it. That's a good tip, Frank."

"Live like it's your last day, but learn like you're going to live forever."

Before he asked me why I waited so long to tell him I didn't like the way he phrased his questions, I said, "Let's get going."

I took a seat across the table from James Swift. It was the farthest I could get, but I'd still stink of cigarette smoke. I pulled the lapels of my sports jacket closer. It felt like they had set the thermostat at sixty-five.

"Thank you for seeing us during such a stressful period."

Mr. Swift said, "We want whoever did this to pay for it."

His wife said, "You couldn't wait until after the memorial service?"

"I'm sorry, ma'am, but it wasn't out of a lack of compassion; I don't want any more time to pass."

She scoffed, and I decided not to ask for a swab of her DNA until after the memorial. Derrick said, "We wanted to do this before the service because if it's all right with you—and you can say no—we'd like to be there."

"Why?"

"Whoever did this may attend and—"

Mr. Swift put his hand on his wife's forearm. "You can come, but you've got to stay out of the way, in the back."

"We'd be there to observe only. We wouldn't speak to anyone."

He looked at his wife, and she said, "Okay, make yourself invisible."

"Thank you, ma'am. Where is it being held?"

Derrick noted the details and said, "Thanks. Now, Detective Luca and I read the case file, but we'd like to ask you about Kate's friends and relationships."

"We figured you would."

I said, "Who were her closest friends?"

Mrs. Swift said, "Katie and Molly were inseparable. They drifted when she started hanging around with Mark Miller, but after the accident, they started getting closer again."

"What accident?"

"The one where Mark got hurt and his mother died."

"When was that?"

"About a year before... before Katie disappeared. You've really got to dig into that. He had something to do with it. I know it."

"Mark Miller was cleared at the time, but we're taking a fresh look at everything and everyone."

"Well, I'd start with him."

"Any other friends we should talk to?"

"She was close to Barbara Quinn and Nancy Toro."

I remembered the Quinn kid from the file but not Nancy Toro. Derrick jotted down their contact information, and I asked, "What about anyone she had issues with? Anyone she didn't get along with? Someone she'd consider an enemy?"

"Katie got along with everybody."

Derrick said, "Who was she afraid of?"

"Afraid of?"

"Yes."

"The only person was Amanda. She was jealous of Katie, and she's a little rough around the edges."

Derrick stole a glance at me. He'd used the tactic and got a reply he wouldn't have otherwise.

After he wrote down the kid's contact information, I asked, "What was her relationship with Bill and Cathy Miller?"

Mr. Swift said, "I guess they were all-right people, and I know it's childish, but it was like they were trying to steal our daughter."

I looked at his wife, who said, "They were good to her. Katie liked playing tennis, and Cathy... she'd played her whole life and gave Katie a couple of lessons. She wasn't uppity, if you know what I mean."

"What about Bill Miller?"

"He was a good guy. Katie said something about us renovating the place in Calusa, and he told her to have me go to his place, and he'd give us the materials at cost. I didn't want to do it, but when we started getting quotes, I had to. We saved a couple of thousand dollars doing it."

Derrick said, "Sounds like a good person to know."

"Yeah, he has a friend that owns a Honda dealership in Fort Myers. He knew we needed a car and gave him a call. The guy gave a great deal."

"Nice contact to have. So, you were friendly?"

Mrs. Swift said, "They invited us over for a barbecue once. We went. I mean it was nice and all, but we're not the same kind of people. They asked us again, actually two times, but we never went again."

I asked, "Did Kate go with you?"

"Yes, we all went."

Derrick said, "What kind of trouble did Kate have at school?"

"Trouble? She was a good student, and not once did the school call us."

I said, "Okay. What teachers was she close with?"

"Oh, she really liked Mr. Marconi. Katie had him twice for English. She was kind of an assistant for him and Mr. Schneider too."

"Barron Collier High?"

"Yes."

We asked a couple more questions but didn't generate any other leads. We had a few strings to pull. One of them was thin and disturbing. I was hoping the vibration at the base of my skull wasn't signaling it as the cause of Kate Swift's death.

13

LUCA

The heat felt good. I slow-walked it back to the car. Halfway down the driveway, Derrick said, "There isn't an ounce of affection between those two."

"Losing a kid will do that to you."

"They cleared the father pretty quickly. You think we should take another look at him?"

"I learned a long time ago never to exclude anybody. We'll check him out again, but I don't believe he's responsible."

We climbed in the car. Derrick started the engine and said, "We didn't get much, but she seems to think Mark Miller had something to do with it."

"It's possible, but something about Bill Miller is giving me a rash."

"I didn't hear them say anything troubling."

"It wasn't anything exact. But Miller went out of his way to befriend Kate's parents."

"He seems like a nice guy."

"Could be a classic groomer."

"You think he might have been abusing the kid?"

"I'm not saying he did, but getting close to the family is what those predators do. It gives them opportunity, and the family doesn't suspect them."

"Man, this guy is major league, with the business and all; it would be sickening if it was him."

"No doubt, but it's something we need to look at. Let's talk with her friends; we'll pick up some intel there. Let's divide it up. You interview Barbara Quinn and I'll pay a visit to Nancy Toro."

———

I TURNED INTO TIMBERWOOD. The neighborhood was off Airport Pulling Road and looked to be all townhouses. The aluminum-sided buildings were more than thirty years old. I drove around Timberwood Circle, stopping in front of a gray, two-storied structure framed by a chimney on either side.

Walking toward the door, a gust of wind had me checking the sky. No threatening clouds, but there was a hint of smoke in the air. It hadn't rained in weeks. I hit the bell, and a second later the door swung open.

"Are you the detective?"

I flashed my badge. "Yes, Detective Luca. Nancy Toro?"

She nodded. "You know, you look like George Clooney."

It had been awhile since I heard that. "I guess I should say thanks."

"He's good looking. Come on in."

The home was dark but had a nice cathedral ceiling in the main living area. The place was sparsely furnished.

"You mind if we sit over there?" She pointed to two stools at the kitchen counter.

"That works for me." It wouldn't be my first interview on a barstool.

"Good. I just moved here, and well, there's a lot to get."

"Good luck with the place. As I mentioned, I wanted to talk about Kate Swift."

She frowned. "She's been gone so long. It's like, weird that they're having the service tomorrow."

I nodded. "You're going?"

"Oh yeah. We were close for a while."

"I didn't find a record of you being interviewed by our department when Kate went missing. Did anyone contact you?"

"No. I know they spoke to Barb, but that's all I remember."

"When was the last time you saw Kate?"

"The day she disappeared."

I cleared my throat. "You're certain of it."

"Oh yeah. No doubt about it."

"When and where did you see her?"

"My mom was driving us home from Baker Park. We used to go for walks there on Sundays, and like, kinda right before the entrance to our community, I saw her."

"You lived in Calusa Bay as well?"

"No, next door to it, in Autumn Woods."

"What was Kate doing?"

"She was talking to Mr. Miller."

"Bill Miller?"

"Yes, him and a friend of his. They were in his car, pulled over, and Kate was on the sidewalk."

"On Goodlette-Frank?"

"Yeah, like a little bit before our neighborhood."

"And you're sure it was Bill Miller?"

"Definitely. He had a red Mercedes convertible. The top was down, and it was him and his friend."

"Do you know who the other man was?"

She shook her head. "No, I'm sorry."

"That's okay. What time was this?"

"I'd say it was about twelve."

"So, to be clear, you and your mother were driving home from Baker Park, and you saw Kate Swift. She was talking to Bill Miller and another man, who were pulled over on Goodlette-Frank in Mr. Miller's car."

"Yeah. That's what I saw."

"Would your mother be able to corroborate that?"

"I'm sure she would. We talked about it when she went missing."

"Is there any reason you didn't go to the police with this information?"

"Why? She was friends with the Millers, and she was seen after that at their house."

That was true, but it was reinforcing the idea that Miller may have had an inappropriate relationship with Kate. Or that he was trying to woo her.

"What can you tell me about Mark Miller?"

She sighed. "It's like there was a curse on Katie. She and Mark were going together for, like, ages. And then with the accident and all, he got messed up and wasn't the same."

"How do you mean?"

"I don't want say anything bad, but he was like a child. He'd throw temper tantrums and, like, want to play with frogs. It was weird, one day you could be a normal teenager, and then..."

"Did Mark have an anger problem?"

"After the accident, he did."

"Do you think it's possible he could have harmed Kate?"

"I thought about that, but he really liked Kate. I can't see him hurting her."

"But he must have been upset the relationship was over."

"Yeah, but Katie felt real bad and let him down easy, you know. She was one of those people that just did the right thing all the time."

"What about anyone that didn't like Kate? Did she have any enemies?"

"Not that I know of."

"What about someone named Amanda?"

She scoffed. "She was a bully."

"She picked on a lot of kids?"

"I guess, but she used to get on Katie's case. I think she was jealous of her."

"Did Amanda ever get physical with Kate?"

"She'd bump into her in the hallways, but other than that, not really. Oh, there was this one time, we were in the parking lot, and Amanda... she was older than us and had her license before we got ours. Anyway, this one day, me, Katie and Barb were walking, and Amanda tried to run her over."

"Just Kate?"

"Yeah, because Katie was on the end, and me and Barb were close to the other cars."

"Kids do all kinds of stupid things with cars."

"I know, but when were in school, Amanda hit Cheryl with her car."

"Intentionally?"

"She said no, but everybody knew better."

"How close was Kate to Mr. Marconi and Mr. Schneider?

She frowned. "She had a bad crush on Mr. Marconi. Most of the girls did, but not me: I thought he was creepy."

"Creepy in what way?"

"I don't want to say anything because I don't have proof,

but I always felt he was trying to, you know, I guess, seduce is the right word."

"Was Mr. Schneider the same way?"

"Kind of. He wasn't as cute as Mr. M. I liked him better, but I kept my distance from the both of them."

14

―――――

MILLER

I pulled into a spot, and Cathy said, "Oh boy, I hope it's not too emotional."

"It'll be okay. It's been nine years."

"I know, but it's never easy."

"Maybe we should start a college grant in her name. It'd be a good way to honor her memory."

"That's a good idea."

I smiled at her. She said, "Come on, let's get going."

"Wait a couple of minutes. I don't want to be one of the first people in there."

"We're not going to be; look at all these cars."

"All right. Let's go."

I grabbed my wife's hand, and we walked toward the entrance of Vanderbilt Presbyterian Church. Pulling open the door, the sun slipped behind a cloud. I hoped it wasn't an omen.

A huge picture of Kate sat on easel at the head of the chapel's aisle. Cathy stopped in front of it. "She was such a pretty young lady."

"I know; what a shame."

I could see the Swifts. They were standing on the altar talking to the minister. As they broke up, the massive organ pipes behind them began droning a depressing song.

Cathy said, "There's the Harrigans."

My eyes swept over the people in attendance as we greeted the Harrigans. Turning to the right, I saw him and froze. What the hell was that detective doing here?

15

LUCA

Stopped at a light on Immokalee Road and Route 41, my phone rang. It was Derrick.

"Hey, Frank, I'm not going to make it."

"Is everything all right?"

"Something is going on with our bank accounts. Lynn logged in this morning to pay some bills, and there was only a dollar in the savings and nine bucks in the checking account."

I didn't like the way that sounded. "Could be a mix-up, or maybe you were hacked."

"Bank of America said it wasn't a hack."

"I hope someone didn't steal your identity."

Derrick groaned. "Oh man. I hope not. The bank wasn't helpful on the phone, so I'm going in person."

"Show them your badge. You should get some respect."

"I hope so."

"Good luck, and let me know what's going on."

Passing the Airport Pulling Road intersection, I turned into Vanderbilt Presbyterian Church's parking lot. Growing up, our church was a traditional one: brick, with plenty of statues. This modern structure looked more like a performance hall.

Two other cars pulled in as I slipped through a side entrance into the church. Mr. and Mrs. Swift were adjusting photos on an easel. They didn't see me. I took up a position to the left, standing out of view, next to a thick column.

I had my eyes on the main doors. There wasn't anything in particular I was looking for, but I received more signals than a Sunset Strip psychic. The way people acted, including their body language, could tip off a good cop.

But this situation required a certain amount of filtering. People, including me, got squeamish at funerals, especially when someone checked out early. It'd be interesting to see what I'd learn.

I was planning to leaf through the book most attendees were signing. It might help to identify someone. At this point, I considered Bill Miller and his brother Mark possible suspects.

Amanda, whose last name was Ryan, was also a person of interest. She had served time in a Lee County jail for reckless endangerment, but there were no details online. I wanted to wait for the case file before interviewing her. A Lee County desk clerk promised to have a marked car drop it off.

I noticed Nancy Toro as soon as she came in with an older woman. Based on her face, I pegged the woman as her mother. They signed the registry and went straight to the Swifts. Nancy embraced Mrs. Swift, whose shoulders began heaving.

I couldn't imagine how painful it was for the parents to see their daughter's closest friend. A chill shot through me when the thought it could be Mary Ann and I, hit me. I shifted my weight, moving my line of vision back to the entrance.

Four older women entered. They could have been former or current neighbors of the Swifts. They signed in and shook their heads at Kate's picture. A pair of men, in work clothes, came in behind them. They bypassed the guest book, took seats in the last row, and studied their hands.

An elderly couple ambled in. As they made their way down the aisle, I wondered whether they were the grandparents. A sudden stream of people caught me off guard. Most looked to be friends of Kate's, some with their parents, others with a spouse.

My eyes followed them down the aisle. No one was getting a free pass, but all of them appeared at ease. Out of the corner of my eye, I detected movement. It was Bill and Cathy Miller.

They were holding hands, walking in step. Miller was a take-charge guy, and the fact he wasn't leading his wife felt off. Was he apprehensive because he was guilty, or was he simply like me at these types of events?

The Millers slipped into a pew after greeting the Swifts. No hugs were traded, and Bill Miller appeared stiff and formal. I studied him as he whispered to his wife. Something hit the floor, echoing through the chapel. I turned toward the entrance: a man I put at around fifty was picking up the sign-in book.

He was dressed in a suit and tie as was standard twenty years ago. He surveyed the room and took a seat behind Nancy Toro and her mother. He tapped Nancy on the shoulder, and she broke into a broad smile. They chatted until the minister stepped up to the podium.

I sauntered over to the entrance and glanced at the open book. The man who'd come in was Richard Schneider, Kate's former teacher. I thumbed over to the previous page. In the middle of the page was the name Freddo Marconi. He was the other teacher Nancy felt was creepy.

The minister asked everyone to rise, and I swept the pews, trying to find Marconi. I had no idea what he looked like and relied on instinct. I came up with two possibilities: a guy with slicked-back hair and light-blue sports jacket, and a taller, handsome man with graying temples, wearing a white linen shirt.

I wasn't a gambler, but my money was on the tall guy. Examining him from the side, I realized it came down to what he was wearing. In my mind, anyone who wears a linen shirt and pants to a memorial is a poser. The exact type of male who'd try to entice a young girl.

The prayer parts were tough, but I couldn't keep it together when the eulogies began. I got teary eyed anytime someone no longer with us was talked about. This was miles worse. I wiped my eyes and hid behind the column. I hummed to block out what was being said.

I wanted to bolt, but I had to know who Marconi was and whether Miller had gotten emotional. I took a couple of steps down to get a view of Miller and his wife. Miller had his chin resting on his chest. He wasn't crying but distracting himself from the proceedings. Was it out of guilt or empathy?

My lower back was starting to act up from standing on the marble floor. I sat in a pew as the minister led the attendees in another song. I wondered what was going through the parents' minds when the minister brought the ceremony to a close.

The first row emptied, engulfing the parents. It was an opening. I headed straight for Nancy Toro. Catching her eye, I signaled her over.

"Real quick, Nancy. Is that guy in the linen suit, Marconi?"

"No. I don't know who that is."

"Is Marconi here?"

She swept her head around. "Yeah, he's like five rows back: dark shirt and bald head."

I snuck a peek. "Thanks. Can you do me a favor and find out who the linen man is?"

"Sure."

"Don't tell the parents I was asking questions. I told them I was just going to observe."

"No problem."

There was that phrase again. It never seemed to fit when it was used. Was it a problem for her to say something?

Though Marconi looked like an accountant, not a womanizer, I learned long ago not to discount anyone. Marconi had aged, maybe badly, but who hadn't?

16

MILLER

I wanted to applaud when the Hallmark movie Cathy had to watch, ended. I said, "And they live happily ever after."

"I thought it was cute."

"It was okay."

Cathy got up. "I'm going to bed. You coming?"

"Not yet."

"Don't stay up late. You've been tossing and turning the last couple of nights."

"Sorry. Trying to decide if we should renew the lease on Airport or build something of our own."

"I thought you were re-upping."

"I'm having second thoughts. We could use more space."

"Don't torture yourself. See you later."

It wasn't real estate that was keeping me up. I was worried about the investigation. That damn detective, Luca, kept probing. He wanted to talk to Mark, and it was looking like I could no longer prevent it.

It was impossible to predict what Mark would say, especially under pressure. I'd been able to protect Mark when the cops came around asking questions about Kate's disappearance. But after the accident and Dad's suicide, the family was swimming in a sea of sympathy.

As the founder of a successful business, Dad was larger than life in the community's eyes. But he never relied on his reputation alone to run interference when he had to. He supported the charitable interests of the most powerful people in town.

It was a smart tactic and one I had ramped up. It worked but there were limits. And I was up against one now.

Trying to distract myself, I flicked through channels, stopping on a commercial for Home Depot. They were pushing their kitchen and bathroom renovation products and services. It was a good spot. Wondering if we should increase our advertising spending, I got up to get a bottle of water.

Coming back into the room, *The Shawshank Redemption* was on. I reached for the remote just as the warden put a bullet into his head. I shut the TV and collapsed into my recliner.

I didn't need the reminder, especially not here, not now. Dad had blown his head off less than five feet from where I was sitting. We completely redecorated the room, even replacing the travertine floor with bamboo wood, but it all came back in a flash.

It was a bright, sunny day. Mark and I had just pulled the boat in. He was tying the boat to the dock as I unwound the hose to wash it down. Wrestling with a tangle, I heard it.

It was a gun. I looked at Mark, who said, "What was that?"

"Firecracker. I think the Bowers are having a party or something. Hose it down. I'll be right back." I handed the sprayer to him.

"I'm coming with you."

"No. Stay here and clean the boat before it gets crusty."

"It's going to get crusty?"

"Yeah, if we don't wash it off right away, it'll cake up."

"I want to see what that looks like."

"Not with our boat."

"But I never saw it."

"All right. Leave one section, the swimming ledge, okay?"

"We can? We can get it crusty?"

"Yeah, but just that one spot."

"Cool."

I jogged to the house. It was quiet. I slid open a slider. "Dad? You all right?"

Silence. I tried again: "Dad! You okay?"

Walking around the kitchen island toward the family room, I froze. The barrel of a rifle. I took another step and gasped. Dad was slumped over. There was blood everywhere. I screamed, "Dad! What did you do?"

I called 911 and sat at the kitchen table crying. We were orphans. How could he leave us alone? There were so many questions needing answers that I couldn't envision what the future held for me and my brothers.

Being the oldest, I was sure everyone would look to me. But without someone like my dad to lean on, I didn't want to be that person. My life had been turned upside down since the accident, and now it was worse. Was I going to be responsible for Mark? What about what I wanted? What about my life?

The sound of an approaching siren made me get up. I looked toward the lake: Mark was on his hands and knees, inspecting the fiberglass. He had no idea what had happened, and I couldn't allow him to be further traumatized.

I washed my face and waited by the front door. The cops and an EMT vehicle pulled into the drive. I ran to the back of the house; Mark was on the boat, dangling his legs in the water.

A police officer had stepped into the foyer. I pointed to the family room. "He's in there."

I followed him and a paramedic to the scene. The medical technician felt my dad's neck for a pulse. He looked at the gaping hole at the top of his skull. He frowned, the lines in his forehead deepening and shook his head. "I'm sorry, he's gone."

The police officer made a call to the homicide department. I said, "This wasn't murder. My dad committed suicide. He was depressed over my mom and the accident—"

"No one is saying it is. We have to rule it out. Whose rifle is that?"

"My dad's."

"Okay. The medical examiner and the crime scene unit are on the way down. We're going to need you to stay out of the house until we say so."

"Okay."

"We'll need you to stick around and talk to Detective Mulroney before you go."

It was the first time I thought of my other brother Greg. I had to tell him about Dad and figure out what to say to Mark. "Okay, my little brother is down by the lake. I've got to talk to him. He doesn't know about this."

The cop looked at me with a crooked eye.

"He's kind of disabled."

"Sorry to hear that, but Mulroney is probably going want to talk to him."

I walked onto the lanai. Mark was polishing the brass; it was never shiny enough for him. It was impossible to figure out how he was going to react, but the knowledge Dad was dead, especially that he killed himself, was going to set Mark off.

He'd lost his ability to accept reality. At Mom's funeral, he'd taken a chair and sat next to the casket, refusing to speak. We figured he was in shock. I mean, we all were, but when the minister came in, he started cursing and knocked down half the floral pieces.

The funeral director tried to calm him down, but Mark attacked him. Greg and I struggled to restrain him, and we shoved him into my car. I took him to my place and missed the burial. He finally calmed down when I took him to McDonald's.

From time to time, he'd ask for Mom and wouldn't accept that she'd died even after I'd show him pictures of the car wreck. There was no way I'd ever show him a picture of what happened today. There was no telling what he'd do.

Inhaling deeply, I headed to the dock. "Hey, bud. Nice job."

"I can't get it shiny. We need one of those machines. I'm gonna get one from the store. We have them, right?"

"The type of buffing machines we carry are not the best for this. We'll look online later."

"Can't we try?"

"Sure. Say, I need a favor. Can you take the boat and go out to Benny's house? Tell him I need to talk to him, in person."

"Now?"

"Yeah."

"But the boat's all clean."

"We're going get a buffing machine."

He smiled. "Okay, okay. Untie the boat."

"Don't rush. Take your time getting out there. Mrs. Macy

is fishing in that rowboat of hers. You make a big wake, and she'll never invite us over for the fireworks."

"I like the fireworks. Can't we get some this year?"

"Why don't we ask Benny? He has connections for the special kinds."

He giggled. "I like the ones that go really high, in the sky."

"Me too. See you later, champ. Remember to take it slow going out."

Shielding Mark had become second nature, but this Katie thing was starting to feel like trying to hold water in your hands.

17

LUCA

After observing the Millers leave, without approaching the Swifts, I watched people file out after saying goodbye to the Swifts. Mr. Linen Suit was fiddling with his phone, waiting for an opportunity to offer his condolences. Marconi and Schneider were on the way out as Linen Man shook Mr. Swift's hand. He was chatting amicably with the couple and suddenly broke away.

I watched him head for the exit and started after him. Instead of upsetting the Swifts, I'd grab his license plate to identify him. My phone vibrated. It was Derrick. I tapped a message to him as Linen left the church.

Scurrying a bit faster than I wanted to, I stepped into the sunshine. Linen was getting into the back seat of a waiting car. I studied the license plate, memorizing it as it drove away.

I sent a text to the office about the car and called Derrick. "Sorry. The memorial is breaking up. Couple of interesting characters. How'd you make out at the bank?"

"Frigging disaster. Someone stole Lynn's identity. They cleaned out our accounts."

"Holy shit! What'd they say?"

"Not much. They're not taking responsibility for it."

"You have any identity protection?"

"Nothing. We're frigging broke."

"Bank of America has to have something they can do."

"They're saying no."

"I'll talk to Mary Ann. She worked in the cyber unit before she got sick."

"I was going to talk to a lawyer about it. Friend of a friend had the same thing happen to him, and it took him three years to straighten it out. They took a bunch of credit cards out in his name and a mortgage."

I didn't want to depress him, but it was going to be a mess. "Sorry, man, you know I'll do whatever I can to help you guys out."

"Thanks. I appreciate it."

"Since we're partners, if you need a loan, I can swing one at, say, ten or eleven percent interest."

"What a pal."

"Seriously, you need some dough, all you have to do is ask."

"I might have to take you up on it because they told us we should cancel our credit cards."

"That's a pain in the ass."

"I know. Look, I'm almost at Barbara Quinn's house. I'll call when I'm done."

"Okay. I'm going to see Bill Miller."

THERE WAS a Chase Bank less than a mile away from Pine Ridge Estates. I pulled up to the ATM and withdrew my six-hundred-dollar limit. Derrick was going to need the money, especially in the short term.

Where were we heading in an electronic society? Derrick had his bank account cleaned out, had no credit cards, and who knew what else would pop up?

There was no doubt crime and criminals were entering a new era. It was a lot safer for the crooks to hack an account than it was to rob a bank. The sad fact was cyber thieves were much savvier than local law enforcement agencies. The feds had capabilities, but an individual getting his identity stolen was at the bottom of their priorities.

I parked and walked up the drive as a garage door opened. Miller had changed out of his suit and was getting in a white Navigator.

"Excuse me! Mr. Miller!"

Miller turned around and frowned. He recovered quickly, pasting a smile on. "Detective Luca. What can I do for you?"

"I have a couple of quick questions for you."

He looked at his watch. It was thick and gold. "They're expecting me at work."

I noticed a couple of shovels hanging on the wall. "This will be quick."

"All right. You want to sit out back?"

"Sure."

I followed him over a stone path, wondering if he used one of the shovels to bury Kate Swift. He had landscapers and money. Why would he need a shovel?

We settled into a corner seating area.

"You have a great view from back here."

"It doesn't get old." He clasped his hands, playing the genteel Southerner.

"Why didn't you tell me that you saw Kate Swift the morning of the day she went missing?"

"What do you mean?"

"Are you denying that you were talking to her on the side of Goodlette-Frank Road?"

"There's no need to be adversarial, Detective. I'm trying to understand what you're attempting to get at. Kate was at my house that afternoon and disappeared after she left. Running into her earlier that day doesn't seem relevant."

"In a homicide investigation, everything is relevant. Tell me about seeing her earlier that day."

"It was nothing. We were coming back from playing golf and she was walking. I pulled over to ask her if she wanted a lift home."

"Did she get in your car?"

"No. She said she wanted to walk. It was near the entrance to her community."

"Who was in the car with you?"

"Benny Alston. He's a longtime family friend. Was close to my dad and works for us."

"Where did you go after talking to Ms. Swift?"

"I dropped Benny off; he lives close by and went home."

"Did you invite Ms. Swift to your home when you spoke to her?"

"No. I told you she came over to return a tennis racket my wife lent her."

"Why were you opposed to building the retainer wall your wife wanted?"

"The wall? What does that have to do with anything?"

"I ask the questions."

His face reddened. "We didn't need it." He glanced at the sliders. "I didn't feel like spending ten grand on another of Cathy's whims."

That could be, but it didn't square with what his wife said. She said she'd been wanting to build it for years. I got the feeling if I kept pushing, he'd look to get a lawyer.

I asked a couple of general questions to take the pressure off him. His face relaxed, and it was safe to go.

Leaving, I had the distinct feeling Miller was hiding something. I'd dig around before our next chat. I also wanted to talk to Benny Alston.

I STEPPED in from the garage. I couldn't smell anything cooking and wondered if I'd have to pick something up. I saw Jessie and a friend through the sliders. They were talking a mile a minute as they floated on chaises in the pool.

Mary Ann was on the couch sleeping. I hoped she wasn't in pain and slid open a slider. "Hey, girls. How's the water?"

"Hi, Dad."

"Hi, Mr. Luca."

"Mom feeling okay?"

"Yeah, she said she was tired, that's all."

"Okay. We'll probably pick up dinner tonight, so, start thinking of a place."

I got changed, and when I came back into the family room, Mary Ann was up. "Hey, you feel all right?"

"Yeah, just a little tired."

"You sure?"

"Yes, don't worry. How was your day?"

"Good, but Derrick and Lynn have a mess on their hands."

"What happened?"

"Lynn had her identity stolen, and they got wiped out."

"Oh my God. They'd better check their credit, see if any

loans were taken out in their names." She sat up. "I have to call Lynn."

"I feel bad."

"It's going to take them years to straighten this out. Their credit is going to be shot. They won't be able to get a credit card."

She struggled to get up. "Stay. Where's your phone?"

"On the counter."

"All right. Decide what you want, and I'll run out and pick up dinner."

I handed off her phone and went into the den. Derrick was going to be distracted. If we were going to solve this murder, we couldn't miss anything. I flipped open the cold-case file and started reading.

18

MILLER

There was no doubt this detective was trouble. I'd have to make sure Greg and I were in lockstep. Any cracks in our stories, and I was sure Luca would drive a truck through it.

I wanted to call Weinstein to run interference but worried how Luca would react to the news he'd have to go through a lawyer. It might provoke him. My plan was to manage this as I'd done for the past decade.

Driving home, I wondered whether Mark sensed danger. He seemed on edge and hadn't come to the office today. I called him four times, and he messaged that he'd call back when he had time.

My cell rang as I turned off Pine Ridge Road. It was my wife. Again. Minutes from the house, I swiped the call away.

As I pulled into the garage, the door to the house opened. Cathy was standing with her hands on her hips. As soon as I got out of the car, she said, "I called you two times."

"Sorry. I was on the way home. What's the matter?"

"I'll tell you what's the matter; it's your brother."

"Mark?"

She frowned. "Who else?"

"What happened?"

"He skinned a rabbit and brought it into the house--"

"A rabbit?"

"It was dead, and the blood dripped all over the floor."

I exhaled. "Let me talk to him."

"Talking doesn't work."

"What do you want me to do?"

"He should be living on his own."

I shook my head. "He can't yet."

"Yet? When, then? I want to know when."

"Take it easy, Cathy. He's got his own apartment."

"Yeah? Well, next time he brings a dead animal in, you clean it up."

"Let me talk to him."

As she stormed away, she said, "Good luck with that."

Mark listened to me, most of the time. People just needed to know he had to be reminded. Often. I climbed the stairs to the apartment we'd built over the garage for Mark.

I knocked and swung open the door. "Mark? You in there?"

The TV was on, but he didn't answer. "Mark?" I stepped in. There was a pile of *Wolverine* comic books on the cocktail table. I wasn't sure taking him to see the first movie was a good idea. If Mark liked something, he'd obsess over it.

I shut the TV off and picked up the gaming console and virtual reality goggles I bought him. My goal was to keep him occupied, but as I sifted through the stack of video games, I wondered about my decision. Mark was playing violent games like *Modern Warfare* and *Grand Theft Auto*.

Much as I didn't want to, it felt like it was time to take him golfing. A new set of clubs would ignite his interest. I didn't want my game to suffer, so maybe a couple of lessons with the pro, then have Benny take him out one day a week.

I poked my head into his bedroom and stepped back. A squirrel tail was laying on a nightstand. I walked in. Dried blood was caked on the end of the tail. Mark had trapped two dozen squirrels and burned them before I found out about it. Was he back at it again?

The closet door was open. He'd hung his clothes in a rainbow-like color palette. They were also organized by size. But under the shortest garments was a pile of dirty laundry.

Wondering where he was, I trudged down the stairs and out the back sliders. Looking toward the lake, I saw him cleaning the boat.

"Hey, Marco. How you doing?"

He turned his head. "Hey, Billy."

"What are you doing?"

"Polishing the brass."

"Looks good."

"No! It sucks. I can't get it cleaner."

"Did you use the buffer?"

"What buffer?"

"I picked one up. Come up to the house; it's in the garage."

He hesitated.

"It'll make the job easier."

"But, but—"

"Trust me on this."

He got off his knees and jumped onto the dock. I asked, "You doing all right?"

He nodded.

"You kind of annoyed Cathy bringing the rabbit in the house."

"I didn't know she'd get mad."

"It's okay. I'll handle her but promise you won't be killing any more rabbits."

"I like their fur; it's so soft. Feel this."

He reached into his pocket and came up with a rabbit's foot.

"You made that?"

"Yep. I used the ax."

"I hope he was dead."

Mark shrugged.

"Can you do me a favor?"

"Yeah, yeah. What?"

"I want to take you for a new set of golf clubs."

"Yay." He jumped up and down. "When can we go?"

"Tomorrow."

"Why can't we go now? I really want new ones. My old ones make me play bad. When we get them I'll be good, really good. Bet I can beat you."

"Oh yeah? I've been practicing."

"Remember that time I made that putt from, like, a hundred feet? You couldn't do that but I did."

"Yep, but I have a new putter now, and you never know, I might get it in, buddy."

"I want a new putter too. Can we go now?"

"I can't."

"Why? Why not? I need new clubs."

"Hold on, tiger. I said I'm going to take you and I will. You just have to wait until tomorrow."

"But—"

"I'm sorry. Cathy's mad about the rabbit thing, and if I take you, she'll say I'm rewarding you or something."

"That's bull—"

I tapped the code into the garage door pad. "Shh, I know it's crazy, but you know how people misunderstand things."

"Can we go later?"

I pointed to the buffer hanging on the wall. "Look at that beauty. I'm telling you; it's going to shine the brass so bright, you'll need sunglasses to look at it."

He ran and took it off its hook. "Cool."

As he ran out of the garage, I said, "Be careful with that."

I didn't like the way he was acting. One slip of the tongue, and there was no turning back, I'd lose everything.

19

Luca

One arm out of my jacket, my desk phone rang.

"Homicide, Detective Luca."

"Frank, when you have time, we need to talk."

"I can come up now."

Sheriff Remin operated in a way that seemed to show more respect than Chester did. Just like asking a person of interest a question, it came down to how you framed it. It was something my mom was a master at. She never told me to do something; she'd work it in a conversation, saying you might want to try that or think about this.

It was a style that proved to be highly effective, but I still had to be reminded about it. When I had my first direct report, I would tell them to do this or that and get pushback or a lack enthusiasm.

I couldn't understand why, but my first wife brought up my mother's approach, and I started saying things like, "Can you help me with this?" Or "If we could somehow do this." It was like magic, and I rarely slipped into domination.

I said hello to two administrators waiting for the elevator

and stepped into the stairwell. The building only had two floors. I wasn't close to being a gym rat, but taking the elevator up one flight struck me as lazy.

"Hey, Florence. How are you?"

Remin had kept Chester's secretary. "Hello, Frank. All's good and you? How's Mary Ann?"

Though she wasn't, I said, "She's doing okay."

"Tell her I was asking after her. You can go on in."

I knocked before entering. "Sheriff?"

Remin peered over his reading glasses. "Come in, Frank. Sit down."

I found it reassuring that Remin's desk was cluttered with paperwork. I took a seat as the sheriff finished reading a document. "The lawyers are taking over."

"I know what you mean."

"What's going on with the Swift case?"

"It's early, sir. We have a couple of leads we're following, including people with access to the burial site."

"The Millers?"

"We don't have anything concrete, but something about Bill Miller isn't right."

Remin sat back in his chair. "The family is well respected, but if you've got something, go after it. No one is above the law."

He was saying all the right things. "Thank you, sir. We're not going to make a move until we're certain."

"Anything else interesting?"

"Like I said, it's early, but we're looking at a couple of the kid's teachers."

"Both lines are going to stir things up."

"We're going to get it right. We also have someone who bullied her, and she's got a record."

"Sounds like progress."

"It'd be nice to give the parents a measure of justice."

He nodded. "Speaking of the parents, they called to complain about your behavior at the memorial."

So other than style, Remin wasn't much different than Chester. "They gave us permission to attend, sir."

"But I'm told you promised to observe only, not to interact with the guests in attendance."

"I only spoke to one woman, someone I visited the day before. I can't believe—"

"The Swifts are living a nightmare. They're making noise out of frustration. I'm mentioned it only to let you know how sensitive this case is."

"It was nothing."

"No need to defend yourself. When I worked homicide, dealing with the families was the trickiest part."

"It is challenging."

"All right, why don't you get back to running down whoever did it?"

Remin seemed supportive. Maybe he was just covering the bases by mentioning it, but it bothered me. Solving a murder case meant ruffling feathers. Remin knew being Mr. Nice Guy was a guarantee to add to the pile of cold cases.

I trudged down the stairs wondering if I'd made the right decision coming back to the force. Looking back was something I tried to stop doing. It accomplished nothing. I had a killer to catch, I thought, emerging onto the first floor.

Sitting at my desk, I plugged Benny Alston into the system. The only thing Collier County had on him was an auto accident back in 2012. I pulled up his driver's license. Alston was sixty-four and had a pockmarked face.

I was about to search the national database when Derrick came in. "Hey, Frank, I think we might have something with the teacher angle."

"What did Quinn say?"

Throwing his jacket over a chair, Derrick said, "She was never comfortable around Marconi or Schneider. Said Kate told her Marconi had invited her over to his place the Saturday before she disappeared."

"Alone?"

"That's what she said."

"Do we know if she went?"

"She doesn't know."

"Maybe Marconi got aggressive, and Swift rejected him, and maybe he thought she'd say something."

"Or they hooked up, and the next day she regretted it. She could've said something to him, and he freaked out."

"This reminds me of another cold case. We uncovered two teachers who'd been preying on high school girls. It makes me sick."

Derrick exhaled. "This is one time I wish we both had boys."

I nodded. "If there's any truth to this, it'd mean Kate Swift was drawn to older men, and that means Miller is in the mix with Marconi."

"And Schneider. Quinn said some girl had made a claim against Schneider, saying he tried to molest her."

"That sleaze is still teaching. How'd he get out of that?"

"I don't know. But ten years ago, you weren't assumed guilty like you are today."

I shot out of my chair. Because of the chemo I'd been doused with, my memory wasn't what it used to be. "The case I mentioned. The teacher taught at Barron Collier."

"Oh my God. They have a history of circling the wagons to protect one of their own."

"What bullshit. Institutions think they can hide a problem, bury it so nobody knows about it."

"As long as someone is willing to dig, it comes out."

"Amen."

"We have a couple of trails to follow. What do you want to hit first?"

"We're starting with Schneider."

20

MILLER

I was reviewing yesterday's sales numbers when Greg knocked on my office door.

"What's up? Silvia said you needed something?"

"Come in, close the door. Looking over yesterday's figures. The lumber numbers are off the charts."

"If we can get a supply, we'll sell it. The margins are pretty sweet."

"People are just happy to get what they can. It's not going to last."

"Oh, I think it will. The mills are telling me they're not ramping up production. Why should they? Everybody's making money."

"It's not a good thing. Something's going to give; prices rose too fast."

"Maybe they were too low, but who cares? Stuff is flying off the shelves." He zoomed his hand like a plane taking off. His nails were too long.

"There's going to be a backlash when demand slows and prices drop. People are going feel like they were played."

"They got no choice. But they can't blame us, it's the mills."

"They don't know anything about mills. They came to Millers', and if they feel they overpaid, they're not going be happy."

"You're a worrywart. We're not the only ones. Besides, we have no choice."

"I don't know. I'm thinking we should cut prices a bit, do some kind of a give-back special or something."

"That's stupid. We have to make the money when we can."

"You know, Dad told me, back in the late seventies, when Carter was president, we had bad inflation. Everybody was hurting, and he said he held the line on prices and got a ton of favorable press. He said it's what helped him build the business."

Greg scoffed, "Different times now."

"No doubt, but loyalty never goes away."

"That sounds like Dad, old school."

"It still applies today."

"You brought me here to get lectured?"

He still resented my being the defacto head of the business. Greg believed he could run the place better than I could. He had better skills when it came to charming commercial accounts, but he was too short-term oriented.

"Sorry if it came across that way. That wasn't my intention. Are we okay?"

"Yeah."

"Look, I'm getting concerned about this detective. He's asking a lot of questions, and he came back to the house yesterday."

"What do you want me to do about it?"

"We have to be on the same page here."

He shook his head. "You know, we wouldn't be dealing with this bullshit if it weren't for you."

"I did what had to be done."

"Oh, stop with that crap already."

"What did you want me to do?"

"You should have told the truth."

"The truth?"

"What's the matter? Isn't that another virtue like loyalty?"

"That's—"

"What would Dad have done? He would've come clean."

I shook my head. "You don't know how the world operates. Dad was no angel; he did what he had to do. If it wasn't for him, we wouldn't have what we do."

"Yeah, yeah, yeah. I've got to go."

"Hang on."

"I can't, the guys from Bonita Bay are on their way."

"Promise me if this Detective Luca wants to talk to you, that you'll let me know beforehand."

"I'm getting really sick of this bullshit." He headed for the door, saying, "I should've never listened to you."

Greg would fly off the handle easily. And that increased the risk. I'd need to think about how to handle him. He lived high. Money was the easiest way to rein him in. The least painful way to get him in line would be to threaten to reduce his income somehow. But I'd need Mark to support me, and that would complicate things.

I tried to think of a way to buy him off. Find a way to either bonus him or create a sales commission for new business. The sales angle was a good one. It was a twofer. Greg would follow me, and it'd be good for business.

21

LUCA

We couldn't find anything on Richard Schneider. Either he was clean, or he was an expert at silencing his victims. It was time to dig into the ugly possibility a teacher had violated the most sacred covenant.

Derrick turned off Airport Pulling onto Cougar Drive. The access road fed both Barron Collier High School and Osceola Elementary. I pushed the thought away a teacher could be abusing even younger kids than a high schooler.

The school was well maintained, but the marine-blue tile wall behind its name dated it to the late seventies. I wondered if the school's perennial appearance on the nation's list of best high schools had influenced administrators to keep secrets.

There were no cameras covering the main entrance. I was about to hit the digital doorbell when Derrick said, "Would you look at this? The door is open."

"Sloppy." I hit the bell and announced ourselves. There was a buzz, and we heard a door unlocking.

Smiling, a professorial-looking man, with a white goatee,

opened the door. "Welcome to Barron Collier High, gentlemen. I'm Marcus Whitmore, the principal."

We shook hands and followed him past display cabinets full of trophies and ribbons. He led us into a conference room.

"So, how can we help you?"

I said, "This is a delicate matter involving at least one of the teachers here."

Eyebrows raised, he said, "Delicate? Can you expound upon that?"

"We're investigating the murder of a former student, Kate Swift."

"That was terrible but before my time."

As expected, he wanted to distance himself. "We know that."

"You're suspecting the involvement of a staff member?"

Derrick said, "It's possible. We'd like any records on both Mr. Richard Schneider and Freddo Marconi."

Whitmore leaned forward. "You think they acted together?"

"We can't comment on an ongoing investigation. We're aware of a claim made against Mr. Schneider in the past regarding an inappropriate episode with a female student. We'll need to review the file."

The color drained from Whitmore's face. "I-I, uh, don't think I can release that to you. It would violate privacy protocols."

I said, "We can obtain a warrant, but that opens the real possibility that this inquiry into Barron Collier will be made public."

"Are you threatening this school?"

"Not at all, Mr. Whitmore. It's a fact; more people would know about it, and something like a high school, well, you know, people like to talk. All we want to do is review the file. We can do that right here, with you supervising."

"He's never given us any trouble since I've been here. I don't know what you're referring to."

I said, "Mr. Whitmore, lying to protect someone can be considered obstruction of justice. Before you say any more, my suggestion would be for you to get the file."

"I'm not protecting anyone. All—"

I tapped my watch. "We're short on time."

He scrambled out of his seat. "I'll be right back."

Derrick smiled. "Why do people go through all of that? Do they think we're just fishing?"

"Human nature. We could work part time if they'd give straight answers the first time we asked."

Whitmore came back with a brown folder marked "Confidential." He unclasped it and slid out a blue folder. "I believe this is what you're looking for. It's from 2011, years before I arrived."

We flipped open the folder as Whitmore said, "The student's name has been redacted."

"You read the report?"

"Uh, no. Someone mentioned it."

The allegations made by a student that Schneider had attempted to kiss and fondle were denied by the teacher. The record reflected that no other student in the teacher's eight years at the school had asserted improper behavior of any kind.

Barron Collier High School wanted to refer the matter to the sheriff's office, but the parents of the child refused to press charges and it died. There were several interviews of other parties but no corroborating evidence.

I handed the file back to Whitmore. "I'd like the contact information for the principal at the time."

He gave it to us and we left. We opened the car doors to let the heat out, and Derrick said, "What do you think?"

I climbed in and put the air on high. "I don't like the pattern Schneider's established."

"I wish we could talk to the girl."

"That would take some doing. We need more before we go there, and I'd hate to dredge the memories up for her."

"You want to talk to Schneider?"

"Call him. The school day is almost over. Tell him to meet us at Noodles. We'll grab a coffee."

THE NAME, Noodles Italian Café and Sushi Bar, seemed like an attempt to appeal to the broadest range of diners possible. I thought it was weird and didn't know about the sushi, but the pasta dishes I had were good.

We sat in the car until we saw Schneider walk toward the restaurant. He peeked in the restaurant, which had to be quiet at this time, and surveyed the parking lot. His shoulders sagged when he saw us.

I said, "Let's sit over there." There was an indoor-outdoor bar. I climbed on a barstool wondering what about this case had me dangling my legs again.

Schneider was jittery as we ordered coffees. I hoped he'd order a decaf but he didn't. He said, "I don't understand why you want to talk to me about Kate Swift."

Derrick said, "You were close to her."

"No, not really."

Putting a drop of milk in my coffee, I said, "You were at the memorial service."

"Just trying to show my respect."

Derrick said, "Tell us about the allegations concerning you and a female student about ten years ago."

"Oh, come on, man. That was years ago, and it was bullshit."

My inclination was to believe him. "We'd like to hear your side of it."

"Seriously, you're digging into some nonsense that happened ten years ago?"

"The fact is, Kate Swift disappeared almost a decade ago. That kicks it out of the nonsense box."

Schneider shook his head. "Look, Ka— I'm not even going to mention the kid's name, well, she's a woman now. She had a crush on me and tried to kiss me. I said no and she tried again. I pushed her away and told her to leave. When she didn't, I went to the office. She panicked and turned it around on me, claiming I was the aggressor."

"How did it end?"

"The school asked her to press charges, but she didn't and that was it."

"Why would you meet alone with a female student?"

"What are you talking about? We meet with students all the time."

"You knew she had a crush on you. Why would you set yourself up like that?"

He frowned. "It was stupid, but I was used to teaching middle schoolers."

Unless something material was uncovered on Schneider, I felt he was truthful. The bottom line looked like he'd misjudged a teenager's estrogen level. It was time to change directions.

"We have irrefutable evidence that inappropriate sexual contact between a female student and a male teacher took place at Barron Collier High."

Derrick choked on his coffee. He thought I was lying, but I didn't state a time frame, and I discovered the transgression investigating the Boyle murder.

Schneider was so white, he looked like a coloring-book image. "It wasn't me. I swear."

"Who do you think it was?"

"I don't know. I really don't."

"We think it could be Freddo Marconi."

"I can't say."

It wasn't the outright denial I expected. "But you're good friends. You'd know."

"We're not close."

"Come on, you came to the memorial with him."

"He's the one who told me they found Kate. I didn't know. He wanted someone to go with and I said okay."

"Why do you think all the girls liked him ten years ago?"

"He was a good-looking guy. I mean, before he gained weight and lost his hair."

"He liked to flirt with them, right?"

He shrugged. "I guess so."

Derrick said, "Come on, tell us what you know."

22

MILLER

I was going over the numbers on constructing a new store on Immokalee Road, east of Collier Boulevard. New communities were breaking ground, and others had already been approved by the county.

By some estimates, there'd be ten thousand new homes in a couple of years. That was a lot of customers who'd need a place like ours. The problem was, being first in the area meant a solid year or two of losing money. I was agonizing over the decision when the intercom buzzed.

"Mr. Miller?"

"I told you, I don't want to be disturbed."

"I'm sorry, sir. But Mrs. Miller called twice, and, uh, she said to get you on the phone."

"Okay. Put her through."

I picked up the phone, wondering what mess Mark had gotten into. "Sorry, hon."

"The police were here."

"They came to the house?"

"Yes. Detective Luca and his partner."

"What did they want?"

"They wanted to talk to Mark."

"You didn't let them, did you?"

"Of course not. You said never to let them."

"Good. Thanks. What did you tell them?"

"That he wasn't home."

"Was he?"

"He was in his apartment."

She had lied for me. "Okay. I'm going to call Weinstein."

"Is Mark in some kind of trouble?"

"No. Don't worry about it. Weinstein will handle it."

"Are you sure?"

"Absolutely. They come again; tell them they need to go through our lawyers. You'll see how fast they stop bothering us."

"I hope so."

"I have to run. I'll see you later."

Hanging up, I found myself wishing I was as confident as I sounded. I came around my desk and paced, wondering if I should call Weinstein. He'd reach out to the sheriff's office to apprise them of his representation. It'd take the immediate heat away, but I knew Luca would read it as sign we were hiding something.

I drifted to the window overlooking the floor of the store. Benny was talking to a mother and a girl behind a cart loaded with flowers. He was supposed to be managing the kitchen and bath renovation exhibit, not flirting.

Hitting the intercom, I said, "Alice, use the PA, and tell Benny I want to see him."

I kept my eyes on him as the announcement was made. He was laughing, and I wondered if he even heard his name. He said goodbye and headed to the stairs.

Benny knocked on my open door. "What's up, Bill?"

"Why aren't you at the renovation exhibit?"

"They're doing fine over there."

"We spent a tremendous amount on advertising. We need to close as many as we can."

"We'll be fine."

"We're not fine. That department is losing money; it's why we are running the promotion."

"Take it easy. It'll work out."

"Taking it easy don't get the job done. Everybody has to pitch in, or Home Depot is going eat our lunch."

"Okay, okay. I'll get over there."

"And, Benny, what's with all the days off?"

"Uh, my sister, she's not doing well. And the drive to Orlando is a nightmare with Route Four."

"Sorry to hear. You didn't say anything about her being ill."

"She'll be all right."

"Hope she feels better. Try to give notice when you have to see her. Greg's giving me a hard time, said the staff is grumbling about favoritism."

"I don't want to step out of line, but if your dad was still around, he'd never say that."

"Boy, I miss him."

"He was one of a kind. In my book, his middle name was Loyal."

"So true. Hey, get on down there before we miss any sales."

"On my way."

I watched him walk out. He moved and looked like a younger man. He had the energy to be productive, but he was a slacker, always looking to do the minimum. Greg was right about him, but getting rid of him wasn't going to be easy.

Pushing Benny out of my thoughts, I pulled out my cell and scrolled for a number.

"This is Jeff Weinstein."

"Hi, Jeff, it's Bill Miller."

"How are you, Mr. Miller?"

"Good, but I need you to get involved in something."

"Kate Swift?"

"Yes, I know the body was found on my property, but I've spoken several times to a Detective Luca."

"You should have called me before speaking with them."

"I know, but I have nothing to hide."

"I understand, but I'd refrain from future communications."

"That's why I'm calling."

"They want to question you again?"

"Not yet, but they came to the house today, wanting to talk to Mark."

"Did you allow them to?"

"No, Cathy told him he wasn't home, but he was."

"That's fine. I'll call Detective Luca."

"You know him?"

"Yes, he's tenacious."

Ugh. "We can't let Mark talk to him. He'll get confused, and who knows what he'll say."

"I'll inform the sheriff's office that I'm representing the family. They'll have to go through my office."

"They can't make him talk, can they?"

"No. No one can be forced to; you're protected by the law."

"Good, good."

"As we did when Ms. Swift went missing, we'll offer a written statement. Unless we're presented with hard evidence that incriminates the family in any way, we'll remain silent."

"But that'll anger the detective. You said he's tough."

"He is. Let's leave it as I said. If we need to address a particular circumstance, we'll do so. But for the moment, everything goes through this office."

"Good. I'll let Greg and everybody know."

23

LUCA

Derrick pulled into the parking lot off Route 41 and parked near the Pelican Bay office building. We were fifteen minutes early for our interview. I sent a text to Mary Ann to check on how she was feeling.

Derrick said, "Do you think it's genetic?"

"What do you mean?"

"What are the odds that Marconi's sister was a suspect in the murder of the kid in Virginia?"

"Long, but what bothers me is Marconi wouldn't even talk to us without a lawyer. He hired a mouthpiece before we asked him his name."

"You know this lawyer?"

I shook my head. "Never heard of him."

Two men in dress shirts were smoking outside the entrance. We circled around them and saw Marconi waiting for an elevator. "Come on." I hustled into the lobby wanting to ride the same car up with Marconi. He looked up, giving a small nod.

We piled in after Marconi. He hit the fifth floor. "We're going to the same floor, Mr. Marconi."

His jaw dropped. "You're... you're the detectives?"

"Yes."

He stared at the floor. The doors slid open, and we followed him into the Law Offices of Martin Colbert. I stood as close as I could to Marconi as he announced himself to the receptionist. It was childish, but I wanted him uncomfortable. Nervous people make mistakes.

Five minutes went by before we were shown into a windowless conference room. Though there were ten chairs around the mahogany table, I had to tamp down my claustrophobia.

Marconi was seated next to Martin Colbert, who stood as we shook hands. Colbert looked directly in my eyes as he did, something I liked in a man. As we sat, I thought about the way it contrasted with the way Bill Miller averted his eyes when we met.

Colbert said, "I'm hoping we can clear up whatever is piquing your interest in my client. Shall we get started?"

I said, "Mr. Marconi, you had a relationship with Kate Swift. Please explain the nature of it."

Marconi looked at his lawyer, who nodded. "Well, first off, it wasn't a relationship."

Colbert jumped in: "I'm fine with the word as it only implies a connection between two people. And since she was a student in one of your classes, we'll let it go."

"Kate was in one of my classes, but it was a long time ago."

"It was more than one, wasn't it?"

"Yeah, I think so. But I taught hundreds of kids."

"I understand, but how many of those hundreds were your teaching assistant?"

"I had several every semester."

"All females?"

Colbert put his hand on Marconi's forearm. "It would be helpful if we kept a narrow focus during this conversation."

"Did you have any male assistants?"

"None of the boys were interested in being an assistant; they wanted to play sports."

"Ten years ago, you had a reputation for flirting with female students."

"That's not true."

"Can you tell us how you came to be called Romeo?"

His cheeks got rosy. "It was a joke. Look at me. You think a young girl would be interested in me?"

"You didn't look like you do ten years ago."

"Kids are kids. What can I tell you? They enjoy teasing."

Colbert said, "Do you have a specific allegation on which you'd like to question my client?"

It was time to regurgitate the line about Barron Collier's sad past. "We do, Counselor. There's irrefutable evidence of inappropriate sexual contact between a female student and a male teacher at Barron Collier High."

Marconi looked like he'd swallowed a golf ball. "It wasn't me."

Colbert said, "Do you have proof this alleged contact involved my client?"

"At this point, it's circumstantial, but we've just begun to investigate. I'd advise your client to be forthcoming about his relationship with Ms. Swift. We know it was more than teacher-student."

Colbert turned to Marconi. "You don't have to say anything. This is completely voluntary; you have the right to remain silent."

Something about Colbert didn't feel right. Though he

jumped in at the right time with his warning, he didn't speak like a criminal lawyer. "Mr. Colbert is right, but keeping quiet is only going to make us dig deeper."

Derrick finally said something. "You went to her memorial service. After ten years, if you didn't have a special relationship, what made you go?"

I was on the fence about the word special when Marconi said, "There was nothing inappropriate about our relationship. Kate was a bright, vivacious woman, and I tried to help her as best as I could."

Now I had to process vivacious and the fact he called her a woman, not a girl. Even Colbert leaned away from his client.

Derrick said, "Besides the scholastic help, what else did you help her with?"

"I can tell that something was bothering her the last month or two before she... she went missing."

"How did you know that?"

"I sensed that Kate wanted to talk but wouldn't open up. I tried to get her to talk, but she said she was embarrassed. I told her she could trust me, and I wouldn't judge."

"What did you think it was about?"

"I'm pretty sure it was a relationship thing."

"How do you know that?"

"Just a feeling."

"What gave you that feeling?"

"Look, I'm around kids all the time. I know when they're, uh, involved with someone else. You can tell."

"Who do you think she was seeing?"

"I honestly don't know, but I'm pretty sure it wasn't someone who went to Barron."

"Do you believe it was someone older?"

"Could be why she seemed embarrassed over it."

I considered it interesting he left the door open on the question. If he was trying to direct us away from himself, he would've shut it down. It made me think of Bill Miller. Again.

"Did she ever mention Bill Miller?"

"Bill Miller? Where her remains were found?"

"Yes."

"Not him but his brother, the one who was hurt in the accident. I remember when it happened."

"Did you know Mark Miller?"

"No. I'm pretty sure he went to Seacrest."

"What did she say about him?"

"They used to go together and that he got injured and wasn't the same. I didn't know him but felt for the kid, and then his father takes his own life. It was like Shakespeare."

When I was forced to read him in school, I did the minimum to pass, but the tragedy connection was clear.

"What can you tell us about Amanda Pearson?"

Marconi frowned. "I don't like talking about a former student. All of us act like idiots when we're kids and she probably changed."

"We're interested in understanding the type of person she was then. What her interaction with Kate was. As we understand, it wasn't good."

"Amanda was a classic bully. There's always one in every class. She was a big girl, and I think she felt out of place. She was at that awkward stage, not a pretty little thing, but big boned, and I guess she felt being aggressive would prevent the kids from teasing her."

We had a few lines to follow but I wavered on whether Marconi was one of them. On the way out, I saw a framed cover of *Gulfshore Business* magazine hanging on the wall.

Colbert was smiling beneath the heading "Corporate Lawyer of the Year."

Marconi hadn't hired a criminal attorney. It didn't mean he had nothing to do with Kate Swift's death, but it was odd. Why hire a lawyer if you have nothing to hide?

24

MILLER

The parking lot for Clam Pass Beach was emptying out. I checked the time; Greg was supposed to meet me twenty minutes ago. I arrived late knowing he'd keep me waiting, but he still wasn't here.

An older couple, carrying beach chairs, made their way to their car. Greg's Range Rover pulled up. We got out of our cars. I said, "Hey, let's take a walk."

"All right, but I don't have much time."

"You ever see the new boardwalk we supplied?"

He shook his head. "I haven't been able to get down here."

"It came out nice. I'm surprised you got the county to go for an exotic hardwood like IPE."

As we passed the tram pickup area, he said, "Piece of cake. It made sense; it's harder than California Redwood and lasts twenty years without treating it."

"Cost effective."

"Looks a zillion times better than any of the plastic products and it's natural."

"How you making out with the bid for the pier?"

"They're not going make a decision for another ninety days. But I'll bring it home, don't worry."

"Good. Look, I hired Weinstein. That detective came to the house wanting to talk to Mark."

"Oh Jesus. This has got to stop."

"Don't worry. We'll be fine as long as we stick together."

"I knew this was going to blow up one day. I just knew it."

I lowered my voice as a tram car passed. "Nothing is going to blow up. Weinstein will protect Mark, and this will die down like it did before."

"This has to end. I can't live with this anymore."

"So, what do you want to do? You want to start talking?"

"We've got to come clean."

"Yeah, and what do you think is going to happen?"

"I didn't do anything."

"You lied to the police."

"That's nothing."

"Yeah, and what do you think is going to happen to the business?"

"What's that got to do with anything?"

Entering the mangrove forest, I said, "You forget the will? Dad gave Mark a controlling interest. He goes down, the business goes with him."

"We'll figure something out."

"You know how tainted the Miller name will be? The press will crucify us for protecting him, for lying, and we'd both probably get jail time for obstruction."

"This is fucked up, and it's your fault."

"Come on, Greg. All I was trying to do was protect Mark, protect the family. Dad would've done the same thing."

"Dad? You mean the guy who killed Mom and blew his brains out?"

I grabbed him by the shoulders and spun him around. "Watch your mouth. It was an accident, and you know it. He felt so bad, he couldn't live with himself. So stop the bullshit."

He shook me off. "Get your fucking hands off me."

"Hold on, Greg. I'm sorry. I just can't stand it when anyone badmouths Dad."

"You took this too far, man. Admit it before it's too late."

"It is too late."

"No, it's not. It's going to get worse. Let's get Weinstein to make a deal for us. We tell the truth, and they'll go easy on us."

"We'll get smeared in the papers. Nobody will shop with us. Would you?"

He shrugged.

"We'll lose it all. And what about the staff? You think they won't bolt once the story breaks?"

"We'll find a way."

"What planet are you on? We'll lose everything."

"The guilt is eating me alive."

"You have to stay strong."

Greg went quiet as we approached the end of the half-mile boardwalk. I said, "You have to trust me on this. This will fade soon. Right now, they found the body, and that brought it up again."

"You think so?"

"I was right the first time. Wasn't I? The cops were asking questions, but it went nowhere, right?"

"I guess so, but it was scary. I didn't sleep for weeks."

"Don't get uptight about it. Just let me and Weinstein handle it and we'll be fine. Don't talk to anyone, just refer them to Weinstein."

"Okay, okay."

I squeezed his shoulder. "Good. Let's head back. Say, Benny and I are going play a round tomorrow at Old Collier. Why don't you come with us? I can get Richie to make it a foursome."

"Benny? He's really getting on my nerves. I don't know how you hang around with him."

"We've been golfing together for years. He's an oddball, but I compartmentalize when I'm on the course."

"I told you, we've got to get rid of him."

"You're right. It's not going to be easy, but as soon as this blows over, I'll pull the trigger."

"Good. You know, we should promote Mario. Let him take over the little that Benny does, and he can help with operations. He's real sharp."

My phone vibrated. I snuck a peek. It was Weinstein. I let it go to voice mail. "Sounds good. I always liked Mario. He works hard and is pleasant to be around."

We hit the parking lot and said our goodbyes. I hopped in my car, hit redial, and held my breath. Why was Weinstein calling?

25

Derrick and I were on our way to see Amanda Pearson. Forgetting to check whether she had a record, I chalked it up to her low standing on the suspect ladder. Though I discounted chemo brain, the omission was forgivable, until I discovered she had a record. It was for assault.

I said, "Make a right onto Immokalee. It's past Seventy-Five; you make a left into Quail Creek."

"I know where it is. Lynn has a friend who lives there."

"You know, it's past where we're going, but back in 1985, there was a double murder of a wealthy family, named Benson, in Quail Creek."

"Really?"

"Yeah, the son killed his mother and his brother. Blew up their car. The sicko watched them get blown away."

"Heartless bastard."

"You got that right. They were worth hundreds of millions. The family made their money from cigarettes."

"Benson and Hedges?"

"I thought the same thing, but it was another company that was bigger than that one."

"All that money and would good did it do them?"

"Amen. Say, did you make any headway with the financial lawyer?"

"He's going to handle contacting the credit agencies, so it doesn't get worse. But he said the banks are going push back on the loans they made."

"How can they do that? It's fraud."

"He said we have to prove it beyond doubt before they'll take the hit."

"How long till your credit is cleaned up?"

"Two, maybe three years."

"That's bullshit."

"Tell me about it."

My cell rang. "It's the sheriff."

"Hello, Sheriff."

"Hey, Frank. Where are you?"

"Headed to see a person of interest in the Swift case."

"Anyone in the Miller family?"

"No, why?"

"We've been notified they retained counsel. We want to talk to them, we have to go through Jeffrey Weinstein. I don't know this lawyer, do you?"

"Yeah, he represented someone in a felony assault charge. He's fair but I don't get it. Why'd they hire an attorney?"

"Might be something there."

"It covers the entire family?"

"He specifically mentioned William, Mark, and Gregory Miller."

"The body was found on the Millers' property, and they won't talk?"

"I'm sorry, Frank, but you'll have to go through the lawyer."

"If they had something to do with this kid's death, I'll nail them, lawyer or not."

"I'm sure you will. Just be sure we don't violate counsel notification, or whatever we get won't be allowed in court."

"Understood, sir."

I hung up and told Derrick what the sheriff said. He said, "What the hell is going on? Marconi, and now the Millers hired lawyers? Is this a big conspiracy or something?"

He knew I didn't believe in conspiracies primarily because I knew the only way two people could keep a secret was if one of them was dead. "To me, something smells. Who'd spend money on a high-priced mouthpiece if you did nothing wrong?"

"I agree with you, but today, the lawyers have convinced everyone you can't go to the bathroom without them."

As we pulled into Longshore Lakes, I said, "It's got to be about Mark Miller. As soon as I tried to talk to him, they shut it down."

Derrick nodded and showed his badge to the guard. The gate opened, and we drove into the community. He said, "That's what it feels like. You know, we're probably wasting our time with Amanda Pearson."

"If we clear her, it's not a waste. It'll help focus the investigation. If it turns out to be the Millers, we'll get them."

We wound our way through the single-family community. The homes were on large lots for Florida, and I pegged them at eight hundred thousand to a million. The deed to the house we were going to was in Amanda Pearson and her mother's names. I surmised the father had passed, willing his half to her.

After passing a series of tennis courts, we turned onto

Shearwater Drive. Amanda Pearson's home sat at the end of the cul-de-sac. A neon-green Dodge Charger was parked in the driveway. I peeked in the window as we walked up the drive. A baseball bat was in the passenger wheel well.

When she swung open the door, I found myself leaning back. Dressed in shorts and a muscle T-shirt, Pearson was Amazonian. "You the detectives?"

Derrick showed his badge. "Yes, ma'am."

"All right, come in. I was sitting out back."

The house had too much furniture but was neat. We followed her onto a screened-in lanai. What I called cages seemed to be on the decline, but nearly every home over ten years of age had one.

We sat around the same fake-stone table Mary Ann and I had. A narrow lake separated the backs of the homes. A couple of kids were splashing around in a pool across the way, yelling "Marco Polo, Marco Polo."

Amanda said, "Damn kids never shut up."

I said, "Sounds like they're having fun."

She shook her head. "So, this is about Katie?"

"Yes. You didn't get along with her."

"You trying to pin this on me?"

"You nearly ran her down with your car."

"Not true. She wasn't paying attention and I almost hit her. It was her fault."

"Was Cheryl Sowski paying attention when you hit her?"

Her eyes narrowed. "Look, man. You're dredging up old shit."

Derrick said, "Every witness said you intentionally hit Sowski."

"You gonna arrest me? After more than ten years? Ain't there a limit of statues or something?"

I wanted to tell her there wasn't a statute of limitations on being a jerk. "You still bullying people around?"

"I don't bully nobody."

"Everyone we spoke to said you did. You were in a number of fights in high school, and each time, you instigated it."

"That's bullshit. You're not gonna frame me for this."

"You were arrested for assault twice."

"It was just once; the other time they dropped the charges."

"You're lucky the judge went light on you. Instead of community service and anger management classes, you could've spent a couple of years behind bars."

"He knew it was bullshit."

Judge Rittenhouse was notorious for cutting young adults breaks. The jury was out on the success of his leniency. "You slammed the victim's head into the bar so many times, you almost killed her."

"She's fine."

"You're lucky the other patrons in the bar pulled you off, or you might be in a federal penitentiary."

"You gonna keep harping on this old shit?"

"Where were you June first, 2013?"

"Man, I told the cops back then, I was home." She shook her head and added, "With my mom."

I didn't like the hesitation before solidifying her where-abouts. A family member, especially a mother, was shaky when it came to alibis. Maternal instinct and emotion clouded judgments in the best of us. "That's what the case file stated."

"So why bust my horns?"

Horns. I couldn't have come up with a better fit for this difficult woman. "Just doing our job, ma'am. We're done. Thank you for your time."

Derrick did a double take as I got up. As soon as we got in the car, he said, "Why'd you end the questioning? You don't think it's her?"

"Not necessarily. I don't like that she's relying on her mother for an alibi."

"Me neither. A lot of people lie for their kids. How we going to verify it?"

"The case file had zero interviews of the Millers' neighbors."

"Yeah, you're right, but I don't get the connection."

I was pleased my memory hadn't failed me. "It'd be pretty hard to miss a woman the size of Pearson. Someone may have seen her on the block. When we get back, hunt down what car she and her parents had back in 2013."

26

MILLER

Weinstein picked up on the third ring.

"Sorry, I was indisposed when you called."

"That's quite all right. I wanted to inform you that Detective Luca contacted my office."

"What does he want?"

"An interview with your brother Mark."

"You told him no, right?"

"I reminded him of the injury he suffered and said I'd get back to him after consulting with the family."

"Consult about what? I don't want him talking to the police."

"It might be a good idea to engage in a dialogue with them."

Lawyers always pulled that garbage; they'd tell you one thing before hiring them and then change their tune. "You said we didn't have to talk to them if we didn't want to."

"Yes, that's true. However, if we propose a written response to their questions, it'll indicate our willingness to cooperate."

"But last time we didn't have to do that."

"We tendered a statement and that satisfied them."

"Why can't we do that again?"

"I offered that, but they refused."

"Why? What changed?"

"Discovering the remains on your property significantly changed the complexion. I understand why they're interested in your brother and you."

"Me? They mentioned me? Specifically?"

"Yes, though the primary focus was on Mark."

"I still don't like it. He's not all there at times, and he'll be misunderstood."

"That's why I suggested written responses. We can control what is communicated to the police."

"What are the downsides?"

"The responses can be entered into the record if this goes to trial."

"Trial? He didn't do anything."

"Let's not get ahead of ourselves. I wouldn't permit him to incriminate himself or anyone else with his answers."

"I don't see the point."

"Your apprehension is understandable, but this is a controlled response. In circumstances like this, with an impaired individual, it shows a willingness to engage and will likely put a swift end to their interest in Mark."

Likely. Running the business, I'd heard him say that before as a reassurance, only to walk it back. I was reminded of it every time I drove by that development on Airport Pulling Road. The Coconut Core Builders owed us over a million and were months behind when the housing market softened.

Weinstein said it was likely they'd pay if we filed suit. Instead, they declared bankruptcy, and we only received fifty-seven thousand. What really pissed me off was the same group reorganized and finished the community two years later.

"How sure are you?"

"These things are difficult to predict." He was backpedaling like an Olympian. "But stonewalling the inquiry is not something I recommend."

I wanted to say no, but deep down I knew refusing would raise suspicions. "All right, but on the condition I'm able to review what is being sent, before it goes to them."

"Good, you made the correct decision. I'll notify Detective Luca."

I hung up, questioning his statement. Letting Greg know about the development wasn't something I looked forward to. He'd be relieved to know Mark was technically talking, but I'd hold back the part it was in writing. I'd have to frame it properly or he'd be looking to run his mouth.

CATHY WAS on her iPad when I came into the house. "Hey, Cathy."

"How was your day?"

"Pretty good. You?"

"Went to lunch with Emily."

"How are they doing?"

"They're going to Italy for a month. We always said we were going to rent a villa in Tuscany. Can we do it this year?"

I had to stay out of jail first. "If not this year, then in the spring. Why don't you start checking around, look at some places?"

"I'll call Anna. They've been there so many times."

"Sounds good. Mark left early today. Everything okay with him?"

"I think so. He was down by the dock earlier."

"Cleaning the boat?"

"Yep. Mr. Obsessive."

"You want to grab dinner at True Food?"

"Sure, I'm dying for the cauliflower dish they have."

"Let me talk to Mark and we'll head out."

Climbing the stairs, the sound of acid rock music got louder. I knocked on the door twice before pushing it open. Wearing headphones, Mark was on the couch playing a video game.

I tapped him on the shoulder and he pulled his headphones around his neck. "You scared me."

"Sorry. How you doing?"

"All right."

"We're going to True Foods for dinner. You want me to pick something up for you?"

"Yech. They just got vegetables and all."

"They have a lot of different things. Eating healthy isn't going to kill you."

"No way."

"You left early today. Anything going on?"

"No, just bored."

"Tomorrow you can come with me. I want to scout out locations for a possible new store."

"We don't need more stores. We should sell video games and stuff. That's where the real money is."

"We're a building and home supply company. Video games don't fit."

"Yes, they do. People can come in, get some light bulbs and outdoor stuff and pick up a game. They don't have to go to Best Buy."

"I'll talk to Greg about it. Look, umm, we're going to need to answer questions for the police."

"The police? Why?"

"Don't worry. Remember we did it last time when Katie went missing?"

He averted his eyes but said nothing.

"Since they found her body here, they have a couple of questions."

His eyes teared up. I put my hand on his shoulder as his voice cracked: "I miss her. Why did this have to happen?"

"It's going to be over soon."

"No! No! It's never going to end. Katie's gone. Forever."

"Take it easy, Mark. We're going to get past this."

"How?"

"Remember, before they found her body, everything was okay, right?"

"What do you mean?"

"We got the new boat. How cool was that?"

"Yeah, it's the best."

"Well, guess what? I have a surprise."

Mark jumped up. "What? What? Tell me."

"You know that boat we saw at the boat show? The one with the blue top that had the twin outboards?"

"They said it's the fastest lake boat ever. In the world."

"Yep. And guess who's going to get one?"

"Who?"

"You."

"Awesome! I can't believe it."

"Believe it."

"When, when can we get it?"

"You remember Mr. Weinstein, the lawyer?"

"He's getting it?"

"No, but anybody asks about Katie, we're going to tell them to call Mr. Weinstein. You got that?"

"Yeah, yeah."

"You keep quiet about Katie, and the boat is yours."

"When am I gonna get it?"

"Real soon. How about we go day after tomorrow?"

"I can't wait that long."

"All right, we'll go down to Naples Boat Mart tomorrow, after work."

I hated bribing Mark, but it was the only thing he responded to.

27

MILLER

One of the things I learned from my dad was the importance of holding daily meetings. Not the big, whole-company types but each department. It was something he said he learned from the Ritz Carlton.

When the big-box retailers like Home Depot and Lowes started to invade his territory, Dad knew competing on price was a race to the bottom. He had a friend working at the Ritz on Vanderbilt Beach, and he asked him how the Ritz got away with such high prices. His buddy told him it was level of service more than the accommodations.

My dad adopted one of the tenets they used: mandating daily meetings before opening, with the staff of each department. It was essentially a reminder, but it engaged our people, and we'd won best in class for two decades running.

I looked at the sign my dad had made. It said it all: "Customer service is nothing more than delivering a product. Anybody can do that. Our goal is to make the customer feel good about buying it at Miller's."

The intercom buzzed. "Mr. Miller, Charlie Riley from Boat Mart is on line one."

He was probably checking in; he saw us at the boat show. I wanted to blow the call off, but I always encouraged customer follow-up. "Hello, Charlie. How are you?"

"Good, Bill. Is everything all right?"

"Yes, all's well. We're thinking of coming in, see what you have."

"Great, let me know. Say, I just got a call from a dealer over in Broward County and thought you should know about it."

"What's this about?"

"Said the police were looking for the Crownline you traded in about ten years ago."

I stiffened. "That's odd. Why'd he call you?"

"The boat business is small; everybody knows everybody. He figured I'd want to know."

"Thanks, but whatever they want with it, it has nothing to do with us."

I shook my head. They located the boat much faster than I anticipated. What did that mean?

A replay of Mark pulling up to the dock, nine years ago, filled my head. Where was Katie, I wondered, surveying the backyard.

The tropical breeze went still. I don't know why, but I knew at that moment, something was wrong. Very wrong.

I stepped off the lanai, onto the grass, and looked around. Not a soul in sight. Mark picked up the hose and was spraying water onto the bow of the boat. He was too methodical. The stream of water too narrow.

He moved the nozzle closer to the boat's surface, never flinching as the water rebounded onto him. I'd have to get a change of clothes for him. He'd have to undress in the garage.

After they dried, I'd put his clothes in the laundry so Cathy wouldn't get mad.

I stood there for a solid five minutes as he pelted the bow with water. It didn't make sense; the only thing Mark was fastidious about were the brass fittings. He'd polish them endlessly, ignoring the lake scum on the fiberglass. I had to remind him to rinse off the entire boat or he'd ignore it.

As he doused the windshield with water, I took a couple of strides toward the lake. A stand of mango trees cut off the view, and I was hoping Katie was hunting for a ripe piece of fruit. She wasn't there.

I headed to the dock. Mark was pelting the leather chairs with water. They were made for the wet world of boating, not for being submerged. "Hey, Mark!" He glanced my way but went back to drowning the cushions.

"How was the lake?"

He shrugged.

"Where'd Katie go?"

Another shrug.

He had shut down. Confirmation that something set him off. I sidled up to him. "Here, give me the hose. I'll do the stern. Why don't you take the skis off and polish up the cleats?"

He handed me the hose but didn't look me in the eye. "You have an argument with Katie?"

The nod and shrug combo didn't say as much as the way he threw the water skis onto the dock.

"You can't toss them around like that. They'll crack, and it'll be hard to—"

He scowled and walked toward the house. "Where you going?"

I dropped the hose and followed him. "Mark, come on now. Everything is going to be all right."

I put my hand on his shoulder and he shook it off. "Don't go in the house like that. Aunt Cathy will go crazy; you're soaked to the bone."

It was as if he were deaf. He walked onto the deck and into the house, dripping wet. I followed behind, grabbing a kitchen towel to mop up after him.

As he stomped up the stairs, I said, "Jump in the shower, and I'll put a couple of burgers on, okay?"

The door to his apartment slammed shut. I went to the front door, peering out the window. No Katie, no anyone. I went back on the lanai, my dread rising with each step I took toward the lake.

It was a Sunday and quiet. I hit the dock and examined the outside of the boat. Nothing amiss. I hopped on board. It looked in order. I spied the hatch and held my breath as I pulled it open. Nothing but life vests.

Breathing a sigh of relief, I eyed the bench seat across the rear and swallowed. I lifted the cushioned lid. The compartment below was empty. Where was the anchor? What happened to it?

I was stricken with a growing horror. My thoughts scrambled as I tried to rationalize the situation. I wanted to call Katie's house to see if she was there, but deep down I knew she wasn't. And calling would leave a suspicious trail.

It was the first conscious act I'd done to manage the unfortunate development. It had worked for a decade. I just had to keep it together until this storm passed.

28

Luca

I was on the phone with Mary Ann when Derrick came into the office. He gave me the thumbs-up with both hands and stood in front of my desk.

"You sure you're feeling okay?"

Mary Ann had slept late and was moving slower than usual at breakfast. She said she was fine, but I knew she didn't want me to worry. "All right, then. I'll see you later."

I hung up and Derrick said, "Is she all right?"

I shrugged. "She said so, but I don't know."

"Why don't you go home?"

"Can't. What did you get on Pearson?"

"Guess who Miller's next door-neighbor saw?"

Hosting a kid's game show figured to be in my partner's future. "Amanda?"

"Yep."

"He knows her?"

"No, but he remembered seeing a big girl that afternoon. Said she was skulking around."

"Skulking?"

"His words. I had to look it up. It means keeping out of sight or acting sinister."

I didn't know that but nodded like I knew what it meant. "What else did he say?"

"Nothing. He said he and his wife were going out, and he saw her when he pulled out of the driveway."

"And nobody talked to this guy?"

"Nope. You want to organize a lineup, see if he can pick her out?"

"It's been around ten years. Unless he knew her, I can't see him identifying her."

"He didn't know Pearson."

"We need a nine-year-old picture of her."

"I'll check with Barron Collier High."

"Perfect."

"Why don't you blow out of here, and make sure Mary Ann is okay?"

"I have to make a stop first. I want to talk to Benny Alston."

THE LOT for Miller's Building Supply was busy. Squeezing into a spot next to the shopping cart corral, I headed inside. A customer service girl with the longest earrings I'd ever seen, pointed to a man talking to a woman. He was sitting on a riding mower, laughing.

"Excuse me, Mr. Alston. Can I have a word?"

Alston eyed me and excused himself. "What can I do for you?"

I flashed my badge and he stiffened. "You want to talk outside?"

We went into the parking lot. As we put on sunglasses, Alston said, "Nice day."

"We could use a little rain."

"If you believe the weather reports, it's going to rain every day."

He was right. Just about every day, the forecast called for rain. It was wrong more often than right. "God created weathermen to make economists look good."

He smiled. "I like that. There's a couple of tables outside the pizzeria."

We sat around an iron table, and he said, "What do you want to talk to me for?"

It was unusual that he'd waited so long to ask what I wanted. "Kate Swift."

Alston frowned. "Oh yeah, they found her on the Millers' property."

"Tell me how well you knew her."

"I didn't really know her. You know, just through the Millers. They were close to her."

"Tell me about the day she went missing, June 1, 2013."

"Uh, we—me and Billy, played golf in the morning. We've been playing every Sunday forever. Then he dropped me off, and I heard she'd gone missing."

"You never saw her that day?"

"No."

It was too bad Alston was wearing sunglasses. He was lying, and his facial expression could be useful. "You sure about that?"

"Oh yeah, we did see her on the way home. The kid was walking, and Bill pulled her over to see if she wanted a lift."

"Did you give her a ride?"

"No. She was near her house."

"You said the Millers were close to Kate Swift. How so?"

"She was there a lot. Kate used to go with Mark Miller before the accident."

"The one that Miller's mother died in?"

"Yeah. It was nasty."

"You were driving. What happened?"

"Some nutjob cut across the road, and I swerved to avoid him. I swear, the guy must've been drunk."

"The other driver was male?"

"Yeah, I think so."

"What kind of car?"

"Oh, I don't remember. It was ten years ago."

"Something that tragic sticks with you."

"Yeah, it does, but it happened so quick, and it was at night."

"How did you know it was a male driving if it was nighttime?"

"I don't get it. Why all the questions about the accident?"

"It involves a person of interest."

"Oh, I get it, you're looking at Mark. Right?"

"What leads you to that conclusion?"

"You know the kid isn't right. The impact from the accident messed up his brain."

"Suffering a traumatic brain injury doesn't make you a killer."

"I know, but he changed."

"How?"

"I don't like to talk about him. I've known the family a long time. They've been good to me."

"We can do this here, or I can haul you in."

"Come on, I feel like I'm ratting the kid out."

"A young girl was murdered; telling what you know isn't a betrayal, it's your civic duty."

"I know but..."

"Spit it out."

Benny leaned forward. "Like I said, Mark used to go with Katie. I don't know how he ever got her interested, but the two of them had something, you know."

"Was the relationship volatile?"

"Tough to say. I never saw anything, but tell you the truth, he was weird even before the accident. I mean he used to catch rabbits and torture them."

"You saw him do that?"

"No, Billy told me. But one time I saw a squirrel he'd nailed to a tree. I almost threw up."

Cruelty to animals was a good precursor to violent behavior toward humans. "And you're sure Mark Miller did it?"

"Yeah. When I told Billy, he said Mark did it a bunch of times."

"In your opinion, did Mark become more violent after the accident?"

"Oh yeah, no doubt. He'd throw temper tantrums like crazy. One time, at the store, he knocked over two displays when he didn't get his way."

"Over what?"

"Who knows? The kid loses it every now and then."

"Do you believe he would harm Kate Swift?"

29

MILLER

Mark bounded into my office. "Can we go now?"

He was forgetful about a lot of things, but I knew he wouldn't forget my promise to get the boat today. "Did you finish filing all the folders away?"

"Yeah, let's go. Come on."

I shut my laptop and smiled. "This is going to look good tied up at the dock."

"I couldn't sleep the whole night."

Locking my office door, I said, "Remind me to make sure to use the old boat as a trade-in."

"Can't we keep both?"

"No, there's no reason to."

"But—"

"Stop it, Mark. One boat is enough. Aunt Cathy will go crazy if we keep the old one."

He sulked as we made our way down the stairs. "Cheer up, man. I bet if I hold out and bust the sales guy's butt, they'll deliver it tomorrow."

As we headed out the door, he said, "We can't take it home today?"

"I don't think so."

"No fair, no fair."

I stopped in my tracks. It wasn't his tantrum. It was Benny. He was talking to Detective Luca.

Mark tugged on my arm. "Come on, let's get the boat."

As soon as we parked in the dealer's lot, Mark bolted out of the car and ran toward the showroom. I pulled my phone out and called Benny. It went straight to voice mail.

Was he still talking to the detective? A gurgle of bile crept up my throat at the thought he was in Luca's car, heading to the station to spill his guts. I'd kill the bastard if he sunk us.

I could see Mark through the window. He was standing aboard the boat we were buying. His smile was as wide as it was before the accident. I hustled inside.

PULLING up the driveway to our house, I said, "Don't say anything to Aunt Cathy about the boat."

"Why? Why can't I?"

"I didn't mention it to her, and she might get mad."

"Why would she be mad?"

"Because when you're married, you should tell your wife if you're going to spend a lot of money."

"But it's your money."

"It is, but do me a favor, will you?"

"Okay, okay." He moved his hand over his mouth.

"Thanks. I'll tell her. You go wash up for dinner."

We entered the house. Cathy was in the family room, and I held my breath as Mark said, "Hi, Aunt Cathy."

"Hello, Mark."

"Did you have a good day today?"

"Yes. It was the best. The best ever."

I said, "Go wash up, Mark."

He bounded up the stairs to his apartment. Cathy said, "He's in a good mood. What did you do?"

"We ordered a new boat."

"Why? The one we have is fine."

"It's old. We got it nine years ago. You're going to love the new one."

"You know I don't enjoy boats."

"You'll like this one. Besides, he really liked it and so do I."

"You can't keep catering to his every whim."

"It was my idea. He never asked or said anything about it."

"You took him to the boat show."

"So? We go to classic car shows all the time, and I never bought him one."

"Okay. I give up."

I massaged her shoulders. "It's not a fight, hon. It's just a boat, that's all. I'm sorry, I should've let you know before I said anything to him."

"It's all right." She smiled. "But this is going to cost you."

"Hey, no fair."

"I'm thinking the black pearl earrings we saw at Saks is a fair trade."

I tried to remember the price. "Earrings?"

"Go get changed before they ratchet up the price tag."

I closed the bedroom door and dialed Benny again. It went to voice mail. "Benny, call me. It's urgent."

JUST BEFORE GOING into Weinstein's office, I said to Mark, "The boat's pretty cool, huh?"

"Oh yeah, when are they bringing it?"

"After we're done here."

"How long is it going to take?"

"If you keep your answers short, it'll go fast."

"Okay, okay."

"Don't say more than you were on the lake with Kate and she had to go home. You docked the boat and she got off. Right?"

"Okay, okay."

"She walked away and you stayed on the boat."

"I did?"

"Sure. You had to clean it, right?"

"Yeah, it gets all sprayed with the lake water."

"Exactly. Come on, let's go in."

We sat around an oval table in the conference room decorated with expensive art. Weinstein smiled at Mark. "You're looking well, young man."

"You too."

"Thank you. Now, I've reviewed the questions submitted by the sheriff's department, and there is nothing to be concerned about. I'll read them one by one, and you think about it before responding. If you want to retract, um, take back something you said, we will. I work for you, and anything you tell me, I can't tell anyone without your express consent."

Mark looked at me.

"It's all good. He's going to help us, and then we'll jump on the new boat."

"You know, we got a new boat. You want to come on it?"

"I'm very busy today, but perhaps another time. Let's get started."

The first five questions were easy, confirming who he was, where he lived and whether he knew Kate Swift. I held my breath when Weinstein asked, "What was the nature of your relationship with Kate Swift."

"We were going to be married."

I said, "You were friends, right?"

"Yeah. Best friends forever."

"We'll go with friends. How long did you know her?"

"My whole life."

I said, "Not exactly. Mark was around ten when they met."

"Okay. They want to know what happened on June 1, 2013."

I said, "Nothing happened. Kate came over, and she and Mark took a ride on the boat. Then, she left and went home."

I looked at Mark, who said, "That's what we did."

"All right. Did you see Ms. Swift after the boat ride?"

"Who?"

"Kate Swift. Did you see her after the two of you went for a boat ride?"

"No, no. I didn't. I swear."

"Okay. I'll organize the response and send it to you for approval."

I stood before he finished. "Great. Let's go."

We went outside, and as I was commending Mark, my phone rang. It was Benny.

30

I answered the call, saying, "Hang on a minute." I covered the phone and said, "Mark, wait in the car."

"But we got to go. I want to go on the boat."

"You will! Now, get in the car before I tell the man to take the boat back."

"You—"

"Get in the car! This is an important call."

"Okay, okay. Hurry up."

Looking like he was about to cry, I said, "I'll be fast, then we'll take a ride on the boat." He hurried into the car, the door slammed, and I said, "Benny. Why the hell didn't you call me back?"

"I lost my phone. I mean, I got it back, but—"

"I saw you. You were talking to Detective Luca. Why? Why didn't you tell me?"

"He showed up at the store. What was I supposed to do?"

"What did he want?"

"Wanted to know about Kate. Asked about the day she went missing and about Mark."

"Mark? What did you tell him?"

"Not much. Just, you know, that we saw her, but I didn't say it right away; he knew we saw her walking home."

"Are you sure?"

"Yeah, what are you worried about?"

"I don't want anybody talking to the police. It feels like they're trying to frame Mark or something."

"You think so? I didn't get that impression from the detective."

I wasn't going to reply about his feelings. "I don't want you talking to them."

"What am I supposed to do? I can't tell them to screw off."

"Let me talk to our lawyer, Weinstein. I'll see if he can represent you as well. These cops are looking to pin this on somebody, and it isn't going to be a Miller."

"Are you sure Mark didn't have something to do with it?"

"What are you talking about? Mark didn't do anything. He and Katie were as close as you can get."

"I'm just saying, you know, after the accident, he just ain't the same."

"Mark's fine. They're picking on him because he's an easy target. They don't care who they blame as long as they can close the case."

"I guess so."

"I've got to go. If the police contact you, I want to know about it."

"Okay."

"I'll let you know what Weinstein says. But in the meantime, don't talk to them."

"What if they come around again? What do I say?"

"That you're busy and have a lawyer. They can't force you to talk; you have rights."

I hung up and wanted to call Weinstein, but Mark had opened the car door. "I'm coming. Let's go see our new boat."

As I drove, I thought about Benny. Greg was right; Benny couldn't be trusted. All these years Dad protected him. How the hell could he talk to the police without telling me?

I was stupid to continue to let the slacker slide. He was dead weight. I wanted to start putting distance between us. I'd need to find someone to round out the foursome and come up with a good excuse. He was a decent golfer, but he was a good-time Charlie and that was it.

We probably had enough in his employment file to justify cutting him loose, but I'd check. I couldn't see Benny filing a complaint with the labor department, but one thing he did know how to do was work the system.

A beeping horn, and Mark telling me the light was green, snapped me out of the thought Benny could throw us under the bus somehow. I never told him anything, but he was too close to Mark. From piecing things together, I knew Mark had to tell him something. It was my fault. I'd used Benny to occupy Mark when I needed time for myself.

I mean, how much can one person be expected to do? I was running a large business and didn't spend enough time with my wife because of Mark. Somebody had to keep an eye on him and it fell on me. Just like saving and running the business. It was all on me, I thought as we pulled up our driveway.

"There it is! Stop the car. I gotta get out."

"All right. Go ahead, I'll meet you at the dock."

Mark ran to the lake, and I pulled in the garage. I stayed in the car and made a call.

"Mr. Weinstein, it's Bill Miller."

"How are you?"

"Okay, but I wanted to let you know that detective went to see a family friend and employee named Benny Alston."

"I'm assuming this is in regard to the Swift case?"

"Yes. Can't we do something about it?"

"The police are within their rights to question him if he knew the victim."

"He did, but I'd like you to represent him, have everything go through your office."

"I'm not sure that sends the proper message to the investigators. It could signal a conspiracy. What are you concerned about?"

"Nothing. I don't like them hassling our employees."

"It's customary. Trying to interfere might backfire, intensifying their scrutiny of your family. It's my learned advice not to get involved. If Mr. Alston decides to engage counsel, I can offer several recommendations."

"I'll let you know. Thanks."

Walking down to the lake, I decided against getting a lawyer for Benny. Beside the obligation of an attorney to protect Benny, it would diminish my influence on him. I had to keep him close, make sure he stayed in line.

31

LUCA

Reading through the interviews that had been conducted after Kate Swift disappeared, it was hard for me to keep my criticism to a minimum. I'd learned it was easy to look back with the benefit of hindsight and see where a fellow officer had forgotten something or overlooked a piece of evidence.

It was bound to happen to me one day, and ripping up a colleague who was dealing with half the facts accomplished nothing. In fact, it was counterproductive and weakened the cooperative spirit that was the hallmark of most investigations.

Movies and television programming were full of cop shows featuring crooked and incompetent officers and law enforcement officials. The reality was much different; I'd run into just two cops that weren't up to the job: one who planted evidence and another who'd shaken down a drug dealer. That was out of hundreds and hundreds of fellow officers.

Both interviews with Bill Miller were as defensive as they got. He barely acknowledged knowing Kate Swift. He also never mentioned running into her on the way home, offering her a ride she supposedly declined.

I didn't like that his answers were exact replicas even though there were nine days separating the interviews. To me, it was a sign they'd been rehearsed.

Minimizing his interaction seemed to placate the detective at the time, but he didn't know the body would be found on Miller's property or that Miller had seen Swift earlier that day.

Adding in that he'd tried to prevent a wall from being built where the body was buried, raised his profile as a suspect. On the other hand, Bill Miller was a prominent businessman and married, with a lot to lose by getting involved with a teenage girl.

On the surface, it didn't make sense. But I'd seen many men go astray, either in a mutual relationship or out of lust. I didn't know Kate Swift, but I'm sure she was as impressionable as most teenagers, and Miller had plenty in the impression cabinet.

Knowing that uncovering a sexual transgression by Bill Miller, with anyone, would catapult him into the lead-suspect slot, I flipped the page to Greg Miller. I scanned past the formalities at the beginning of the interview with Bill Miller's brother.

His brother hadn't been at the house the day Kate Swift vanished, and the initial interview was short and unproductive. However, the second time he spoke to the detective, he claimed to have seen Kate walking on Goodlette-Frank Road at four o'clock.

The timing of that sighting had to be why the detective didn't concentrate on Bill or Mark Miller. I checked the date of the second interview: June 11. I flipped back to Bill

Miller's second interview. It was conducted on June 10. Had they fabricated Greg seeing Kate?

I reread the transcript. Greg Miller had been in Atlanta for the weekend. He parked his car in the short-term lot at Regional Southwest Airport and said he noticed Kate as he drove home.

Checking his address, Greg lived close to Royal Poinciana Golf Club. Why wouldn't he have taken the Pine Ridge Road exit if he was coming from the airport? I scanned the text. Delta Airlines was mentioned. It was nine years ago, and warrant or not, who knew what kind of data was kept by the airline or parking lot.

While I contemplated a verification method, Derrick swept into the room, saying, "The neighbor ID'd Pearson."

"He remembered her for sure?"

"He said no doubt. Said she reminded him of his niece. He even dug out a picture of the girl, and she does look like Pearson."

"Hmm, so we know Amanda Pearson was there that afternoon."

"And she was skulking around."

"You like that word, huh?"

Derrick smiled. "Yeah. My mother always said to use a new word as often as possible so you won't forget it."

"She's right."

"Say, how's Mary Ann feeling?"

"A bit better, thanks."

"You hear back on that new drug?"

"We're going Tuesday."

"Fantastic."

"Yeah, I'm waiting to hear back from the drug company on cutting us a break. The insurance company is not covering it."

"Bastards."

"It's all right. I just hope it works. If it does, we'll figure it out. Let's get back to the case."

"What do you want to do with Pearson? Bring her in?"

"She's tough and has been arrested before. I can't see her cracking unless we have something concrete."

"What about pressing some of her friends?"

"Good angle but start with anyone who's been in trouble or has a pending court hearing. Maybe she bragged about it to them, and if we're lucky, whoever she told may be receptive to cutting a deal."

"I'll go see Sanchez, have his guys put a tail on her, see where she hangs out."

"Good. Look, the Millers are heating up."

"What's going on?"

"Couple of things. I was going to tell Remin we're ready to bring Mark Miller in, but something in an old interview needs checking out."

"What do you need?"

"Greg Miller backed up his brother's claim that Swift left their house. He claimed to have seen Swift on Goodlette-Frank, walking home around four. It just feels too convenient to me. He never mentioned it in the initial interview."

"He was away, I think in Atlanta."

"That's what he said. So we need to check with Delta. We don't need passenger lists at this point, but check the departure and arrival times into Fort Myers for what flights they had on June first back then."

"I'm on it."

"Thanks. I'll go see Remin."

I hustled down the stairs after seeing the sheriff. After hearing what Benny Alston said about Mark Miller, Remin was on board with bringing Mark in. Leaving my jacket on, I dialed Weinstein and told him his client had to come in.

Weinstein was matter of fact about it, surprising me. We set up the interview for tomorrow morning.

32

MILLER

My phone vibrated. It was Weinstein. I got up from the table. "Sorry, hon, I've got to get this. We're in trouble with the Collier Group; they're threatening to pull the contract."

"Go ahead. I'll clean up."

I stepped onto the deck. "What's going on?"

"I've set up a meeting with Detective Luca."

"Have you lost your mind?"

"They want to question Mark."

"No fucking way."

"Take it easy, Bill. It's going to be all right."

"Says who? Mark isn't up to it. He'll say something, and we'll be screwed."

"Don't tell me the details, but are you concealing his involvement?"

"No, no. I'm worried he'll say something stupid and the police will run with it."

"We can invoke the Fifth Amendment, refusing to answer questions in which Mark might incriminate himself."

"So, he doesn't have to answer anything?"

"No, the Fifth Amendment doesn't offer protection from questioning, just a remedy for self-incrimination."

"What if he says something about, uh, Greg or me that makes it look like we're involved?"

"He'd have to answer."

"I don't like that. He's, uh, not really stable, if you know what I mean."

"Then I'd suggest we explore the possibility of having a judge rule on his competency."

"What would that entail?"

"Mark would undergo psychiatric evaluation to determine whether he has sufficient capacity to observe, remember, and narrate events, as well as understand his duty to tell the truth."

"Ugh, I'd hate to put him through all that."

"I understand. You should also be aware that it's not without consequence."

"What can happen?"

"It will heighten their suspicion, and if there is something there, they'll keep digging until they find it. It doesn't protect him from prosecution."

"What do you suggest?"

"I think we should proceed with the interview. I'm going to lay the ground rules over how it's conducted. I'll decide what questions he'll answer and end it if I feel it's leading to incrimination."

"Can we do it at my house?"

"The interview?"

"Yes. Mark will be less, uh, agitated."

"That would be unconventional. If we do it at our offices, I believe they'll be amenable to the change in venue."

I was torn between the familiarity of our home versus the perceived invasion of his safe space. "Okay. Set it up."

———

WEINSTEIN'S OFFICE was on the ground floor of a glass office building on the corner of Route Forty-One and Neapolitan Way. I pulled into a spot and before shutting the car off, turned to Mark. "Now, remember what we talked about?"

"I know, I know. Listen to Mr. Weinstein."

"And don't say anything about what happened to Kate. All you know is she came over and you took a boat ride. Right?"

Mark nodded. "Uh-huh."

"After the ride, she left, and you stayed on the boat to clean it."

"Like I always do, right?"

"Exactly."

"They ask what happened, you say you don't know. Okay?"

"Yep."

"After this is over. We'll go to Dick's Sporting Goods and get some new water skis."

"Really?"

"Definitely. Just make sure you don't say anything more than you took Kate on the boat for a ride, then she left, and you washed the boat."

"You have to clean the boat; the lake water gets on it."

"It does. All right, let's get this over with."

Weinstein met us in his office. After greeting us, he said, "They're waiting in the conference room. Mark, you need to keep your answers short. A simple yes or no will suffice for many questions. If I feel the answer you're giving is problematic, I'll put my hand on your forearm. When I do, you should stop speaking. Understand?"

"Yeah, okay."

"If you're uncertain of how to answer a question, ask for a break. They have to allow us to confer."

"What about if I have to piss?"

"Just let us know and we'll pause the session."

I liked the way Weinstein took command, but I said, "Remember, you took Kate for a boat ride, and when she left, you stayed at the dock and cleaned the boat."

Mark nodded and Weinstein, eyebrows still raised, said, "Shall we?"

I was surprised Detective Luca was alone. He stood and we shook hands. He smiled at Mark. "There's nothing to be afraid of here. I have a couple of questions to ask, that's all."

He was playing good cop, hoping to gain my brother's confidence to nail us to the wall. I touched Mark's arm, guiding him into a chair between Weinstein and I.

Luca slid a recording device to the center of the table and after hitting record, recited formalities. The first couple of questions were softballs. I tensed when Luca asked, "What time did Kate Swift come to your house?"

Mark looked at me. I said, "Around two."

Luca glared at me. "If you're not going to allow him to answer, I'll have to ask you to leave the room."

"What's the matter, Billy?"

"Nothing, Mark. It's okay."

Luca said, "Who was at the house when Kate came over?"

"Uh, me and Billy."

"What did you do with Kate?"

"We went on the boat. I gave her a ride; we used to always go for rides. She liked it—"

I kicked Mark's leg, and he looked at me. Weinstein said, "Next question."

Luca cleared his throat. "How long was the boat ride?"

"Uh, I don't know. Like, normal."

"Where on the lake did you go?"

"All over, like we always did."

"How did you decide to end the boat ride?"

"Uh, I don't know; we just did."

I could hear the detective's phone vibrating as he asked, "Did you argue or fight with Kate while you were on the boat?"

"Uh, I wanted her to drive, like she used to, but she wouldn't. I kept asking but she didn't want to."

"You were angry with her?"

Mark shrugged. "I don't know."

"Did you try to force her?"

"She wouldn't take the wheel. I kept asking her."

"Did you hit Kate when she refused to drive?"

When Mark said, "On the boat?" I jumped up, grabbing Mark's forearm. "It's time for a break."

Luca narrowed his eyes but remained silent. He stole a glance at his phone as Weinstein said, "Please give us a moment. Can I get you anything?"

"No."

We retreated to Weinstein's office, leaving Mark with his secretary. Weinstein closed the door, saying, "You were mistaken to interrupt the questioning."

"You said you were going to control what went on. You didn't do anything."

"Mark was not going to incriminate himself. Even if he forced her or even struck her, it doesn't prove he killed her."

"Are you crazy? They find out he did something, they're not going to let up."

"I disagree. She got off the boat and left your property. You saw her leave. Your brother Greg saw her an hour later, near her home. Whatever happened on the boat didn't lead to her death."

He didn't know that I never saw Kate leave my home or that Greg had lied to back me up. "I don't know."

"You hired me to represent you, and my advice is to let me handle this."

"Are you sure?"

"Yes."

"All right."

When we entered the conference room, Luca was on the phone. He hung up and said, "Something has come up. We'll have to continue this another time."

Watching the detective leave, confirmed that stopping the interview was the right move. Who knew what Mark would have said, if we went along with the way Weinstein wanted to handle it?

33

Phone in hand, I hustled to the car, pressing dial. Derrick answered on the first ring. "Hey, I ended the interview. They're hiding something, but fill me in on what we got."

"Forty-eight-year-old female, found shot dead on her lanai in Park Shore. Her name's Sylvia Taras."

"Who found the body?"

"Husband, Paul Taras."

The fact it was midafternoon was a flag. "We know what he does for a living?"

"Not yet. Why?"

"If he works a nine-to-fiver, he'd better have a good reason for being home at two in the afternoon."

"Yep, and it's the spouse."

"We start with him. You call Bilotti?"

"Yeah, he's on the way."

"I'm minutes away from Park Shore. What's the address?"

"Seventeen Turtle Hatch Road."

"Meet you there."

I made a U-turn on 41 and headed toward the crime

scene, thinking about the Millers. The kid was off a bit, but he seemed bright and competent enough not to be managed by his brother Bill.

There was no doubt. Bill Miller was protecting someone. The question was whether it was his brother or if he'd been responsible for Kate's death. Bill Miller was afraid of what Mark would say, but I put it at fifty-fifty whether it was self-incrimination he was concerned about.

I wondered about the possibility forensics might be able to get evidence from the boat. It had been exposed to the elements and Bilotti had said getting to Saturn was easier. But I had an idea.

I turned down Neapolitan Way, catching a glimpse of the sign for Hogfish Harry's. I loved the grouper dish they made with brussels sprouts and leeks. I made a mental note to tell Mary Ann I wanted to go there for my birthday and turned left onto Belair Lane.

Park Shore was a neighborhood in the middle of a complete makeover. Modest homes were being replaced by contemporary homes that were too big for the lots. I wondered if the Turtle Hatch crime scene was on the western side, backing up to Venetian Bay. Those homes were always expensive, but these days, a couple of million would only get you the dirt.

The Tarases' house wasn't on the bay side, but it was still impressive. Prices had ratcheted up so fast, it was hard to put a number on the coastal-looking home, but it was more than I could afford in three lifetimes of busting my tail.

Two marked cars blocked the gray paver driveway. I pulled behind Derrick's SUV. He was talking to a uniformed officer at the entrance.

He came down to meet me. "Hey, Frank. I was the second to arrive and didn't touch anything."

"Good. Does it look like a robbery gone wrong?"

"I don't think so. I checked, and there's nothing obvious to suggest a break-in or invasion."

"Husband?"

"He's sitting in Leonetti's car. You want to talk to him?"

"Not until I see the scene."

"Let's go, then."

I signed in, and we entered the home after donning gloves and booties.

Derrick said, "This is some place."

We stood in the double-storied foyer. "Nice. Feels like it's been remodeled."

"Must've cost a ton."

My eyes swept across the main living area. A waterfall-marble island anchored a kitchen open to the family room. Light flooded in from a bank of sliders that made up the rear of the house. "These kinds of people don't drink the same coffee we do."

"What? Oh, I get it."

"Where's the body?"

"Outside, by the outdoor kitchen."

The homes were tightly packed in Park Shore, and greenery provided more privacy than I expected. It was a plus for the homeowners but presented a problem for me.

Slumped over, the victim was lying on a chaise lounge. Blood-soaked, her beige top had two small-caliber bullet holes in the upper chest area. Kneeling, I touched her arm; rigor mortis had begun to set in.

I checked the ground for shells but came up empty. "Look around. See if you can find any casings." The back of the chaise lounge was intact. It looked like the bullets were inside the victim.

I put the back of my hand to the glass of water sitting on

the side table. It was warm. "Bilotti will confirm, but it looks like she's been dead about three hours."

"So, that'd put the shooting at around eleven."

"Call Sanchez. Ask him to have a couple of officers go door to door, see what the neighbors might have heard or seen around that time."

I circled the body. She was well kept, looking younger than her age. A paperback, featuring a bare-chested man, had fallen into her lap. There were no glasses.

"Make a note to see if she wore contacts."

"Got it. Gianelli's here. And the doctor is right behind him."

"Good. Let's document the scene before the doc does his thing."

Derrick escorted the photographer to the body, and I met Bilotti in the kitchen. "Hey, Doc."

"Hello, Frank. What do we have?"

"Looks like a homicide. Two gunshots to the chest."

"Been awhile since we've had one."

"I know. But bad timing. We're closing in on that cold case."

"The female remains from the Miller property?"

"Yes. If it's what it appears to be at this point, it'll be a satisfying one to clear."

"A win for the good guys."

"You know, Doc, with all the advances in forensics and cameras everywhere imaginable, you'd think we'd be solving more murders than ever, yet the unsolved rates have gone from twenty percent to forty over the last couple of decades."

"That's a nationwide statistic, and labs are buried with samples."

"I know, it's not helping."

"They should put you in charge; you'd make a dent in the numbers."

"Thanks, Doc, but with all the gang-related killings and serial killers, I wouldn't want the job if it existed."

Bilotti smiled. "Looks like Gianelli is done."

"Good. I'm counting on you to make this an easy one for me."

The medical examiner stepped onto the lanai and surveyed the scene. It was one of the things I liked and disliked about his methodology. He approached it like a homicide detective, but I was impatient and wanted to get on the hunt for whoever did it, not watch him waste time.

Bilotti moved slowly, like someone twice his forty-five years of age. I whispered in Derrick's ear that rigor mortis must be contagious, and he started chuckling. Elbowing him, I stepped in front of him as Bilotti took the corpse's temperature.

I said, "I think she either knew the shooter or was completely surprised."

Bilotti nodded. "No defensive wounds, and she doesn't appear to have been attempting to get up."

"We're going to talk to the husband; he found her."

34

MILLER

I got dressed for work feeling rested. It was the first night I'd gotten a decent sleep in a while. We hadn't heard from the police, but you couldn't miss the news on the shooting in Park Shore.

I popped a Nespresso pod in the machine and smiled. It was crazy to say but I was grateful; the murder had become a priority for the sheriff's office. I'd deny it, but I was hoping we had a serial killer on the loose.

The detectives who investigated Katie's disappearance were more trusting than Detective Luca. They respected the Miller name that Dad had worked so hard to build. Luca sounded like a New Yorker, and I was worried he wouldn't give up as easily as the others did.

I stepped onto the lanai. The TV was on. Cathy was sipping a coffee and watching the news. "Good morning. You slept in."

I pecked her cheek. "Finally got a decent night's sleep."

"I know, you were snoring like a foghorn."

"Sorry."

"It's a beautiful morning."

"I know. I was thinking of taking the convertible in."

"It's a top-down day. You better take advantage of it; a tropical storm is due to blow in tomorrow night."

"We could use the rain. What are you up to today?"

"I'm going to lunch with Evelyn. We want to try that new place on Fifth."

"What restaurant?"

"I think it's called Maritime or something like that. They took over the space that used to be Annabelle's, then was Café Lurcat."

"Right, I knew they were about to open. I think Roger put some money behind those guys. If it's good, we'll go next week."

"Okay. But let's go alone. I'm tired of your brother tagging along."

I didn't like the way she said "your brother" but she was right. We needed alone time. I'd ask Benny to stop by and check in on Mark. "Sounds good. I'll pick up some tacos for him. See you later. Say hello to Evey for me."

———

GREG SAID, "I don't like the entrance being off-center." He pointed to the drawings for the new store we were standing over. "Either make it dead center or all the way to the left. People are trained to go right."

"Good point. It 'orphans' the seasonal section. And that's where the good margins are."

"We want shoppers to pass through it. They'll see something they'd normally wait on buying."

My cell vibrated. "Let me get this. It's Weinstein."

"Hello, this is Bill."

"Hello, Mr. Miller. How are you?"

"Good. We're in the middle of something. Can this wait?"

"Not really."

I collapsed into my chair. "What's going on?"

"I received a call from Detective Luca. He's making inquiries regarding the boat that you had at the time of Kate Swift's disappearance."

"What does he want to know?"

"Who it was sold or given to."

"That was nine years ago."

"There's nothing to be gained by being uncooperative."

"Damn it, Weinstein, did I say I wasn't going to cooperate?"

"If you'd like, you can call me when you, uh, have the time."

"I will. Goodbye."

Greg said, "That didn't sound good. What's the matter?"

I took deep breath, reminding myself to calm down. "He got a call from the detective looking for information on the boat we had back when Katie went missing."

"Shit! He knows something."

"Take it easy, Greg."

"He knows it happened on the boat. You said the detective was asking Mark if he hit her on the boat."

"He was fishing for information."

"He's got to be looking for blood or DNA or something."

"Nine years have gone by. What the hell could they find?"

"You traded it in, right?"

"Yeah, the Boat Mart took it in. Who knows where it is? It could be anywhere, the Keys, Miami..."

"Or right here."

"It doesn't matter. Let them look it over if they want."

"Oh no. This is bad. They can find traces of DNA years

later. And blood, they spray that stuff on it, and it shows up no matter how old it is."

"You're watching too much TV. It's not as easy as they make it seem. So what if they find her DNA on the boat? And blood? Whatever was on it has been mixed up with fish blood, chum, and who knows what?"

"Okay, okay but it's not a good sign. This detective isn't going to stop until he figures it out."

"He's not going to do anything. Just like the old investigators, he'll give up; you'll see."

"I don't know; we should come clean; tell them what we know. Mark's got issues; they'll go easy on him."

I got in his face. "You want him to end up in some hellhole of a mental institution? They'll drug him up so much, he'll be drooling on himself. Is that what you want?"

"No, but there's gotta be a way to end this crap. Let's talk to Weinstein, see what kind of a deal he can cut."

Though I hadn't, I said, "I already did. The both of us could be charged with obstruction and perjury."

"We can make immunity a part of the deal."

"Our reputations, the Miller name, it'd be ruined, forever."

"Yeah? Well, I'm not spending the rest of my life behind bars as an accomplice after the fact."

Greg headed for the door.

"Hold on. Let's relax. Nothing has changed. So, don't do anything stupid. I'll feel out Weinstein again if you want, okay?"

He nodded. "You will?"

"Yes."

"I think it's the way to go."

"We'll see what he says. Meanwhile, let's get back to the drawings, all right?"

"Okay."

As we went back to the table, I said, "Accessory after the fact? You didn't talk to a lawyer, did you?"

"No, I was watching *Bosch* last night and they said it."

I was relieved, but my mind was still racing. Greg was going to be tough to keep in line if things heated up, and I thought they would. I'd think it over before calling Weinstein.

Now, I was leaning toward giving them the trade-in information they wanted. The sound of distant thunder reminded me of the storm coming in. Another heavy downpour could only help dilute whatever evidence was there, if there was anything at all.

35

LUCA

Paul Taras had a tan that a man of leisure would have. His hair was professionally dyed, and he wasn't carrying any excess weight. He wasn't smiling, but when we were introduced, his teeth were too perfect to be natural.

Standing on the balls of his feet, Taras looked me in the eye as we shook hands. "I can't believe this. It's insane."

"Tell me what happened."

"Nothing happened. I came home and found her, uh, she was unresponsive. I tried to find a pulse and called nine-one-one."

"What time did you come home?"

"Around noon. You can check the time of the call. I was only here a couple of minutes, maximum."

"Do you work?"

"Yes. How do you think I pay for all this?"

"What do you do?"

"What does that have to do with what happened?"

"Routine questions. We need background in order to conduct an investigation."

"It not work related. I'm the managing partner of Krypto Might. We sell and manage digital wallets."

"For crypto currencies?"

"Yes. I don't see the relevancy."

"What were you doing home in the middle of the day?"

"My hours are flexible and I work remotely, two days a week, minimum."

"Did you notice anything missing in the house?"

"I really didn't check. I didn't even go into my bedroom."

"Let's take a walk through the home."

He led the way but hesitated as he stepped into the foyer. We went room to room. Nothing seemed amiss. We got an eyeful of diamonds when he opened his wife's jewelry drawer.

"Everything seems to be here."

Derrick asked, "Do you own a firearm?"

"Yes."

"What kind gun is it?"

"A pistol."

"Caliber?"

"I-I don't know. I think it's a thirty-eight."

That was small caliber, like the one that killed his wife. "We're going to need to take it with us."

"What? You think I did this?"

"It's protocol, Mr. Taras."

He walked into his closet and opened a drawer. I was pleased to see he stored it in a gun safe. Taras put his finger on the reader and it popped open. It was a Colt and a thirty-eight.

Derrick pulled a plastic evidence bag out, and I lifted the pistol up. Before I dropped it in the bag, I sniffed the barrel. It had been fired recently. Taras was staring at me. "It's been used. We went to the Alamo. Me and a bunch of guys a couple of days ago."

And you didn't know the caliber of the handgun? "Guys night out?"

"Kind of. Look, I'm telling you, I had nothing to do with what happened to Sylvia. You're wasting your time. The real killer is out there, so focus on finding him."

There was no use in trying to confirm his story. If we found out this was the murder weapon, he was cooked whether it checked out or not.

"You want to gather a few belongings, a change of clothes? The house is going to be off limits for a day or two to let the forensic team go over it."

"Oh yeah, right. Let me get an overnight bag."

Derrick stood with Taras, and I went to see what Bilotti was up to.

The medical examiner was combing through his hair. I said, "Anything?"

"Nothing I can see here."

"Any sign of sexual activity or molestation?"

"Nothing obvious. Her tennis shorts don't appear to have been removed. We'll perform swabs back at the office."

Office? Not the description I'd use for an autopsy suite. "And run blood panels." A soon as I said it, I knew Bilotti would consider it an insult.

Eyebrows arched, he looked at me over his glasses. "Anything else, Doctor?"

"Yeah, the name and address of the shooter would be nice."

"I suggest you leave before a mistake is made and you're loaded into a body bag."

I smiled. "Appreciate it, Doc. I didn't mean to interfere but—"

"But it's what you do, right, Frank?"

"Just a little anxious to catch the killer."

"Bye, Frank."

"See ya, Doc."

I stepped back inside the kitchen. Taras was wheeling a piece of luggage out of the master suite. Derrick beckoned with his hand. "Frank, Mr. Taras mentioned something you need to know."

We met in the family room. "What's going on?"

"I asked Mr. Taras if he knew anyone that would do something like this. He said no, but then, why don't you tell him?"

Taras said, "Well, we moved in here less than two months ago; it's actually a day over six weeks."

"It looks like you've lived here forever."

"We're kind of anal, more me than Sylvia, plus we used a white-glove mover, which really helped."

I wanted to ask how much that cost but said, "What did you tell Detective Dickson?"

"When he inquired whether we had any enemies, I said no, but I started to think, flipping through all the contacts we have, and it hit me that maybe it was a mistaken identity type of thing."

This guy was working hard to deflect attention away from himself. "And?"

"Three nights ago, we had just gone to bed. I was just about to shut my lamp off when the doorbell rang."

"What time was this?"

"Just after eleven. It was weird. I even asked Syl if I was hearing things. But she heard it too. I went to the door, and two men were standing there.

If he told me he opened the door, his credibility was taking a hit. "What did they want?"

"Frankly, I was afraid to open the door, so I asked through the door what they wanted. They kept asking for an Olga. I told them no one by that name lived here, but they kept insisting. Finally, I said we'd just moved in, and if they didn't leave, I was going to call the police."

"They left?"

"Did you see their car?"

"I'm sorry. They were parked by the curb and it felt like they had the wrong house, that's all."

"Was the former owner named Olga?"

"I don't know; the house was owned by a trust."

"What did these men look like?"

"They looked a little East European to me."

Well, that narrows it down. "They had accents?"

"Only one of them spoke. He was bigger, wore a dark tracksuit. The other man kept looking in the sidelight. It was kind of spooky, to be honest."

"Any facial hair, tattoos?"

"The big guy, he had a beard. The other was clean shaven."

"Did they or anyone else return?"

"No. Just that one time."

"Give Detective Dickson the contact information for the Realtor and attorney who handled the sale of this home."

36

LUCA

I dialed Derrick's number as soon as I started the car up. As I cranked up the air, he answered, "Hey, Frank. Everything good?"

"Just finished with Alston. He said Mark Miller can be violent, and he thinks he could've had something to do with Swift's death."

"No wonder they won't let us talk to him."

"That's what it looks like, but we'll start with the written bullshit and take it from there. Where are you?"

"Just left Fifth Third Bank. Opened a new account there, but it's only got a hundred bucks in it."

"I'll give you a check for a thousand tomorrow. Is that enough?"

"Oh man. You guys are doing too much for us."

"Don't worry about it. When you get straightened out, I'll collect from your deadbeat ass."

"Seriously, you sure? You guys don't need it?"

"No, we're okay. You get a picture of Pearson as a kid?"

"Yeah, two of them. I'm going to run it by the neighbor in the morning."

"Good. I'm on my way home."

———

THE HOUSE WAS QUIET, making me nervous. My pee alarm went off. Again. I was two hours past the deadline to relieve myself. I ran into the kitchen. Through the sliders I saw Mary Ann and Jessie lying poolside in chaise lounges. I waved at them and went into the bathroom.

I sat on the bowl. It only took ten seconds to get a flow. But it was painful. I couldn't keep ignoring my doctor's orders, or I'd end in the hospital getting new plumbing. Again.

Mary Ann was outside, which I took to mean she was feeling decent. It was a better feeling than taking a piss. Washing up, my phone rang. It was Dr. Bilotti.

"Hey, Doc, how you doing?"

"Good, Frank. You have a moment?"

"Sure. What's going on?"

"When you told me about the flare-ups Mary Ann has been experiencing, I took the liberty of reaching out to a couple of contacts."

"You did?"

"Yes. There's a promising drug; it's experimental at this point, but it may be something to consider."

"That's good news, Doc. What is it?"

"It essentially works on reducing inflammation. It's quite technical, but in short, it's an antibody agent."

"Sounds interesting."

"It may not work but it's worth investigating. I'm told

about thirty percent of patients respond favorably with reduced symptoms and a slowing of the progression."

There was a one in three chance it would help Mary Ann. Not great odds. "We've got to try this."

"I agree but it's expensive."

"I don't care."

"I understand, but you should be aware the cost is four thousand dollars a shot."

"Four grand? That's insane. How the hell do they get the nerve to charge—"

"Hold on, Frank. The pharma company has been developing this for six years. I believe they have eight hundred million in the project, and the last two efforts didn't pan out."

"Why does it cost so much?"

"Long story but years of research to identify compounds and then large-scale clinical trials to prove efficacy. It takes time and money."

I sighed. "I know it costs a ton. How do we get it for Mary Ann?"

Bilotti gave me the information we'd need. I thanked him and jogged out to the lanai.

"Dr. Bilotti just told me about a new drug for MS."

"Mom can get it?"

"Yep. It's kind of experimental, but there's a good chance it will work."

Mary Ann said, "Experimental? What about side effects?"

I was so blinded by hope that I'd never asked. "It depends on the individual. The doctors will explain it all."

"Mom, this is great news. I'm so happy."

"I bet it's not covered by insurance."

"Don't worry about that now. Let's see if it works first."

HANGING UP THE PHONE, I tossed the document the Millers' lawyer sent over onto the credenza. Before going to see the sheriff, I placed the thousand-dollar check on Derrick's desk.

The sheriff's door was open. I knocked and Remin waved me in. "Come in, Frank. You want some coffee?"

"No thanks. I had three cups already."

"Everything all right?"

"Yes, sir. Why?"

"I heard Mary Ann is, uh, having difficulties."

Gossip in organizations spread quicker than venereal disease. "She's had a couple of episodes, but she'll be okay. She's tough."

"They don't come stronger than her. I remember when she stayed on that robbery case until she nailed every one of those lowlifes."

I laughed. "As you can imagine, she doesn't let me get away with much."

Remin smiled. "Give her my regards. If you need some time off, wrapping up the Swift case would clear the deck."

And I'd let the thought Remin wasn't a political animal creep into my assessment. "Is the Swift investigation what you wanted to see me about?"

"Yes, but it has nothing to do with Mary Ann. Family comes first."

I wanted to remind him he'd just tied the two together but held my tongue. I was worried about Mary Ann's health, and who knew what the future held? I nodded instead.

"I wanted to let you know Project Help filed for a permit to hold a rally in Cambier Park in support of the Swift family."

"Project Help? They're focused on sexual assault victims."

"Primarily, but they have a support group for the loss of

loved ones. There may be a family connection as to why they're getting involved but I don't like it. It puts too much attention on the department."

"Did they organize anything when the kid went missing?"

"I don't know, but that's a good question. The best response is for us to solve this."

Us? "We're working on a couple of credible leads. One of them involves Mark Miller. He was close to the victim and one of the last people to see her. Someone close to the family is pointing the finger at him."

"How close?"

"Relationship goes back to old man Miller. Couple of decades. I think there's something there and why they hired Weinstein. We received their responses, but it was as sterile as a pediatric intensive care unit."

"Bring him in. Call Weinstein, and tell him we want to question him."

37

LUCA

I'd been exchanging nonstop texts with Derrick as we waited. Mary Ann said, "You didn't have to come. You have too much going on."

"It's okay."

"You don't have to worry about me; I'll be fine."

"You? I'm not worried about you. I'm only here to see what a four-thousand-dollar shot looks like."

She elbowed me. "Very funny. When is the drug company going to get back to you?"

I shrugged. "They said within a week. They're bringing it up to a panel that decides on relief cases."

"I hope they do something; we can't be paying this out of pocket every two weeks."

"If it helps, I'll find a way. If they cut us a break and the insurance company picks some of it up, we'll be fine."

"Jessica wants to take design classes at Parsons."

"In New York?"

"They're online. But not cheap. She wants to build up college credits."

"How much is that going to run?"

"About two thousand a credit."

"What? For an online class? It's a total scam. We should be arresting them for grand larceny."

"Mrs. Luca? We're ready for you."

We were shown into a cramped examination room. Mary Ann reached for my hand. I stroked it. She was as strong as they came, but my heart hurt for her. I was in the midst of reassuring her when there was a short knock, and the door flung open. A tall woman in a white lab coat extended her hand to Mary Ann.

"I'm Felice, the physician assistant who'll be administering the shot."

For four grand we're not getting a doctor? I said, "We're concerned about side effects."

"Like all drugs, there is a chance of an adverse reaction. Most people do fine, but some experience headaches, sluggishness, and nausea."

Mary Ann said, "Okay, I expected something. That's it?"

"In rare cases, there has been clotting issues and lesions."

"How rare?"

"Less than five percent of recipients."

Mary Ann nodded as I calculated the one in twenty odds my wife would develop a serious condition.

"Ready?"

Mary Ann said yes. I stuffed my objections back in my mouth.

The shot was over in ten seconds. Even Warren Buffet didn't make four hundred bucks a second. Or did he?

We left with a lighter wallet, a pound of paperwork, and a ton of hope.

After I dropped Mary Ann at home, I sped to the office. I

hung my jacket up and slipped behind my desk. Derrick had stuck a Post-it on my desk; Sheriff Remin wanted to see me.

He'd called when we were in the exam room, and I'd forgotten to call him back. I grabbed my jacket and took the stairs to see him.

Remin looked at his watch and threw a chin to a chair.

"Sorry. I, uh, was with Mary Ann at the doctor's."

"Everything all right?"

"Yes. She's okay. We're hoping this new drug helps."

"Good luck with it."

"Thanks. What did you need?"

"You didn't submit a report on the Park Shore shooting. I need to make a statement. Tell me about it."

"Sorry, I had a lot of paperwork to file in the Swift case."

"That's a nine-year-old case. Park Shore takes priority."

"I know, sir. But just so you know, we're closing in on the Swift murderer."

"Good. Park Shore?"

"Sylvia Taras, wife of a man who owns a tech company, was shot in the chest twice with a small-caliber firearm. We seized a thirty-eight pistol that belonged to the husband. Dr. Bilotti is performing the autopsy as we speak."

"Is Dickson attending?"

"Uh, no. He's developing background on the husband."

"I see."

"There was no signs of forced entry, and the victim didn't appear to take a defensive position."

He nodded.

"The husband is the one who found her. He called for help."

"I don't have to tell you, I need this wrapped up fast. The Park Shore Association is demanding additional patrols.

Their lawyer suggested the county find a way to gate the neighborhood. Can you believe it?"

"That's an overreaction."

"It is and it's why not being able to have this office issue a proper, timely statement to reassure the community is so important."

"I understand. You know the numbers on spousal involvement in homicides. If it's what it looks like, you'll be able to—"

"Make sure I'm kept up to date. The timing of this murder is terrible. That group is planning another vigil for Swift. I was hoping we could stamp it solved."

"We're closing in. Detective Dickson and I are going to work both cases simultaneously."

"He's also preoccupied. Dickson's been dealing with the identity theft."

Mary Ann's illness was a preoccupation? "He's doing fine. We have this under control, sir."

"I'm told he's also scheduled for time off."

"It's a quick trip to Tallahassee; there's a lot of paperwork that the state needs regarding the fraud committed under their names."

"You're going to need help. I'm thinking of reassigning Hubert to help you with the Swift case."

"It's not necessary, sir. We've got it under control."

"Dickson also has vacation time scheduled."

"That's for the following week. They're going to Baltimore to see Lynn's mother; they're concerned that she's showing signs of dementia."

"That's unfortunate."

I wasn't sure if he was referring to the timing or his mother-in-law's condition.

Remin stood. "I have a busy day."

I took the stairs slowly, replaying the conversation. Was the sheriff crumbling under the pressure of the first homicide on his watch? The body was barely a day old. What did he expect?

The Swift case had been cold almost a decade before the remains heated things up. It didn't make sense. Remin wanted me back on the force, and now he wants to take a case off me? He was a homicide detective before moving into management.

Collier didn't have many homicides, allowing us to focus on one case at a time. But that was a luxury, and at times we not only had another murder to deal with but worked burglaries and narcotics at the same time.

Did Remin forget working multiple cases was something we knew how to do?

38

LUCA

"How you feeling?"

Mary Ann said, "I'm fine."

"You're not feeling anything unusual?"

"No, the same as before the shot."

"Good."

"They say it takes a couple of shots to see if it works."

Sure. They wanted you to spend sixteen or twenty grand before you knew it worked. "I know, but remember she said the side-effect parts can be cumulative as well. So, anything doesn't feel right, we've got to see the doctor."

"I know. Do me a favor and stop worrying so much. I'm going to be fine."

"I'm sorry. I can't help it. I keep wondering if something happens to you, who's going make me lasagna?"

"You'd better watch it, wise guy, or I'll go on strike, and you'll be eating peanut butter and jelly sandwiches."

I laughed. "The kid in me misses those. Hey, I'm getting another call. I'll see you later."

"Homicide, Detective Luca."

"Hi, there. This is Officer Reno from the Broward County Sheriff's Office."

"Hello, what can I do for you?"

"We chased down the request you made on a 2010 Crownline boat, hull number OOB31981102010. What do you want done with it?"

"There's a connection to a homicide that happened around ten years ago. I can't imagine there being anything forensics would be able to get from it but two things, if you can."

"Ask away, Detective."

"Have them check for human blood, but tell them not to go crazy."

"Okay, and the other thing?"

"Take a couple of pictures of the boat. Make sure you get the name on the back and hull number."

"When we cataloged it, we took a bunch of pictures. Give me your email, and I'll send them over."

"Thanks. If you need anything in our area, ring my bell. It'd be my pleasure to reciprocate, Officer Reno."

I hung up and chuckled to myself as Derrick came in. "What's so funny?"

"They located the Millers' old boat."

"But you said there was no chance of any usable DNA being found after nine years on the water."

"I know, but my goal was to screw with Bill Miller's head. When he finds out we have it, he's going lose a little sleep, if he's hiding something."

"You going to make like we got actionable DNA from it?"

"Haven't made my mind up yet."

He slid behind his desk, saying, "You're evil."

I smiled. "Sometimes, you got to fight evil with evil."

Derrick tapped on his keyboard. "How's Mary Ann reacting to the new drug?"

"Just talked to her; so far, no side effects."

"Good. We're hoping it helps."

"Me too. I hate to say it, but it'll be worth the money if it pushes the progression back a decade or two."

"It will, buddy. I feel good about this."

I scoffed, "Glad you do."

"Hey, got an email from Delta. They had two flights from Atlanta into RSW back in 2013. One arrived at one-oh-seven and the other just after six in the evening"

"That's the scheduled ETA, or actual arrival?"

"Those are actuals."

I reached for the murder book and flipped through to the interview with Greg Miller. "Greg Miller said he saw Kate Swift at four p.m., on the way home from the airport."

"Unless they lost his luggage or his car broke down, he should've been home no later than two."

"If that. This family probably flies in the front of the bus, and I'm betting he didn't check luggage. He said it was an overnight trip."

"He's lying."

"And he never mentioned the sighting until the next day. He's covering for his brothers. It corroborates Bill Miller saying he saw her leave the house."

"They're trying to distance themselves."

"It's curious, at best, that nobody saw her leave the Miller residence but Bill and, supposedly, Greg Miller. Not one person saw the kid walking home. Goodlette-Frank isn't the busiest road in town, especially on a Sunday, but you'd think someone would've come forward to support what the Miller brothers want us to believe."

"We have to grill Greg Miller."

I nodded as he reached for the ringing phone on his desk. He answered it and said, "It's Dr. Bilotti."

I picked up the call, telling myself to be extra nice. "Hey, Doc. How are you?"

"Good, Frank, I completed the Park Shore autopsy and just sent the preliminary report to you."

"What did you find?"

"She died of a bullet wound that clipped her aorta. She could have survived the other shot."

"You retrieved the bullets?"

"Yes, they were both thirty-eight caliber."

"Matching the pistol we seized from the husband."

"The bullets are on the way to the lab, and I've ordered a complete blood panel workup."

"Thanks. I'm going to get the handgun fired into the tank. We'll see if the ballistics line up with what you dug out of the victim."

"You may get lucky, and this case will be the quick solve you wanted."

"More like, need, but don't jinx me, Doc."

"You'll get it done, Frank; you always do. How's Mary Ann?"

"Good, no reaction but no results either."

"You know it's going to take time to determine the efficacy for her."

"Time and money."

"Was the company able to grant a measure of relief?"

"They say they're working on it, but the max they'll do is a twenty percent discount."

"Hmmm, still expensive."

"No doubt. I wouldn't tell them this, but I'll pay retail if it helps her."

"You know, I always thought you hit the jackpot with Mary Ann, but now, it sounds like both of you were lucky to find each other."

"As you know, it's work, but I've never been happier."

"That's something we need to celebrate. I have a magnum of a 2010, Conterno Barolo Riserva that's been begging for an excuse to open."

"I don't know much about Barolos except they're expensive, and you have to wait to drink them."

"You'll love this one. It's starting to be drinkable. You tell me when, and I'll decant it a couple of hours ahead of time."

"You know, Doc, if I wasn't already married... Seriously, I appreciate the offer, and I'm going to take you up on it as an academic exercise to further my education."

Bilotti laughed. "Just say the word."

Hanging up, I asked Derrick to retrieve Taras's pistol from the evidence locker and bring it to the basement for a ballistics test. He left immediately, and I printed a copy of the autopsy report.

I scanned the summary. The bullets were the most useful information, but the time of death, which Bilotti pegged between ten thirty and eleven thirty, was going to play a role if the bullets didn't match the gun in the home.

Closing my eyes, I thought about the victim's husband. He was intelligent and had money. The combo had often led people, particularly men, to think they could outsmart law enforcement. The ringing of my desk phone jostled me. It was Sanchez. One of his patrol officers had just spoken to a woman who wanted to talk to me.

39

MILLER

I arrived at Weinstein's office early. Greg believed I had a doctor's appointment and that I'd meet him there. Regret was coming on faster than rain in a summer afternoon downpour.

I was on the fence about retaining another lawyer. Weinstein was frustrating my efforts to direct things. I was paying him but he wasn't listening; he had his own ideas on how to interact with the police. If my foot could reach my butt, I'd have kicked myself for allowing him to convince me.

But the truth was, Detective Luca wanted to speak to Greg, and he said yes. I wanted to stop it and asked him as gently as I could but he resisted. My best shot was with Weinstein, but he thought talking to a family member who had nothing to hide would temper the grand conspiracy angle.

Arguing against the logic would raise more questions. I wasn't so sure anymore.

"How are you, Mr. Miller?"

"Good. A little nervous."

"There's nothing to be concerned about."

He should only know. "You know, I didn't think this was a good idea but you were very persuasive."

"It's the correct move."

"I'm afraid they'll increase scrutiny of my family. This gets out and our business will suffer. You know how people like to talk."

"We're on the way to putting this permanently behind us."

"I still don't understand what they want with Greg. He wasn't even there that Sunday."

"As discussed previously, he made a statement he saw the deceased late on the day she went missing. Detective Luca, being new to the case, is naturally interested in hearing the details of the sighting."

"He's going to start there, but he'll go off on a witch hunt. You have to keep him in check."

"He'll explore; it's what an investigator does. But that's why you have me. I'm going to protect Greg."

Greg? He wasn't the one needing protection. "I'd appreciate it if you didn't allow him to go on a wild-goose chase."

"You're overly concerned. Is there something you'd like to share?"

"I'm responsible for Mark and the business. I don't trust the police. There's tremendous pressure on them to solve this case and the Park Shore murder. Did you see what the sheriff said? He promised he'd get justice for the Swift family."

"It's a customary statement."

"Well, I just don't want Mark to get framed for it."

"If he had no involvement in her death or disappearance, you have nothing to fear."

Weinstein's secretary announced Greg's and Detective Luca's arrival. We met them in the foyer and retreated to the conference room. Luca eyed me suspiciously as I whispered to Greg to keep it short.

Detective Luca put a recording device on the table. "This interview is being recorded for everyone's protection."

When Weinstein said, "We don't object," I wanted to stomp on his foot.

Luca stated our names, the time and location, and began, asking Greg, "I want to talk to you about the events of June 1, 2013."

Greg said, "Just to be clear, that's the day that Katie Swift went missing, right?"

"Yes. It was a Sunday."

"Yeah, I remember flying back from a quick trip to Atlanta."

"On June third you contacted Detective Thomas, who led the investigation and reported that you'd seen Kate Swift on Goodlette-Frank on the afternoon of June first, the day she went missing."

I held my breath as Greg responded: "Yes, that's right. I was driving home and saw her walking."

"At the time, you said the sighting was around four p.m."

"That sounds right."

"Sounds? Or is the time you reported accurate?"

"It was about four in the afternoon."

"And what were you doing on Goodlette-Frank at that time?"

"I was on the way home from the airport."

"Got it. That would put you on the southbound side of Goodlette-Frank. Is that correct?"

"Yes."

"In your statement, you said Ms. Swift was on the north side of Goodlette-Frank."

That detail bothered me at the time but no one questioned it. I picked at a nail as Luca asked, "How fast were you traveling when you saw her?"

"I don't speed, but I'm not an old man either, so, say, forty-five miles an hour."

"That's the maximum speed limit. Going at that speed and identifying someone on the other side of the street is challenging."

"It was her; I'm sure."

"You stated she was on the northbound sidewalk?"

"That's right."

"Even if you were in the left lane, with the median and two lanes separating you from the sidewalk, that amounts to more than forty feet away. And you were traveling fast. Are you positive it was her?"

"Yeah, my eyesight is good."

"Detective Thomas interviewed you on June second, but you never mentioned seeing Ms. Swift. I don't understand why you failed to tell him."

"I don't know. I just didn't think it was a big deal."

"You don't have children, do you?"

"None."

"A young girl was missing, her parents frantic to find her, and you didn't consider that a big deal?"

Weinstein cut in. "We're cooperating, Detective. There's nothing to be gained by badgering Mr. Miller."

"Fair enough, Counselor. I'm just trying to understand why your client omitted critical information while a search for a teenager was being undertaken."

"I'm sorry, all right? I realized my mistake and called him the next day. I'm really sorry about it, but it had nothing to do with what happened to Katie."

My spirits lifted with Greg's response. It was exactly what I would have said.

"I think you're right. It had nothing to do with Kate Swift's disappearance."

What Luca said stunned me. Weinstein said, "We're pleased you acknowledge that. Are we finished here?"

"No. Your client never saw Ms. Swift."

"Excuse me?"

"Mr. Miller took a flight from Atlanta. The flight arrived around noon. Unless your client walked home, he'd be home by one, not four."

I blurted out, "You can't call him a liar."

"He made up the story to corroborate your story. Someone is hiding something, and I'm going to find out who and why."

Weinstein said, "Let's take a step back and calm down."

Luca reached over and clicked off the recorder. "Thank you, gentlemen."

40

LUCA

Rita Corso lived diagonally across from the Tarases. I parked in front of a home with so much cast-concrete ornamentation, it looked like it was designed by Gaudi. Circling around a massive fountain, I headed to the entrance. As the doorbell chimed endlessly, I stretched my neck to see the top of the honey-colored door.

A bird of a woman opened the door. "Detective Luca?"

"Yes, ma'am."

She stuck her hand out. "Rita Corso, nice to meet you. Come in."

The interior looked as if Liberace had decorated it. My eyes didn't know what to focus on: a concert-sized grand piano, the chandelier, the wall of gold-gilded mirrors, or the bank of sliders overlooking a statue-lined pool.

"Nice home, ma'am."

"Thanks. Please call me Rita. Like I said, I'm heading out; my daughter and her family are in town, and we're having lunch at the Ritz."

Naturally. "That's fine. What did you want to tell me?"

"Well, I'm not one for talking about people; everybody lives the way they want, you know. I don't judge."

"I understand. Go on."

"Sylvia moved in just a couple of weeks ago, and I always personally welcome new neighbors by bringing them a bottle of champagne."

"That's nice of you."

"I knew something was off. Being married forty-three years, you develop instincts about these things. You know?"

I nodded, and she continued, "She didn't say much that first time, but I felt something and rang her bell two days later. I could tell she was having problems with him."

"Who?"

"Paul."

The way she said it sounded like she just stepped into a pile of dog poop.

"What did she say was going on?"

She pursed her lips. "He was cheating on her."

"Do you know with who?"

"She said her name was Cissy, but I don't know her last name or, frankly, if it's a nickname."

"Any idea how long the affair has been going on?"

"Sylvia indicated it was several months, maybe even a year. Did you know about this?"

"No. Thanks for bringing it to my attention."

She smiled. "I knew it. You know sometimes you get this feeling, even though you don't want to do something, you just have to?"

All the time. "I know what you mean. We'll consider this information as we investigate. You didn't know her long, but was there anybody you think could have done this?"

"No. I'm not saying 'he' did it, but he's a snake."

I nodded. "What can you tell me about the previous owners?"

She made a face. "Didn't like them one bit. Kept to themselves but real flashy, kind of like, Miami types."

I wanted to ask about the difference between ornate and flashy, but I understood her. "The home was owned by a trust. Do you happen to know the names of the people who lived there?"

"They were Latino. All we knew was, Caesar and Lorena. Like I said, they were private. When I brought the champagne to them, they didn't even let me in the house. It was rude, and I never forgot it. They never even sent a thank-you note. Can you believe it? No manners at all."

This was an interesting, if not unexpected, revelation. It could provide the motive for Taras to kill his wife. If the ballistics test confirmed the deadly bullets were shot from Taras's pistol, it was solved.

I got back in my car knowing the prosecutors would love being presented with the motive, opportunity, and weapon used. And for me, it meant being able to pursue the Millers full time again.

The sun was out, but the sky was darkening toward the east. By the time I turned onto Route 41, huge drops of rain began beating on the windshield. Two minutes later, passing Bellini Restaurant, the sun broke out and the rain stopped. I gave a passing thought if it was a bow to my Italian heritage, but knew it was just the tropical weather we had in Southwest Florida.

I knew better than to count on the ballistics match, but it was a good excuse to switch back to the Swift case. I called the office: no messages from either the real estate agent or the lawyer the Tarases used to buy the house. It felt strange, but people never liked talking to a cop. I pressed the accelerator and sped to the station.

Sliding behind my desk, I plugged the Tarases' address in Collier County's property records. The previous owner was The Inter-Costal Trust. The name alone screamed East Coast to me.

Searching the public records database, I came up with the trustee for The Inter-Costal Trust, Blaine Blanco. I said the name out loud. Twice. It sounded like a stage name. The address was listed as being on South Miami Avenue.

I popped it in the address search. It was an office building in an area of downtown Miami known as Brickell. Blaine Blanco had no criminal record, which wasn't surprising and neither was the fact he was a lawyer. He was an actor after all.

My cell buzzed; it was Derrick. "Hey, where are you?"

"Just getting to Orlando. Frigging bumper to bumper."

"You should have taken three-oh-one."

"Waze took me to Route Four. Anyway, what's going on?"

"Waiting on ballistics. In the meantime, I'm digging into the trust that the Tarases bought the house from. The trustee is a Miami lawyer named Blanco."

"You have contacts in Miami-Dade, right?"

"Yeah, a couple of good ones. I was going to make a call when you buzzed."

"I wish I was there to help, partner."

"Take care of this identity business. The work is going to be here when you get back."

"I'm bored out of my mind."

"Drive safe. I've got to go; the phone is ringing."

It was the lab. They had the ballistics results. I grabbed my jacket and headed for the door.

41

MILLER

I felt my jaw hanging as Detective Luca walked out. He was smug but had a right to be. Weinstein trailed behind him, his small talk fading. I turned my attention to Greg; he was shaking his head.

Before I could compose myself, he started mumbling: "I knew it. I knew it."

I leaned over, whispering, "It's going to be all right."

"No, it's fucking not."

"Take it easy; we'll talk when we get out of here."

"I should've never listened to you. You made everything worse."

"I did what I had to do. It was for Mark, for all of us."

"Stop it! Stop the bullshit!"

"Come on, Greg. Don't make a scene."

"I'm going to come clean."

"You can't start changing what you said; it'll look—"

"I can't keep doing this. It doesn't matter anyway. They know I lied about seeing her."

He was right. Maybe coming clean about that would help.

"Let's talk to Weinstein. See what he says." I lowered my voice: "But just the part about seeing her."

"I don't know; we should say something about Mark."

"What? What do you want to say?"

"That he did it."

"Are you crazy? You want him to go to jail?

"They're going to find out he did."

"And that you lied to protect him. You'd be an accessory or something. You want to go to jail with him?"

"No, but—"

Weinstein came back in and closed the door. "Well, that didn't go as expected. Do we have something to discuss?"

I said, "Greg might have made a mistake with the dates and all."

Greg said, "I think I got the dates mixed up. Detective Luca is probably right. I think it was the weekend before. That's why I didn't say anything the first time I spoke to them."

"If you want to retract your statement, we have to be clear about the circumstances surrounding the misunderstanding."

I said, "Greg told me he had a dream about seeing Katie the night she went missing. Remember, Greg?"

"Uh, yeah. When I heard she was missing, and talked to the cop, I couldn't stop thinking about her. I felt bad; we knew her a long time. When I went to sleep, I dreamt I saw her, and everything got jumbled up in my head."

Weinstein's eyes moved between my brother and I. "So, you saw her, but in your dreams?"

"Yeah, it felt real. I mixed things up. I've done that before..."

"We have to be positive when we amend the statement. Are you confident in this, uh, new revelation?"

"Yes. That's what happened. I can't get in trouble for what I said nine years ago, can I?"

"If they can prove you said it to protect someone, it would be classified as obstruction—"

"But it was a mistake, an honest one. I mixed things up."

The skeptical look on Weinstein's face was understandable. I just wanted out of there. I needed time to think of the ramifications of this. Weinstein said, "If they come up with evidence you were engaging in a diversion, the authorities will apply pressure to discover the truth."

I said, "Why don't we take a break? This is stressful for everyone and taking a step back would be good."

"It'd be my preference to get ahead of this. The sooner we correct the record, the better it will reflect on Greg and the rest of the family."

Greg said, "Okay. I'm okay with doing this now. The sooner it's over with, the better."

I had to say, "Okay. But I have to use the bathroom." I looked at Greg. "Anybody else have to go?"

Greg stood and followed me into the men's room. I bent down, looking under the one stall as Greg stood in front of a urinal. I took the next one. "Let's keep this simple. Tell them the mix-up was because of a dream."

He shook his head. "I can't believe you came up with that. I wanted to tell the truth. I'm sick of this bullshit."

"It's perfect. Just hang in there a little while longer. We'll be out of here in a flash."

"I don't know. Weinstein doesn't buy it."

"It doesn't matter what he believes; he's paid to represent us."

"I don't like it. It'd be lying again. They'll find out and I'll really be in trouble, and I didn't do shit."

"They'll never find out."

"They found out about this."

"It was a dream. If you stick to the story, they can't prove you didn't have a dream about Kate."

He looked at me and zipped up. I knew I had him. He would play ball.

Weinstein read back Greg's statement. "Is that what your recollection is?"

"Yes. That's what happened."

"I'll have copies printed for your signature." He used the intercom, and a crack of thunder shifted the talk to the weather until a woman in a blue pantsuit came in. She handed her boss a handful of pages.

Weinstein compared the sheets and read the top copy. He slid the copies across the desk. "Feel free to read it and sign at the bottom."

Greg signed three copies and handed them back. The lawyer witnessed the execution of his signature and said, "I'll have this messengered to Detective Luca."

I started to get up. "We appreciate your help in clearing this up."

"One moment please." Weinstein looked me in the eye. "It's exceedingly difficult to protect you if I don't know the facts." I opened my mouth, but he threw up a hand. "Keep in mind that anything you tell me is bound by attorney-client privilege. We can't continue to alter statements without negative consequences."

"We realize that and how this, uh, episode, makes my family look. It's embarrassing."

"I understand your responsibility to shield your family, but in these circumstances, it may not be the most prudent position to stake out."

"What is that supposed to mean?"

"It's early in the investigation. The sheriff's department

hasn't yet expended considerable resources on the case. That represents an opportunity to explore a deal."

"A deal? No way. We have nothing—"

"Excuse me, Mr. Miller. It's my duty to advise you of your legal options. In the early stages of an investigation, negotiating a plea with favorable terms is easier. But the window of opportunity is closing."

"Thank you. We appreciate the advice, but it doesn't apply to us."

42

Luca

Driving out of the parking lot, I hit the voice-activated call button. "Call Vinny Longo." It was something I rarely used and, after three more attempts, knew why. I pulled over and dialed the number.

Longo and I knew each other from John Jay College. After going to the academy, he spent time in New York's Hell Kitchen. I don't know if being a cop in Jersey was easier or if he saw the light before me, but Longo made the move to Miami after only two years.

"Lieutenant Longo."

"Lieutenant? You're a big shot now."

"Who's this?"

"Frank, Frank Luca."

"Yo, Frankie. How are you?"

"Good. All's well, my man."

"How's your kid doing?"

"Jessie is no kid. She's seventeen, getting ready for college."

"Holy shit."

"Tell me about it. How you doing, bro?" As soon as it came out of my mouth, I realized how easily we changed our speech to fit relationships.

"Vinny Junior is fourteen now."

I couldn't remember his wife's name. "How's the old lady?"

"Natalie's good. She's doing real estate."

"Good timing."

"She's making way more than me."

"You better bank some of it."

"We are. What's going on?"

"Looking for information on a Blaine Blanco."

"The lawyer?"

"Yep. You know him?"

"He had a frigging billboard on one-ninety-five. I saw his face every morning the first two years I got down here."

"What do you know about him? Any seedy, big-money connections?"

"He's a criminal mouthpiece for sure but let me make a couple of calls. I'll get you the lowdown on who he's hooked up with."

"Thanks, bro."

I called Derrick. "How's the drive going?"

"Don't ask. It's stop and go. Just got to get out of Orlando. What's up?"

I thought about playing the guessing game Derrick seemed to enjoy so much. "Got the ballistics back."

"And?"

"No match."

"Are you kidding me?"

"It would've been too easy."

"I didn't tell the sheriff yet."

"You want me to call him?"

"I better call him myself on this one. I just wanted to let you know."

"Thanks. Now what?"

"On my way to see Taras. Let's see what he says about cheating on his wife. I also reached out to my buddy Longo; he's with Miami-Dade. He's checking into the lawyer behind the trust."

———

PULLING into the new industrial area off Old 41, I surveyed the parking for Crypto Might. There were only a handful of cars, and it was the middle of the day. It made me wonder how he was paying for the multimillion-dollar Turtle Hatch home.

Pushing through the glass door, I got a kick out of the Superman reference they used in their logo. Then it hit me; I thought he said they were into digital wallets. Did I remember that correctly, or was another bout of chemo brain hitting me?

The door wasn't locked, and I hadn't picked up any outdoor surveillance cameras. I stood at a counter waving to a woman wearing neon-blue headphones. She was glued to her screen, and it took her a solid minute to notice me.

Pulling down her headgear, she said, "Can I help you with something?"

"I'd like to see Mr. Taras."

"And you're...?"

"Detective Luca, Collier Sheriff's Office."

She frowned. "That was horrible what happened."

I nodded. "Is he in?"

"Yeah, I'll get him."

There were five other people in the office. It was quiet. Everyone was wearing headsets. No one had desk phones.

Taras came into the bullpen area, beckoning to me with his hand. I headed to the office he disappeared into.

Approaching, I heard him talking. His back to the door, Taras was looking out the window, talking through his headset. He used so many acronyms, it was hard to understand what he was saying. Turning around, he pulled off his headgear.

"Sorry. We're upgrading encryption on the entire suite, and there's no shortage of disagreement amongst coders."

"This digital wallet thing sounds too technical for me."

"I'd be happy to give you a primer."

"No, thanks." I patted my rear pocket. "I'll stick with a traditional one."

"I don't know how long you'll be able to. We forecast fifty percent adoption in the next five years and penetration levels approaching eighty percent in ten."

"Really? I guess a little info wouldn't help. But give me the one-liner version."

"Digital wallet sounds intimidating, but in simple terms it's just a payment tool that stores credit and debit card information, negating the need to enter a card's details, swipe it or even carry it with you to complete a transaction."

"My wallet has a lot more than credit cards in it."

"Digital wallets contain information to validate a person's identity as well."

It was a scary thought walking around without my wallet, but it'd be good to ditch the two inches I sat on. "It's interesting. I expected to see more people working here."

"We have over a hundred associates working remotely in the States and another two hundred around the globe. I'm here because I want to be. I'm lucky to live and work here."

We did have something in common. "I'd like to ask you a couple of questions about your wife and what happened."

"Whatever I can do. But before we get started, do you have any idea when I can get back in my home?"

"I'll check with the crime scene unit, but think they're all done at this point."

"Good. I'm not particularly anxious to be where Sylvia was attacked, but nice as the Ritz is, I'd like to be home."

"I understand. Did you meet the previous owners of the Turtle Hatch house?"

"No. Never met anybody from the selling side. Our Realtor and lawyer took care of everything."

"Okay, I'll check on when you can get back in as soon as we're done here."

He nodded. "Do you have any leads on who did it?"

"Nothing solid."

"You think it was those men who came to the house?"

"We're looking into that."

"Is it dangerous to return to the home?"

"We don't believe so."

"What about my firearm? When can I get that back?"

"We'll release your handgun as well. It cleared the ballistics test."

He had a smug look on his face. "I understand it's natural to look at the husband, but you're wasting your time on me."

I heard that more times than someone saying they had to use the bathroom. "How long were you married?"

"Almost twelve years."

"No children?"

He shook his head. "That was my fault. I felt I was too buried in my work to be a good father."

"How was the marriage? Your relationship with Sylvia?"

"It was actually very good. We had our ups and downs, but we were doing good, especially since we moved to Park Shore. She really wanted the house."

"Any extra-marital affairs?"

"Sylvia? Never. At least I hope not."

"And you?"

"Look, I'm not proud of it. I did have a little something going on, but it's over."

"With who?"

"Oh, come on. It was over when Sylvia was murdered. I don't want to get her involved; it's not fair to her."

Was it fair you were screwing around on your wife? "How long ago did the affair end?"

"Uh, right before we moved in."

"And that was just a month ago."

"About that."

"What's her name?"

"Do I have to?"

"Yes."

"Her name is Cecilia Newly, but everybody calls her Cissy."

43

MILLER

I parked and swung open the door to the employees' entrance. "Afternoon, Mr. Miller."

It was one of the disabled kids we hired in the outreach program we'd started three years ago. "Afternoon, John." I stopped before entering the store. "Hey, John. I'm hearing great things about you. Keep up the good work."

"I promise to. I really promise."

"I know you will. Say, come see me next week. I think it's time you got a raise."

"What?"

"Sshh, don't tell anyone. Just come knock on my door."

"When?"

"How about Monday?"

"You sure?"

"Yep, have a good one."

Walking through the plumbing aisle, I caught a glimpse of Mark. He was rearranging the sink display. I watched him for a couple of seconds. He was making micro adjustments to a pedestal sink. I resisted the urge to tell him it looked good and cut through the paint department.

The thought of Mark serving time in an institution, never mind a prison, brought me down. I wondered what Weinstein might know. The way he said things, almost challenging me, was concerning.

I would have asked him what he knew, but Greg was there, and I couldn't risk having him spouting off.

Collapsing into my office chair, I knew deep down I didn't want hear what they had. They knew Greg lied, that meant there was no one to back up what I'd said about seeing Katie leave the house. It was serious because without convincing evidence that she left, they'd naturally point the finger at Mark or me.

It was my word against theirs, and I was what they called an upstanding member of the community. But it was clear I could have fabricated it to protect myself or my brother. If the damn body, or what was left of it, hadn't been found on my property, we'd be home free.

I was certain he'd weighed the body down, sinking it into the muck at the bottom of the lake. After seeing a movie where the gases in a body forced it to the surface, I looked into it. You needed something like fifty pounds per hundred pounds of weight. I searched for the weight of the anchor. It wasn't enough, but the chain was gone. He must have wrapped it around her. I remembered looking up the weight of chains and sat back in my chair.

The thought they could find my searches by looking at my browser history had me holding my head in my hands. How long did they keep that information? I'd heard nothing ever got deleted from the internet.

Once they found my browsing history, they'd focus on me instead of Mark. My cell rang. It was Benny. I swiped it away. A text pinged. Benny said he needed to see me. That it was important. Why wasn't he working?

I sent a text telling him I was in the office. Three minutes later, he knocked on my door.

"Hey, Bill."

"What's going on?"

"I got another call from Detective Luca. He wants to talk to me."

"What did you tell him?"

"Well, I blew off the first call, but he just called again, so I told him I was working."

"Damn it. Why doesn't he leave us alone?"

"He's breaking your chops too?"

I nodded. "Mark and Greg, as well."

"I thought so. You haven't been yourself the last couple weeks."

"Sorry. It's the stress."

"You don't need to apologize to me, buddy."

"Thanks. I'm worried the police are trying to pin Katie's murder on Mark."

"What do they have on him?"

"I don't really know, but he was the last person to see her alive."

"I get why you said you saw her leaving."

"What was I supposed to say?"

"You could've asked me. I could've walked to your house and said whatever was needed."

I had thought about it but he wasn't family. "Thanks, but I figured it was covered."

He eased himself into a chair. "You're like your father; you feel like you have to manage things."

"Who else is going to do it?"

"It's a tough spot to be in."

"Tell me about it. I appreciate you get what I'm up against."

"But, you know, you can't control everything. It wears you down."

"It's not been easy."

"Sometimes you have to let something take its own course. This feels like one of those times."

"What do you mean by that?"

"I know you're trying to protect Mark and all, but I'm just saying you can't fix everything."

"Mark?"

"Come on, Billy. We've known each other forever. And I'm close to Mark. I can read between the lines."

I didn't like where he was going. "Anyway, just forget about it. It's going to be all right."

"You know Mark told me some things about what happened."

I gasped. "What are you talking about?"

"Come on, Bill. About what happened to Katie."

"What did he tell you?"

I held my breath as he said,

"The day after she went missing, he said they'd had a fight and that he did things he wished he hadn't."

I was torn between wanting to know what he said and wanting to shut this conversation down. "They had a little argument; I think it was about going too fast."

"He said it was about getting married."

"Married? They weren't even eighteen at the time."

"Did Mark say anything else?"

"Not directly."

"What's that supposed to mean?"

"I could tell he was hiding something."

"You're a psychiatrist now?"

"No, but he was beating around the bush. Stepping all over himself when I pressed for details."

I stood. "Pressed? Who do you think you are pressuring my brother? He's not right, and you know it."

"I'm sorry, man. I didn't press; it's the wrong word. I was just trying to get information."

"Information to do what?"

"I don't know. Look, you're taking this the wrong way. I'd never do anything to hurt him. Me and Mark are close, you know."

I wanted to fire him right then and there. I took two breaths and said, "I'd really appreciate it if you didn't talk to that detective."

"What am I supposed to tell him?"

"You want a lawyer? I'll pay for it."

"No, it's not necessary. I can talk to him and tell him nothing. I won't say anything about what we just talked about."

"I'd prefer you didn't speak to him."

"I'll dodge him for a while, see what happens. If he keeps on me, I'll talk but tell him nothing."

"You're sure you won't say anything?"

"A hundred percent."

"Good, thanks. Look, I have a busy day ahead of me."

As soon as Benny left, I closed the door and sat down. I ripped my tie off. Benny was a trusted family friend who'd saved my father from going to prison for vehicular murder. He'd kept the secret for more than ten years, and he'd be okay talking to the police if it came to it.

However, I was nervous. Benny wasn't the only one who seemed to know something; Weinstein gave the same impression. It felt like Detective Luca was closing in. I hit the intercom button and told them to hold all calls. I needed time to think.

44

Luca

I came back in the office. Derrick said, "What's the matter? Sheriff gave you a hard time?"

"He's pressing for a solve on the Turtle Hatch case. He used to be a homicide dick: the case isn't a week old; he should know better."

"Bet it was that piece in the *Daily News*. You see it?"

"What did they say?"

"The headline was dramatic, something like, Murder Halts Park Shore and Moorings Home Sales."

"Halts?"

"It was BS. They quoted one Realtor who said a client went into contract before the murder and is thinking of backing out."

"You got to love the way the news sensationalizes things. You know, I think Remin's sister-in-law is a real estate agent."

"I can't see why a Realtor would talk this up. It hurts them."

I smiled. "Maybe he has listings downtown to push."

"Maybe. What did Remin say?"

"He wants us to set aside the Kate Swift case and focus on Taras."

"Makes sense."

"I know, but we can do both."

"For sure."

The phone rang and Derrick grabbed it. "It's your buddy Longo."

"Hey, Vinny. How's it going?"

"Good. I checked around on your boy Blanco. He's up to his hips with some of the baddest asses in town."

"What kind of scum we talking about?"

"He represents a major drug supplier, guy by the name of Frisco Runyon. They call him Frying Pan Frisco, 'cause nothing sticks to him."

"Any history of hits?"

"Frisco sits on top of a gang that's been connected to several homicides. Two of his guys were on the verge of being arrested and disappeared. We think they fled to Colombia."

"Sounds like they have someone inside, feeding them information."

"IA is all over it; they've been busting balls for months."

"Can you send me photos of Frisco's known associates?"

"Everyone?"

"Not the little fish. The guys we're looking for have money."

"Got it."

"And, uh, if you know any enforcers from a rival gang, send those over too."

"We have an endless supply of punks. Give me an hour. I'll go up and talk to the task force."

"Thanks, pal. I owe you."

"No problem. We've been thinking of taking a ride over

one of these weekends. I'll let you know, and you can buy me dinner at one of those swanky restaurants you got there."

"You're on. Mickey D's or Wendy's, your choice."

"You still got it, Frank. We'll talk soon."

Hanging up, I said, "Longo's going to send over photos of some gang members Blanco represents and a couple of rival enforcers."

"If any of the neighbors say that's who was living there, we may have something."

"Yeah, and if Taras can ID the men he said came to the house—"

"But why kill the wife? If they were looking to hit the owner, it doesn't fit."

"They could've come expecting him, or maybe they wanted to send a message."

"Frigging ruthless."

"No doubt. Meanwhile, Taras's playmate is about to get off work. Let's see what she has to say."

"I feel bad going away. It feels like things are about to break wide open."

"Family comes first. You go and do what you have to. You're only gone a week or so. I got it under control."

———

CECILIA NEWLY LIVED in a high-end community called Grey Oaks. I hadn't Googled the address, expecting her to live in one of the cheaper condos. The gate directed me to an enclave of single-family homes surrounding a lake. When I pulled up to a custom-built home, I wondered how a customer service rep for Hertz was living there.

I couldn't see this place being under a million and a half.

I'd have to check whose name was on the deed. My bet was the taxes were being paid by Paul Taras.

The mahogany door had to be ten feet tall and was rounded at the top. I hit the bell and took in as much as I could.

A sweet voice called out, "I'll be right there."

As I said, "Take your time," the door opened.

"Sorry." Cecilia Newly was every inch the five feet ten inches her license said. Short blonde hair framed pouting lips.

I pulled out my badge, but she didn't look at it. "No problem."

"Well, come on in."

She had an athletic build. The V shape of her torso pegged her as a swimmer. "Nice place. How long you been here?" The furnishings weren't high end, and the pictures hanging were the same type of stuff we had.

"About eight months." She led me to a white-on-white kitchen. She pointed to the island. "You mind sitting at the counter? I want to get dinner started. I have a yoga class in an hour."

"It's fine." I tool a stool facing the back. "From here, it looks like the lake and pool are connected."

"Yeah, they did a good job with the infinity edge."

"You know, a friend of a friend is looking to rent something like this. Do they rent here?"

"Uh, yeah, that's what I'm doing."

"Who's the landlord? Paul Taras?"

"As a matter of fact, he is. Why?"

"Just curious, since I understand you two were in a relationship."

"We still are."

"That's not what he said."

"You must have misunderstood."

"How long has your relationship been going on?"

"Off and on about three years."

I'd forgotten to put my phone on vibrate and it rang. "Sorry." I took it out to silence it. The call was from Benny Alston. What did he want? I swiped it away, but it weighed on me.

"Did you know the deceased?"

She smiled. It was a nice smile; I could see what attracted Taras to her. "Not really, but she knew me."

"Did Paul Taras say he was going to leave his wife?"

"The marriage was over a long time ago. She wouldn't give him a divorce."

That was something to check into. "Did he ever give you the impression he wanted her out of the way?"

"You mean like, killing her?"

"Yes."

"No, he wouldn't do that."

"Are you sure? Don't protect him, because if he did it to one woman, he'd do it again."

She chuckled before saying, "Paul doesn't have the balls to do something like that."

It was one of the weirdest responses I'd ever heard. "Does he have it in him to hire someone to do the dirty work?"

"Maybe." There was that smile again.

"Where were you the morning Sylvia Taras was murdered?"

"I was working."

"At Hertz?"

"Yes. I know you think Paul pays for everything, but I'm very independent."

There wasn't much more I needed from her at this point. I'd check on her alibi and whether Paul Taras had wanted a divorce. I was anxious to call back Benny Alston.

45

Luca

Eyes on the mini mansions as I walked down the driveway, I thought over what Cissy Newly said. She rebutted what he had said, claiming the relationship was ongoing. She also indicated it had started years before.

Was Taras trying to remove the love affair as motivation? The divorce comments, if truthful, would prove he was lying. What else was a lie?

I opened the car door, letting some of the heat escape, and pulled my phone out. Starting the engine, I put the AC on high and hit dial. Adjusting the vent to hit my face, I waited for Alston to answer. He didn't. It went to voice mail. I left a message.

It was getting late. Mary Ann was getting her second shot tomorrow morning. She said I didn't have to come, but much as I wanted to put the time into hunting down these killers, the feeling something bad was going to happen dogged me.

I called the office to check on the photos Longo said he'd be sending. I smiled. My buddy had made good. A plan in my head solidified: I'd swing by the office now to pick up the photos. After Mary Ann's doctor visit, I headed out with the pictures to see if the neighbor recognized anyone.

I'd save Taras for last. He had questions to answer. I smiled at the idea of throwing him a curveball. Why not have a little fun and see how he reacted?

I OPENED the car door for Mary Ann. "Let me help you."

"I can get in the car, Frank. I had an injection, not surgery."

"I know, just trying to be helpful."

Making a turn onto Livingston, I said, "You feel anything?"

"It's only been twenty minutes."

"The doctor said it's cumulative, that a bad reaction could be coming sooner and sooner with each shot."

"It's only the second one."

"So you feel good?"

"Yes, Frank. I'm fine."

I opened the driver's door after parking in our driveway. Mary Ann said, "You don't have to get out. Get to work." She leaned over and pecked my cheek. "Talk to you later."

"See you." I waited until the garage door closed behind her before backing out of the driveway.

I swung around the landscaping truck and pulled in front of the house I'd dubbed Mini-Bellagio. Last night, I divided the photos into two lots: the men who could have lived in the Taras home and possible enforcers.

I splayed out the ones I was going to show the neighbor and chose the one who parted his hair down the middle. It was a little game I liked to play to see how sharp my intuition was. In reality, it wasn't instinct. It was guessing, but still fun.

Pictures in hand, I got out of the car and walked up the driveway. The house didn't seem as ornate; it was still too busy but it was well done.

Rita Corso pushed open the door. "Hello, Mrs. Corso."

"Nice to see you again, Detective."

"I appreciate your time, ma'am. This shouldn't take long. As I mentioned, I want to show you a couple of men who could've been living in the Taras home before the Tarases moved in."

She closed the door behind me. "Do you think they're the ones who did it to Sylvia?"

It was interesting that the closer people were to a homicide, the more reluctant they seemed to be to choose the words killed or murdered. I guess it brought the brutality too close to home. "While I can't discuss an active investigation, I can say that we look at every possible connection in a crime like this."

"The community appreciates the diligence, Detective Luca."

"It's our duty, ma'am." I took the pictures out of the envelope. "There are four men I'd like you to look over. See if any of them look like the man who used to live there." I handed her the first picture. She shook her head immediately. "No. His eyes are too close together."

I exchanged the photo for another one. She looked at it intently, bringing it closer to her eyes. "This man looks familiar. I can't say for sure it was him though."

"That's fine." I took it back and gave her the one I'd picked out.

"No. His hair was combed straight back."

I'd guessed wrong. "Here's the last one." As I handed her the picture, she said, "That's him. That's Caesar."

"Are you sure?"

"Yes, it's him."

"Thank you. That's all I needed. You've been a big help."

"Umm, he wouldn't know I identified him, right?"

"No worries, ma'am. This is between us."

The man's real name was Roberto Caldera. He was one of the right-hand men in Frisco's gang. I wasn't sure what it meant though. Caldera was a bad guy. The only possibility that made sense was a rival gang put a hit on him. They didn't know Caldera had sold the home, and killed Sylvia Taras by mistake.

If it turned out to be the case, it would put a entire new look on being in the right place at the wrong time. It was another reminder that anything could happen.

Seeing Paul Taras took on a new meaning. Getting an ID on one or more of the enforcers from Taras would take the case in a direction I hadn't anticipated.

I hopped in my car. Resisting the urge to put my strobes on, I turned left onto Route 41 to Taras's place of business. The traffic was light but the action in my head busy. Approaching Wiggins Pass Road, my cell rang.

It was Benny Alston. I answered. As he spoke, I pulled into the parking lot housing an Italian eatery named Limon-cello. It was one of those places we would've liked to try but somehow never remembered to go. That was going to change. Based on what Benny just told me, I'd never forget where I was when I heard it.

46

"Mr. Miller? Mr. Weinstein is on line one."

"Tell him I'm in a meeting."

"I did, but he said it was important."

I exhaled. "Okay, give me a minute." I checked the time and said, "Sorry, guys, we'll pick this up tomorrow, say, at ten?"

"That works."

As they gathered their things, I stared at the flashing light. What did he want? The door closed. I took a deep breath and picked up, "Hello, Mr. Weinstein. This couldn't wait?"

"I'm afraid not."

I wrapped my fingers around the chair's arm. "What is the problem?"

"Detective Luca called, and he wants to bring in Mark."

"He can't do that."

"We need to cooperate. Based on what he revealed, if we refuse, he'll get a subpoena compelling Mark to appear."

Revealed? "Wh-what did he say?"

"He has a witness who claims Mark admitted to causing Kate Swift's death."

A witness? "Who? Who said that?"

"We don't know at this point."

I jumped out of my chair. "It's bullshit. He's just saying that."

"He said it's someone close to the family."

The thought of a traitor took my breath away. If it was Greg, I'd never recover. "Close to or part of the family?"

"He said close. I don't believe it's a family member."

"What are we going to do?"

"We'll prep Mark as best we can and give them their chance to interview him."

"Oh no. No. He's... Can I be there?"

"No, but don't be concerned. I'll be with him."

"This is a disaster."

"Take it easy, Mr. Miller. If I feel he's incriminating himself, I'll end it, and we can consider our options."

"What options?"

"We can explore his competency if the court rules he's unable to understand the questions or the implications of his replies and possibly the state of mind he was in when the event took place."

"You're talking as if he, uh, did it to Kate."

"I'm not insinuating anything. The fact is an allegation has been levied, and it must be defended."

"This is crazy. We have to find out who the rat is."

"What we have to do is address the allegation. If this goes further, we'll have an opportunity to discover who the witness is."

I collapsed into my chair. This was a disaster. Not only was Mark going to jail, but I'd also probably be in the next cell for trying to protect him. What was I going to do?

47

LUCA

It wasn't like me to relish delivering a progress report, but Remin wanted to be kept updated, and I had more information than usual.

I could hear him ripping somebody a new body orifice. My bet was it was Squad Sergeant Romero. I'd heard one of his guys got into it with a citizen who'd nearly run him down. Restraint was good policy, but sometimes even the best were tested beyond reason.

He barked for me to come in. Normally, I would've been uncomfortable, but I was bearing gifts to cheer the sheriff up.

"How are you, sir?"

"I'm sure you heard me." He shook his head. "The only blessing is, there doesn't seem to be a recording of the, uh, interaction. Yet."

That seemed unlikely. It may have been recorded by someone with an appreciation for the tough circumstances officers were put in. "It's never easy out there."

"I don't get it. They guy tried to run down a cop. What's wrong with people today?"

That question was right behind what the meaning of life was. "I wish I could answer that, but we've made significant progress in both the Park Shore murder and the cold Swift case."

"I can use good news."

I explained the call from Benny Alston. The sheriff said, "I wasn't comfortable with how Mark Miller was handled. If I was around back then, I would've applied more pressure."

"It would appear that the prominence of the family and the kid's condition made things delicate."

"You've always been loyal, Frank. But they didn't do enough. The only thing I'll give them was it was a missing person case at the time."

I nodded. "We're going to interview Mark Miller, and we'll be respectful, but I intend to lean on him."

"You've got my support. It'll be interesting to see where this goes. I wish I would have known about this case sooner. We can't allow the public to think a family like the Millers are above scrutiny."

"I agree, sir. We go where the evidence leads us."

"You mentioned the Taras case: what do you have?"

I told the sheriff we ID'd the previous owner, and the chances are that it could have been a case of mistaken identity.

"That would be as sad as it gets."

"I know, but I'm not done with the husband. There's significant distance between what he says and what his lover said. She's claiming the relationship was ongoing and that he was looking for a divorce."

"We have to make this case our priority."

"I can handle both, sir. We're closing in on the Swift case, and I'd hate to lose the momentum we have."

He stroked his chin. "Dickson's on vacation. You could use some help."

"It's just a week, sir. I've got everything under control."

"When are you bringing in Mark Miller?"

"Tomorrow."

"All right, see where that goes, and get back to Park Shore."

WEINSTEIN and his client Mark Miller were in the interview room. On the video feed, the lawyer was chatting with his client. Mark seemed jumpy but not overly so. Normally, I'd screw around with the temperature in the room, letting it get uncomfortable. It was childish, but I felt like it gave me an edge. Given what I knew about Mark, it didn't feel right and I passed.

I gave a knock on the door and stepped in. Weinstein stood, introducing me to Mark. Lawyers and I didn't usually mesh, but Weinstein was a strong defender of his clients' rights yet played it straight.

Mark kept clicking his jaw, which distracted from his good looks. His voice was a bit meeker than I expected, but being in an interview kept most people off kilter.

I hit the record button and after reciting the formalities, said, "Thank you for coming in today, Mr. Miller."

"My name's Mark."

"Right. Thanks for coming, Mark. I have some questions. If you need a break at any time, just ask."

He looked at his lawyer, who said, "You just tell me, Mark. I'm here for you, and everything is going to be all right. Are you ready to begin?"

Mark nodded and I asked, "Excellent. You remember the last time you saw Kate Swift?"

He nodded.

"You'll have to speak your answers. Do you recall the day?"

He traced a circle on the table with his forefinger and kept going over it. "Uh-huh. Katie came over; she had white pants on. I like white pants. Do you?"

"Yes. What did you do when she got there?"

"We zoomed all over the lake."

"On your boat?"

"Yep."

"What time of the day was it?"

"I don't know. It was real sunny, like afternoon time."

"How long was she there?"

"I don't know. We went around the lake, like we always do. It's so much fun to buzz all over the place."

"Did you or Kate go into the water?"

"No. I always have my bathing suit on but not Katie. I wanted her to drive, like she used to do."

"Did you get mad when she didn't want to steer the boat?"

"Anybody who's the captain has fun. I wanted her to have fun like she used to."

"Were you mad at her?"

Mark shrugged. "I don't know."

"Kate wasn't enjoying herself?"

"A little, I guess."

"Are you sure you weren't upset at her?"

"I never get mad at her. We're best friends, forever."

"Someone said you admitted to them that you were mad at Kate and that you were fighting with her."

He wagged his head. "Not true. It's not true. We never fight."

Mark was talking as if she were still alive. Was he shutting out what had happened? "It's okay to fight. Everybody argues from time to time. My wife and I get into it every now and then. Do you see by saying you never fought with Kate, it's hard to believe?"

He turned to Weinstein. "Why are they saying this?"

"It's okay, Mark, don't get frustrated. Just answer truthfully."

"But I am. Mommy said to tell the truth and I do. Except one time, I ate all the cake Aunt Cathy made, and she was real mad, so I said I only had, like, two pieces."

I had experience dealing with someone with a brain injury. Before I came down to Naples, a marine who'd been hurt in a car accident was a murder suspect. It was impossible to figure out if he'd killed the man who'd bullied him.

That said, something about the way Mark was talking and acting seemed genuine. My thoughts shifted to his older brother Bill. Almost from the start, I'd considered him a suspect.

"Okay, we believe you. Now, that day, June first, was a Sunday. It was sunny, and Katie came over. Who else was there?"

"Nobody. Just me and her."

"No one else was at the home? Where you live?"

"Billy was there."

"Your brother?"

"Uh-huh."

"And that's all? Nobody else?"

"Oh, Benny came over too."

"Benny Alston?"

"Yes."

"What time was that?"

"I don't know. I-I can't remember."

There was a knock on the door. The sheriff stuck his head in. "Detective Luca, I need a word."

This was unusual. Was he interfering? I paused the recording and excused myself. I stepped into the hallway, and Remin put his hand on my shoulder.

"I'm sorry, Frank, but Mary Ann called. She's being rushed to NCH."

"Why are they taking her to the hospital?"

"I don't know. Schneider's waiting in the lot; he'll drive you there."

I stood there, shocked.

"Get moving. I'll take over the interview."

48

MILLER

I paced the room. Weinstein promised to call me as soon as they were done with the interview. It was after one. What the hell was going on?

Maybe he forgot. I picked up the receiver to call him, when my cell buzzed. It was Weinstein.

"What took so long?"

"Well, it went longer than expected, but part of it was the sheriff took over."

"The sheriff? Why? What's going on?"

"It was unexpected but don't read too much into it."

"What happened?"

"Detective Luca had a personal emergency, and Sheriff Remin relieved him."

"Wouldn't they just postpone it?"

"The sheriff is interested in the case."

"Interested? What the hell does that mean? I want to know what went on, every frigging detail, and where is my brother? Is he all right?"

"I dropped him off at home. He was a bit traumatized."

"Traumatized?"

"That wasn't the best choice of words. These interviews can be grueling but he's fine."

"He better be. Now, tell me what happened."

"As I mentioned, Detective Luca conducted part of the interview before leaving. He questioned Mark in a, shall we say, softer approach. Mark handled himself very well, and though it was early, I thought the interview would conclude well."

"Are you going to tell me what the hell happened?"

Weinstein cleared his throat. "Luca asked several questions about Mark and Kate being on the boat and whether he was angry with her that day. Pretty standard questioning. He asked who was there, and Mark identified you."

"Of course I was there. It's my damn house."

"Just providing the details you requested. Luca pressed on who else was there, and Mark said Benny Alston was there."

"He wasn't there. He must've been confused; we went golfing earlier."

"That could explain it, but Sheriff Remin came into the room and called Detective Luca outside. We took a short recess, during which the sheriff reviewed the interview up to that point."

"Why didn't you walk out?"

"You're well aware we went there to answer their questions."

"Yeah, yeah, yeah. What happened with the sheriff?"

"He was forceful in his questioning, and I think it unnerved Mark because he started from the beginning, reframing questions the detective had already asked."

"Didn't you object?"

"Of course I did, but it's a customary strategy used by law enforcement to see if someone changes their response. In this case, Mark did."

"What did he say?"

"He stated that he was upset that Kate was in a rush."

"Disappointed is what he probably was. That doesn't mean anything."

"That alone, of course not. He admitted to trying to scare her when she declined the opportunity to pilot the boat."

"What did he do?"

"He tried to tip the boat over."

"What? Why would he do that?"

"I assume he was frustrated. It's problematic as it displays a recklessness that fits the narrative they're trying to build."

"Oh Jesus. Don't tell me there's anything else."

"There was one more thing. He said Kate was upset at getting wet from the way he was driving and she got mad at Mark."

"They were just kids having fun for Chrissake. I can't see them making a big deal out of all this."

"I believe you should prepare yourself for more scrutiny."

"Me? Or Mark?"

"Both of you. Mark asked for you several times, and the sheriff pressed him on whether you were telling him what to say."

"That's ridiculous. I'm his older brother and just about his legal guardian. Of course he depends on me."

"I'm sure he does. However, Mark insinuated that you bribed him in order to keep him quiet."

"Bribed him? That's crazy. He was probably confused, that's all."

"He claimed you bought him a new boat as a reward."

My knees buckled. "That's ridiculous."

"Did you get a new boat?"

"Yeah, but it had nothing to do with anything."

"How recently?"

"I don't remember exactly."

"After the remains were discovered?"

"Yeah."

"Hmmm."

"What are you 'hmming' about? You don't believe me?"

"I'm paid to represent you. What I believe is not important."

"What's that supposed to mean?"

"I'm trying to understand the facts surrounding this case. Knowing so enables me to provide the best counsel I can. It has nothing to do with belief."

"You know everything there is to know. Mark had nothing to do with Katie's death."

"Noted."

The way he said "noted" annoyed me. I was paying him four hundred dollars an hour, and he was appeasing me. "What is our strategy going forward?"

"We wait. We'll know soon enough if the sheriff is going to issue an arrest warrant."

"Arrest warrant?"

"Yes."

"They don't have anything to arrest him on."

"All the police need is probable cause. They'll have no problem getting a judge to sign a warrant."

"This is crazy. What are we going to do?"

"If they issue a warrant, I'll negotiate a surrender. We have to avoid a public arrest. The press wouldn't be good for you."

I hung up in a state of disgust. We had no relationship

with Sheriff Remin. What was he doing in the middle of the case anyway? My family's luck was terrible as it was, and now a detective's personal emergency had Mark on the cusp of being arrested. How the hell was I supposed to manage bad luck?

49

LUCA

The thought Remin was sticking his nose in my case should've eaten away at me. But as long as Mary Ann was going to be all right, the sheriff could sleep in my spare bedroom. Schneider pulled under the ski-slope-shaped canopy over the entrance and I bolted out.

I was hesitant about calling Jessie. She'd be mad I waited, but I needed an understanding of what was going on. It was final exam week, and I didn't want her bolting out if it wasn't serious.

Hurrying through to the emergency wing, it felt serious. A nurse escorted me through a large room separated into areas with curtains. The sound of someone vomiting was unmistakable; it was my wife.

The long list of side effects cycled through my mind in a split second. Throwing up was an adverse reaction. What scared me was remembering that it could be signaling a larger problem.

Hand on Mary Ann's back, a nurse was holding a pan by

my wife's face as she spit up whatever was left. She had an IV in her arm and was ghostlike.

"Hey, Mary Ann, how you feeling?"

"Like crap."

She looked bad, but I'd learned what to say to a woman. "You look fine. What does the doctor say?"

The nurse said, "We took blood and urine and are running tests."

"Did she tell you that she's on an experimental drug for her MS?"

"Yes, we have a call into her neurologist."

"Vomiting is a side effect. I read about it."

"It may be the cause, but we need to run tests. She's experiencing pain in her abdomen, which may be related to her appendix. We're going to take her for an ultrasound as a precaution. I'll be right back."

I held her hand. "You feeling any better?"

I got my answer as she pitched forward, retching into the pan. She fell back on her pillow.

"Hang in there. They'll figure out what's going on."

"You didn't tell Jessica, did you?"

"No. I wanted to see how you were first."

"Don't say anything. I don't want her worrying."

"I'll tell her when we know something."

The nurse and an orderly came in. Ignoring me, they wheeled my wife away for an ultrasound.

I went to a waiting room filled with crying kids, worried parents, and wheelchairs. Checking the time, I tried to remember Jessie's schedule. She tutored grade-school kids twice a week, played soccer, and took dance classes on top of her social activities. She needed to know, and I needed company.

Pulling my phone out, a text chimed in. It was Derrick.

He was asking about Mary Ann. Word spread fast when trouble hit a fellow officer or his family. The lack of privacy annoyed me at times, but the brotherhood was comforting. Exhausted, I settled into a chair

The pain in my back woke me up. I studied Mary Ann's chest. She was sleeping. I stretched and grabbed my phone. It was ten thirty. I told the nurses' station I was going home to take a nap and shower. I'd be back at six.

MY CELL RANG. It was Sheriff Remin. "Hello, sir."

"How's Mary Ann?"

"She's doing good. She's home already.

"Good. What happened?"

"It ended up being a case of food poisoning."

"That can be nasty."

"I was worried it was the new drug she's been taking. It's experimental with a slew of side effects."

"How is her MS?"

"It's gotten a bit worse. She's had a series of flare-ups which is why we decided to try the new drug."

"Hope it works. Tell her I was asking about her."

"Will do, sir. How did the rest of the interview with Mark Miller go?"

"You ask me, he did it. I'm going to present what we have and get an arrest warrant."

"You want to arrest Mark Miller? For the Swift homicide?"

"Yes."

"What did he say?"

"We'll go over it when you get back in. In the meantime, take care of your family."

"But—"

"No buts."

Staring at the phone, I tried to figure out what the hell had happened. What did Mark Miller say to convince the sheriff to arrest him? Had I been wrong in believing he wasn't involved?

I replayed the short interview I'd conducted, wondering if I'd missed something. Mark had been the last or next-to-last person to see Kate Swift alive. That made him a suspect. Mark had a brain injury that could cause erratic behavior. Maybe it was him.

Derrick needed to know. As I pulled my phone out, Jessie called out, "Dad, I have to go to school. Can you help Mom? She needs to go to the bathroom."

My first duty was to Mary Ann, but she was going to be fine in a day. Whatever the sheriff was planning could last a lifetime.

50

Luca

Derrick had his hands full. I wanted to ask him to come back early but couldn't get up the nerve. As soon as I dropped the idea, he called. "Hey, Frank, how are you?"

"To tell you the truth, I had a little scare there." For some reason, I found myself using sayings that I despised. What exactly did "to tell you the truth" or "I've got to be honest" mean? That you were lying the other times you opened your mouth?

"What happened?"

"Mary Ann was rushed to the hospital. I thought it was the experimental drug, but it turned out to be food poisoning."

"Ugh, what from?"

"It looks like it was undercooked chicken."

"I got food poisoning once from clams, and I wanted to die, it was so bad."

"Me too. That's why I never eat clams casino."

"I don't touch it either."

"How's it going?"

"Not the best. We're looking into a place to put her aunt. She can't live alone any longer; it's a mess."

"Sorry to hear."

"It's okay. What happened with Mark Miller?"

"Mary Ann got sick in the middle of the interview and the sheriff took over, and now he wants to arrest him."

"Why? What did he say?"

"Nothing much when I talked to him. I think Remin is looking to scare the kid into talking."

"Oh man. I'm sorry, I should have been there to back you up."

"It's all right. When I get in, I'm going to see the sheriff and find out what the hell is going on."

PUTTING your glasses on your head when not using them was something a lot of people did. But Remin had a habit of pushing them to a position on his forehead. I thought it looked weird and it was distracting.

The sheriff had a foot resting on an open drawer as he spoke on the phone. He waved me to sit as he talked with somebody about his campaign to hold the position he inherited from Chester.

I tried to keep out of the political side of things and thought stability was as good for the department as competency. But if Remin was going to meddle, I was changing my mind.

Before hanging up, he told whoever it was to remember he was a regular Joe and that should be the focus of any advertising. It was a common theme. Politicians liked to espouse it but never lived it.

"Sorry, Frank."

"No problem."

"How's Mary Ann?"

"Doing great, thanks."

"What's on your mind?"

He barged into my case, and he wants to know what I want? "The Swift case. You said you were thinking of arresting Mark Miller."

"Yes, that's right."

"I'm confused, sir. What evidence do we have?"

"What he said during the interview."

"What came out?"

"There were several discrepancies, but it's more like what didn't surface. He's hiding something, and his brother is abetting him. We bring him in, isolate him; he'll crack."

"Are you sure?"

"Did you forget, I was a homicide detective before getting this job? And I don't mind saying it was in a district with ten times the cases we have in Collier, thank goodness."

Did he just take a shot at me? "My solve rate—"

"Take it easy, Frank. No one's challenging your abilities. You concentrate on solving the Park Shore murder. I've got this one."

"You're taking the case from me?"

"Not taking, assisting you. You're busier than Cher's plastic surgeon at the moment.

I tucked the analogy away for future use. "But I can handle it. Hold on, is this about Mary Ann?"

"No, Frank. As soon as you nail the Park Shore killer, you'll get this one back."

"I can do both."

"My decision is final."

What was going on? "I'd like to review the interview with Mark Miller."

"You're not on it, at the moment."

"But we're close on the Taras murder, and I'd like to be up to speed on Swift."

"Be my guest. But not on the county's dime. We need you focusing on Park Shore."

Ready to rip my badge off and toss it on his desk, I forced myself to say, "Yes, sir."

Trudging down the stairs like a kid who'd lost his center-field position on the eve of the championship, I tried to understand what happened. The only thing that made sense was his campaign. He'd use the Swift case to show he was active in bringing justice. A worker bee rather than a queen. It had to be.

Remin was right: I was busy, maybe not like a Hollywood plastic surgeon, but Derrick was out, my wife had needs, and we had a fresh murder to solve. But deep down, he wanted the publicity, if it turned out right. If it blew up, I knew it'd land on my desk, and Remin would be as far away as the generals who ordered the storming of Normandy.

I had to see the video or at least read the transcript. Reading, I could skim. It would go faster. I'd go see Paul Taras, show him the pictures of the enforcers to see if he could match any of them to the men who came to his house. After that, I'd stop in on Mary Ann. If she was okay, I'd head back to the office, close my door, and dive into the transcript.

51

Luca

It was hard not to think I'd made a mistake coming back to the force. I couldn't chase killers as a private investigator, but I also dealt with a lot less bullshit. The bills had gotten paid, and I was around the house more. Speeding along on Route 41, I thought the only thing I'd have to figure out was health insurance.

Heading west on Neapolitan Way, I saw the sign for Ciabo. It was a restaurant I'd been to with Bilotti. He knew the owners, and they were cool with him bringing in wine. The doctor always made sure the owner got a taste. I wasn't sure if it was just his good nature and love of wine, or was it insurance against being charged a corkage fee?

Going to a head doctor had its benefits. Dr. Bruno had me acting less irrationally these days. She said to take a step back, think things through to avoid doing something I'd regret. She'd given me tools to use and I owed her for helping me become more even-tempered.

After I was done with the interview, I'd call Bilotti. He'd talk me off the ledge. I made a left onto Crayton Road and slowed as Turtle Hatch Road came up. I was about to turn when a car swung out and passed me. I did a double take. It looked like Cecilia Newly.

Taras pushed open the door. He had on white linen pants. It made me think of the man who attended Swift's memorial service.

"Come in, Detective."

"Thanks. This shouldn't take too long."

I followed him into the kitchen. A laptop was open, and a huge monitor occupied a third of the stone table.

"Working from home today."

"Busy?"

"Can't keep up. The demand for our products is off the charts. We can't rest though, got to stay ahead of the cyber thieves."

I wanted to tell him good luck with that. "Digital wallets, who would've believed it would be such a hit? The pace of change is scary."

"Nothing to be frightened about. Get informed and you'll be fine. As offered, anything I can do to help get you up to speed, let me know."

He wasn't too obvious in his attempt to build a relationship but I'd be on guard. "Thanks. I'd like to see if you can identify the men who came here a couple of nights before your wife's murder."

"Sure. The more I think about it, the mistaken identity theory seems more probable."

I pulled four pictures out. Three were Miami gang enforcers and one was an officer who worked in the evidence room. I handed off the first picture. "Recognize him?"

He looked at the image. "Can't say I do."

I exchanged it for another. "Hmm, looks familiar."

"Was he here?"

"Not sure."

"Let's move on." He took the next one.

Taras nodded. "It's him. This is the guy."

"You sure?"

"One hundred percent."

"All right, take a look at the last one. It could be the other guy."

"Nah, the other guy had a bigger nose and more hair."

"Okay. That's very helpful."

"You think it's them?"

"We'll see."

"Please keep me posted. I've got to get back to work."

"I have a couple of questions that need clarification."

He looked at his watch. It was one of those expensive ones, not a smart watch you'd expect a techie to wear. "I have to prepare for a Zoom meeting."

"It won't take more than five minutes."

"All right."

"You said the relationship with Cecilia Newly had ended."

"Yes."

"Not according to her. She said it was ongoing."

"It's over as far as I'm concerned, but she's hanging on."

"When was the last time you saw her?"

Taras hesitated. "As a matter of fact, she was just here."

"So, it is ongoing, then."

"It's more complicated than that."

"Explain it."

"Look, the relationship ran its course, but Cissy won't let go, if you know what I mean."

"I get it. How long were you two together?"

"Just about a year." He added a hedge: "I'm pretty sure."

"Ms. Newly said it was more like four years."

"She's exaggerating." He added another hedge. "I mean,

we first met about four years ago but it was nothing steady. We'd see each other from time to time but it was no affair."

I was pretty certain his dead wife would have disagreed. "Stepping out on your wife for four years or however long you've been doing it with Ms. Newly or others is a long time. Wouldn't it be easier to get a divorce?"

"I didn't want a divorce."

"You have a prenuptial agreement?"

"Look, this questioning is venturing into private territory. I don't see the point of answering any more of these kinds of questions. I wasn't a perfect husband and I'm not proud of some of the, uh, things I did, but I had nothing to do with Sylvia's death."

It was yet another proclamation of innocence by a person of interest. I'd heard it countless times: some were accurate but too many weren't. I was undecided where Taras's statement would fall.

With the car door open to let out the heat, I stood looking at the Tarases' home. It was a beauty and expensive. He was a self-made millionaire, and that meant he was smart in some areas of life.

Driving along Crayton Road, I tried to figure out if Taras was trying to throw me off his trail. The man he fingered as the guy who came to his home was a cop. Was he another notoriously unreliable eyewitness, or had I gotten lucky with his diversion tactic?

52

MILLER

The ballroom was full of people, and they were loud. It was time. I turned to Sally who was the Ritz's banquet manager. "I think the room is about ready. Let's kick this off."

"It would be my pleasure, Mr. Miller."

Surveying the crowd as she got a few steps ahead of me, I hoped they'd drunk enough to surpass last year's haul. I climbed the stairs to a stage as she quieted down the room. My cell vibrated. I snuck a peek. It was Weinstein.

I heard my name, and a round of applause broke out. I forced a smile and walked to the podium.

"Good evening. I'm honored that so many of you came out to support the Golisano Children's Health Center. Your continued generosity is a testimony to the goodness in the people of our slice of paradise. Give yourself a hearty round of applause."

As the crowd patted themselves on their backs, I wondered what Weinstein wanted. Was it bad news? The crowd simmered down, and I continued, telling them they'd given the organization the confidence to break ground on a new facility in East Naples.

After a short video of sick children to tug heartstrings, I finished: "Nothing we do is possible without your help. I'm making a plea on their behalf, and who could deny these children? Let's show them our support by smashing the amount we raised last year."

The cheering made me feel good. The hospital would do very well today. Smiling, I waved at the attendees, trying to estimate what the take would be. My chest pocket vibrated. I hurried offstage.

I shook a few hands and chatted with the co-chair next to the silent auction tables. Excusing myself to use the men's room, I headed out. Pulling my phone out, I walked to an alcove by an empty conference room and hit dial.

"Sorry, I'm chairing the Golisano event."

"Good luck with it. It's an excellent cause."

"It sure is. What's going on?"

"I'm afraid they've issued an arrest warrant for Mark."

I leaned against the wall. "Oh my God. Isn't there anything we can do?"

"No, but we'll mount a vigorous defense."

"I can't believe it."

"Fortunately, they're agreeable to allowing Mark to surrender."

"How soon does he have to?"

"I set it for noon tomorrow."

"This is a disaster. I have to tell Mark."

"Would you like me to?"

"No, no. It's better coming from me."

"I understand."

"What's going to happen? Is he going to be released on bail?"

"After he's processed, he'll be arraigned and enter a plea."

"It's got to be not guilty."

"If that's what he wants."

"He doesn't know what he wants."

"If that's the case, we should go for a competency hearing."

"No. I don't want to drag him through that. They'll use it against us, and he'll end up in an institution."

"It may be useful to take a step back and think this through."

"I don't need to. He'll be released, on bail, right?"

"The prosecution won't contest that too vigorously."

"They better not. How long does all this take?"

"Generally, arraignments are from a couple of hours after processing to the next day. It's dependent upon how busy the court is."

"He can't stay overnight."

"It's something we're unable to control."

"Of course we can. Who do you know down there? Start making some calls."

"It doesn't work like that."

"It sure does. You think celebrities go through the system?"

"I'm—"

"Pick up the phone; I've got to go."

My mind raced. How would I break this to Mark? He'd go at noon. What could it take—an hour to take fingerprints and whatever else they did? Even with two hours of bureaucracy, that would be around two o'clock. What time did the court usually do hearings? Most TV shows I watched held them at night.

I didn't want him alone for too long. I'd accompany him and Weinstein to the station and would sit in court when he was arraigned. If we could keep him from being stuck overnight in a prison cell with who knew who, he'd be all right.

Breaking the news wasn't going to be easy. What could I promise to get him? It had be something good. Something he could focus on. I saw Sally step into the hallway. She walked toward me, bringing the reality I had a half-drunk crowd of donors to woo.

"Are you okay?"

"It must have been something I ate. Had to, uh, make a bathroom run."

"You feel better?"

"A little bit, but I don't know how long I can last."

———

HEADSET ON, Mark was on the floor, playing a video game. He nodded as I came into his field of vision. I held a finger up and he paused the game. "How you doing?"

"Not this game but the one before, I killed it."

The word sent a shudder through me. "Better than my all-time best score?"

He put his headphones back on. "Uh-huh."

"Hold on. I have to tell you something."

"What?"

"Now, don't be scared because it's going to be all right."

"What?"

"Well, you know all this talk about what happened to Katie and talking to the police."

"Yeah?"

"Well, they want to talk to you again. But it's going to be a little different this time."

His eyes searched my face.

"Tomorrow we'll go to the station, and they're going to book you in."

"Like on TV?"

"Kind of. You'll have to stay a while, then see the judge before you can come home."

"You going to be there, right?"

"I can only be with you some of the time. Now, don't get nervous, but you'll have to wait for the judge in a cell."

"In jail?"

"It's not a real jail, just a place to hold people before the judge gets to talk to them."

"No! I'm not going!" He went back to the video game.

I shut the TV off.

"Hey, leave me alone."

"Mark, this is serious. Calm down and listen to me. I know you don't want to do this, but if you do, how about I get you something? Something really special."

"Like what?"

"We could get another boat, this one for fishing and go out on the Gulf."

"I like the lake."

"Okay, I was thinking it's time you got your own house. We could build one right close to the lake."

"I like my room."

"How about one of those new virtual reality setups? We can get one of those new curved monitors and—"

"Really? Can I get it? Can I?"

"Of course. Now, when you're inside the police station, don't say anything to anybody about Katie? Okay?"

"Okay. When can I get the VR kit?"

"After the judge does his thing, we'll go straight to the store."

"When's that?"

"By this time tomorrow, you'll be playing on a new setup."

53

LUCA

I poked my head outside. Mary Ann was reading on the lanai. She looked up. I said, "How you feeling?"

"Good. I nodded off for about fifteen minutes and feel like a new person."

"Great. You need anything?"

"No. You leaving?"

She read me better than the mystery novel on her lap. "Want to stop by and talk to Remin about the Swift case."

"I'll see you later."

I expected her to ask me about the case, but that was the major difference with the two of us. When we were both on the force, if an order came down from above, she'd accept it and move on. Now, confronted with MS, Mary Ann had shrunk her world down. She was worried about her family, health, and maybe the house.

Me? It was hard for me not to play the planet's policeman. I knew it was a losing proposition, but if everybody gave up, what kind of a world would Jessie inherit?

I PUSHED food around my plate as Mary Ann and Jessie chatted like teenagers. The good feeling my wife was almost at full strength had faded, replaced by a growing fear my opinion didn't count with the sheriff. I'd lost the argument over arresting Mark Miller.

Mary Ann didn't see it that way. She may have been right, but if he wanted the damn case, he should've taken it from day one. Once I walked into a carnival, I wasn't going home without a stuffed animal.

"Dad? Dad, you there?"

"Uh, yeah. Just thinking."

"He's mad at the sheriff over a case."

"What happened?"

"Nothing."

"I hate it when he does that!"

"Okay, okay. I was working a case, you know the old one where that kid, Kate Swift went missing and they found her remains?"

"Of course. What happened to her?"

"We're not sure yet but the sheriff seems to think differently than I do, and—"

"He overruled you?"

"Yeah."

"Ouch."

As Mary Ann said, "He'll recover," my cell rang. It was Bilotti.

"Hey, Doc. How are you?"

"Good. I heard about the Swift case."

Everybody knew I'd been booted off the case. "Yeah, well. I'm not happy about it, but he's the boss."

"Indeed. How's Mary Ann?"

"She's doing great. We just finished eating."

"Want to come over and drown your sorrows in that Barolo I mentioned? We'll have the house to ourselves."

I looked at Mary Ann. "Nah, I can't. I want to stick around, just in case."

Mary Ann said, "I'm fine, Frank. Go ahead and do whatever you two are cooking up. Just make sure you Uber it."

HAVING a friend like Bilotti is one of the treasures of life. Life moved so fast, people took each other for granted. Until they're not there anymore. Nobody is perfect, and we annoy each other at times. I wasn't good at it, but I was trying to focus on the better qualities of those I knew, not their pimples.

I was happy in my own skin. Couldn't fathom living someone else's life. I could imagine my life with a lot more money but didn't want to be a rock star or anyone else. Climbing out of my Uber, I thought if I was forced to choose being someone else, Bilotti was a good choice.

"It's good to see you, Frank."

"Thanks for having me over."

He smiled. "Figured you could use a griping session."

Right there I realized he was a better friend than I thought. He knew Mary Ann's MS could flare up with stress, and he didn't want me brooding around the house.

I followed him into the kitchen. "You got it all wrong. I only came for the wine."

"I decanted it as soon as we hung up."

"The whole magnum?"

"No, I can't drink like I used to. I had the Conterno in a seven-fifty format as well."

A pair of glasses and an empty bottle of wine sat next to a glass pretzel filled with wine. "I love that decanter."

"It looks good but it's not practical. Difficult to pour and fragile as heck."

He grabbed the decanter and poured a small amount in each glass. Bilotti put two fingers on the base of the glass and swirled the wine. He stuck his nose in and inhaled deeply. "Oh, this is a beauty. Getting some rose, a bit of tar..." He took a sip, closed his eyes, and went silent.

I took the opportunity to swirl my glass and took a sniff. I didn't get what he did, but maybe there was a hint of chocolate, and it was kind of earthy. It wasn't a fruit bomb but lighter, elegant.

"The finish is long. About forty seconds. How you like it?"

"It feels lighter, right? And I don't know, but maybe a little chocolate in it?"

"Could be. Don't feel pressure to identify what you're tasting. Just be aware. It'll come to you."

That meant no chocolate. "It's the nebbiolo grape, right?"

"Exactly." He took a sniff, then a sip. "This is heavenly."

I took another taste. "It's good but seems to have changed."

"Absolutely, this will develop over the next hour, if the wine lasts that long. Let's sit inside."

He took the decanter, and we sat in a the family room. Pictures of his family, including a daughter he'd lost and trips taken, surrounded us. He asked, "You feeling okay?"

"Sure."

"You're under a lot of pressure with Mary Ann and what went on with the sheriff."

"Mary Ann's all that counts." I said it, but it wasn't completely true. "Remin... I don't know what to say."

"What happened?"

I brought him up to speed.

"I have to agree with you, he's ex-homicide, feels it's not overstepping. If he gets a solve, he has something to campaign on. He must know it's looking like Blazer is going to run."

"But he's an outsider."

"Charlotte County isn't Virginia."

"I know. Let me ask you, I'm worried about this kid. Well, he's not a kid, but with the brain injury, he seems to act like one. Is it real?"

"We don't know enough about the brain, but we know a serious injury can cause personality changes. The brain regulates emotions and impulses."

"Anger and aggression?"

"Yes, and it could trigger a lack of self-awareness and even violence."

"So sad."

"Indeed. You're getting low; let me pour you some more."

As Bilotti filled my glass, my fear over arresting Mark softened. Was it the alcohol or what the doctor had said concerning brain injuries?

54

Up all night, I considered whether it was time to throw in the towel. No matter how hard I tried to shield him, Mark was going to be arrested. There didn't seem to be anything I could do to stop it. Even the competency angle had been shut down.

I didn't want to go down that road but put my fear aside to keep Mark from having to go into the legal system. But when I called Weinstein last night, instructing him to go that route, he said Mark would still to have to surrender tomorrow. He'd go through the same process: before competency examinations and hearings.

Certain Mark didn't understand what the day was going to be like, I put a pod in the coffee machine.

"You're having another cup?"

It was my fourth. "Still feeling foggy."

She lowered her voice. "You did everything you could. Too much, if you ask me."

"I feel like I failed him."

"That's ridiculous." She looked around. "If he did it, he deserves to go away for a long time."

"He's my brother."

"That doesn't matter. Anybody who kills has to be held accountable."

It was tough to admit, but Cathy was right; if he killed Katie, he had to pay the price. All I'd wanted to do was help him. I couldn't totally abandon him, but now I had to focus on protecting myself.

I kept my eye on the clock as I went through emails. In the middle of typing a reply to our HR manager, the time ticked to nine o'clock. I made a call.

"Mr. Weinstein. It's Bill Miller."

"Good morning. What can I do for you?"

"I'm wondering if there's a chance I might be in a bit of trouble."

"Related to the Swift case?"

"Yes, but I had nothing to do with what happened to her."

"But you're concerned over what you may have done in an attempt to protect your brother?"

"Was it that obvious?"

"At times."

"Do you think I'm at risk?"

"That depends. Did you help hide the body?"

"No, I'd never do that."

"Get rid of a weapon?"

"No."

"Any direct involvement?"

"None."

"Everything you did was after the event?"

"Yes. I never really knew she was, uh, dead. I had a bad feeling, but that's all it was."

"Did Mark tell you he did it?"

"No but I put two and two together..."

"But you had no direct knowledge of the murder."

"That's right, none at all."

"Given what you've said, there may be interest in you, but I believe it would be for obstruction."

"Explain that to me."

"Withholding or fabricating information is a prosecutable offense. As an example, if your claim to have seen the young lady leave your home proves false, it would fall under fabrication. Your attempts to shelter Mark would qualify as impeding and misleading an investigation."

Weinstein never believed me. "They don't prosecute those types of things these days."

"They certainly do. While it's not an everyday occurrence, examples must be made to keep the charge from proliferating."

"And I'd make a good example?"

"Unfortunately, that may be the case."

"What are the penalties?"

"Providing false information is a first-degree misdemeanor in Florida, punishable by up to a year's imprisonment and a fine."

"They wouldn't put me... would they?"

"Unlikely, but depending on how serious the breaches are, it's possible."

I couldn't tell Cathy what I was worried about and stepped onto the lanai. The way the lake shimmered when the sun rose in the east was magical. I wished there was some wizardry I could deploy to get us out of this jam.

Standing on the dock, I rationalized that with our legal firepower, we were in good shape. Despite the appeal to make an example out of me, the chances of going to prison for even a day, were remote.

The things to worry about were Mark and the media attention he would bring to the family business. When Dad took his own life, I hired a public relations firm. I didn't know if it would help, but we needed to change what was talked about when it came to the Miller family.

They did a media blitz, focusing on the struggle my dad had to undertake to make his business a success in the age of big box retailers. It portrayed us as the underdog, and business jumped 20 percent.

I pulled my phone out. Staring at the screen, I debated the slim odds we wouldn't need them. Scrolling, I hit dial. It was time to get them involved.

———

WEINSTEIN PULLED his car to the rear entrance of the station. He parked. "You ready, Mark?"

Mark looked at me. I said, "He's better than ready. This is going to be all over in a couple of hours. Less time than it takes to play a round of golf."

Mark nodded.

I reached for the door handle. "Remember, after this, we're going straight to get that virtual reality setup." I squeezed his knee. "Come on, let's get this over with."

He smiled thinly and got out. Two uniformed officers burst out of the rear door, and Mark scrambled behind me. "Don't let them get me."

The officers turned left, getting into a patrol car. I said, "Take it easy, it's going be all right."

Weinstein held the door open and I led Mark in. It was quieter than I expected. We sat along a wall. I put my arm around Mark as he rocked back and forth.

A pair of officers approached. Weinstein stood and introduced us. I pulled Mark to his feet. The smaller policeman said to me, "Step away, sir." I shuffled away as the officers stood on either side of my brother.

"Mark Miller, you're under arrest for the murder of Kate Swift."

One cop read him his rights as the other slapped cuffs on him. I put my fingers in my ears as Mark screamed. My stomach lurched.

Mark refused to walk. As the officers dragged him away, I knew I'd never forget this for the rest of my life.

55

LUCA

By time the Uber car pulled up to my house, I was back in a full-blown funk over the impending arrest of Mark Miller. The comfort in what Bilotti had said about a brain injury's impact on impulsive and emotional behavior had faded.

Now, the ruminating over confabulation was consuming me. I'd never heard of the term before. Bilotti explained the condition caused the brain to make up stories to fill gaps in memory.

If Mark was confusing reality, he shouldn't be arrested but assessed for competency. Why wasn't Weinstein pushing for a declaration? It didn't make sense.

I sat up. Was that the plan all along? To claim whatever Mark said was a mishmash of reality and fantasy? My wine buzz dissipated several notches as I considered the possibility of such a legal stance. It was a brilliant idea.

We'd need physical evidence, and all we had was circumstantial. They were friends; he was the last person to see her, and her remains were found on the Miller property.

That was a lot of circumstantial evidence, and combined

with what Alston said Mark told him, it could sway a jury. But where was the truth?

––––––––––

REMIN HADN'T RESPONDED to my email request for a meeting. I called his secretary. The sheriff was out, giving a presentation on sexual predators. I grabbed my jacket and headed out to see a friend of Paul Taras. Instead of going to my car, I hustled across the campus and pushed through the doors of the court building.

"Hey, Frank. You testifying again?"

"Nah, going to see Mason." I emptied my pockets and went through security.

A Collier County attorney, Lee Mason, was one of those people whose eyes were yellowed in the white areas. He stood and grinned. "How are you, Frank?"

"Good. You and Emily?"

"We're heading to Sanibel on Saturday."

"Enjoy. We haven't been there in a long time. It's a great spot."

"Yeah, we're looking forward to it. What's going on?"

I lowered my voice. "The Swift case. I need to know if an arrest warrant was issued for Mark Miller."

"Remin didn't tell you?"

"He said he was going to get one but he's MIA."

"Whiting signed it late yesterday. Miller's surrendering at noon."

My stomach dropped. "Thanks, I've got to go. Enjoy the vacation."

––––––––––

I DROVE, my thoughts ricocheting like a professional hitting a break shot on a pool table. The sheriff was moving too fast. Would Mark Miller turn into another Barrow? I couldn't take the chance. The question was how to reinsert myself into the Swift case.

The simplest answer was to solve the Park Shore murder. But the reality was it was never easy to figure out a killing without a witness or hard physical evidence. Stopped at a light on Bonita Beach Road, I made a call.

"Longo, it's Luca."

"Franko, how's it hanging?"

He didn't need to know my troubles. "Pretty good. Say, looks like a witness ID'd Roberto Caldera as the previous owner of a home where the murder occurred."

"He's a badass."

"Can you check around, see if anyone put a hit out on him?"

"There was some kind of dustup about two months back at a restaurant in Little Havana."

"The Cuban part of Miami?"

"Yeah, Caldera and one of his girls were at the table that Favret, he's the top dog in Little Haiti, usually sits at."

"How many 'Littles' you guys got over there?"

He laughed, "Just those two, bro."

"What happened at the restaurant?"

"Favret told Caldera to get his ass off his table. Caldera drew a weapon and Favret pulled his out. After some dick measuring, the old woman who owns the place begged them to back down, and Favret told Caldera to watch his back and walked out."

"It's like the Wild West over there."

"It's gotten better, just some neighborhoods got to be avoided."

"Were any of the pictures of the enforcers out of the Haitian community?"

"You said they were Latino or white."

"They could've outsourced it, to get some distance from the tiff they got in. Can you sniff around?"

"You got it, bro."

I wondered how we were ever going to break the cycle of ethnic gangs. It was all about assimilation. It was tough to come to a new country and adjust to a new culture and language. The natural inclination was to align yourself with those from the same country who'd made the move. It made it easier, but I was convinced the insular nature held you down in the long run.

Passing Coconut Point, I pulled into a parking lot of an office building. Outdoor Concepts was on the second floor. I expected a showroom filled with chaise lounges and firepits, but it looked like any other office.

Kurt Houghton was tall, with a premature head of gray hair. His handshake was firm, but there wasn't a hint of a smile on his face.

"Let's go to my office."

The walls of his office were lined with pictures of their stores.

"I didn't realize you had so many stores. How many locations you have?"

"Forty-two. We're shutting down the last couple in Michigan. My dad started up there, but they just don't do the business the southern ones do."

"Makes sense."

"How can I help you, Detective?"

"It's about your friend, Paul Taras. I'm interested in his relationship with his wife."

"Paul is a good guy. We've known each other since we were ten, but we don't see as much of each other these days."

"Why is that?"

"We're at, uh, different stages of our lives. My wife and I have two kids and Paul and Sylvia never had kids, and you know, they were having issues."

"Can you expound?"

"Paul is one of the most ambitious guys I know. He's always reaching for the next thing, and Sylvia, she's more, I hate to say this but... down to earth."

"I'm aware of his affair with Cecilia Newly. How serious would you characterize it as?"

"Oh, it was serious. Paul was considering divorce."

"Did he see an attorney about it?"

"He said he was, but, uh, we never spoke about it again."

"How long ago was that?"

"Just a month or two before she was murdered. I still can't believe it."

56

LUCA

I lifted my head. It sounded like a wild animal had been attacked. I got up and opened my office door. Someone was screaming. I looked at my watch. It was 12:10 p.m.

It had to be Mark Miller. Hustling toward booking, I heard him shriek, "No! Billy! Save me!"

I closed my eyes before rounding the corner. Between the backs of Bill Miller and his lawyer, I saw Mark being dragged away. Swallowing hard, I exhaled. I took a step toward the stairwell and stopped. I couldn't storm up to the sheriff's office; it wouldn't accomplish anything.

Retreating to my office, I invoked something Dr. Bruno taught me. She said to think through what I wanted to say in a confrontation situation. She even suggested rehearsing lines to stay focused on what I wanted to say and keep my anger in check.

It was easier said than done but it worked. The problem with this situation was Remin was my boss, and though I had a feeling Mark Miller wasn't the killer, it was certainly possible. My beef was he'd moved too fast. I couldn't be anywhere near another Barrow-type case.

Closing my eyes, I ordered my thoughts. I had to shake the emotional reaction I'd had seeing Mark dragged away. What I needed was clarification on why the sheriff acted and to get my hands back on the case.

It only took me ten minutes. I was going to keep it simple. Repeating the KISS acronym, Keep It Simple Stupid, I headed upstairs.

Remin was coming out of his office. He didn't have his jacket on. I stuck a finger in the air. He said, "Wait in my office. I'll be a minute."

I scanned the top of his desk. My eyes settled on the file from the cyber unit. It was marked Miller. What was that about? I turned to see if anyone would see me taking a peek. Remin was coming in. "Sit, sit."

"Thanks. I won't take much of your time."

"You have an update of the Park Shore case?"

"Uh, yeah. More inconsistencies in the husband's story. He even explored getting a divorce, though he denied it when questioned."

"Not surprising, if it turns out he was involved."

"I don't think he's the triggerman though. He was the one to report it."

"Time to dig in."

"We're sifting through the tips that came into the hotline, and I'm still exploring the Miami-gang-mistaken-identity angle."

"Still a lot of ground to cover. When is Dickson due back?"

"Three more days."

"All right. Keep up the good work."

He reached for the phone, signaling the chat was over. I said, "What's going on with Miller?"

"He'll be arraigned in the morning."

"I'd like to be there when the next interview is conducted."

"You have more than enough to deal with right now."

"I know the players, sir."

"I'll think about it."

"I couldn't help notice the cyber file. What's that about?"

"They were able to uncover websites this kid visited years ago. Guess nothing really gets deleted."

"What did they come up with?"

"He was interested in the speed of body decomposition and what temperature a fire needed to be to turn bones into ash."

"When was this?"

"A couple of years back." He shook his head. "People think they're smarter than us."

It was true, but I wasn't sure Mark Miller believed that. I wasn't sure of much about the case except it needing me to be involved.

THE ONLY WAY I was going to get back on the Swift case was to solve the Park Shore murder. And even then, I worried Remin would squeeze me out if it would benefit his campaign.

I pulled in front of the Tarases' home and surveyed the ritzy street. The houses were large though not spaced out. One of the tips that had come in was from a woman who said she saw a female by the Tarases' home at the time she heard a gunshot.

It was either a neighbor or someone taking a walk or riding a bike. We had a couple of officers revisiting the homes on the street. I'd asked a car to sit just off Crayton Road for the hour before and after the time of the shooting.

Most people had routines and exercised at the same time of day. Chances were, we'd find who it was. Wild cards were someone walking to the beach, a tourist or short-term renter in an Airbnb.

Paul Taras pushed open the door, and a welcome blast of cold air hit my face. He looked over my shoulder. "Would you like to come in?"

"Sure. Working from home again?"

"I have admin items to deal with, and they're dealt with best without distraction."

I stepped into the foyer. Classical music was playing in the distance. "Nice option to have."

"Working remotely is spreading. The only thing holding it back is the fear companies can't manage productivity. It's a baseless fear. We have the tools to effectively manage it. It's all about mindset."

"It's a good trend, but some jobs, like mine, can't be done remotely."

"True to a point, but can you envision this interview taking place via Zoom?"

I didn't want to show my age or put him on guard by saying no. "That will take some imagination."

"Maybe, but those who embrace new technologies make the transition much easier than those who resist or delay adoption."

He had a point but I needed context conducting an interview. Watching a video of a crime scene couldn't compare to being on the scene. Seeing, smelling, and getting a sense of the scale were impossible looking at a screen. I also thought about the inability to read body language on a Zoom call. "I guess we'll see how quickly it spreads." Before he had a chance to respond, I asked, "How is Cecilia?"

"I believe Cissy is doing well. But you'd have to check with her."

"You tried to give me the impression it was over with her."

"Whether you choose to believe me or not, it is."

"You said divorce wasn't something you were interested in."

"That's correct."

"Yet you discussed getting one, with friends."

His ears flattened. "I realize you have a job to do, Detective, but I can't say I'm pleased you're interrogating my friends over my personal life."

"You were looking into getting a divorce but your wife wouldn't agree."

"That's not true. I never mentioned it to Sylvia. I was frustrated with our relationship and needed to explore options."

"Did you contact a divorce lawyer?"

"No. There was no need. We worked on patching up the relationship."

"While you were still seeing Cecilia?"

"Look, as far as I'm concerned, it's over."

"But she feels differently?"

He shrugged. "She's clingy."

"Expand upon that."

"She became increasingly possessive. Perhaps I was blind to it, but she began demanding more and more of my time. I have a growing business that needs my attention, and it's one of the things I truly enjoy, but she was jealous."

"Do you think she could have been involved in the murder of your wife?"

"Cissy? No, I can't see that, no way."

"All right. I'll leave you to your work."

"What about the previous owners? They were unsavory characters."

"I can't discuss it, but we're looking into the possibility they're involved."

57

MILLER

Weinstein left an hour ago. There was no chance of Mark being released tonight. I don't know why I hung around but I had. Actually, I knew what it was. It was the guilt.

It was irrational, but I couldn't shake the blue feeling. What happened wasn't my fault, I kept telling myself, but the thought I should have supervised him and Katie was circling in my head.

Trying to be fair with myself was tough. Mark was an adult. He had issues, for sure, but he'd been productive at work and was quiet, most of the time, at home. What I couldn't push into a closet was the fact I looked the other way when signs of instability surfaced.

And there was the violence toward animals. It was disturbing, and the research said it was a forerunner to larger problems.

The wooden bench was irritating my butt. I stood. It was time to leave. Whatever or however I'd contributed, I had to deal with the situation confronting me.

Heading to my car, the energy bars I bought from the

vending machine began climbing up my throat. Was it the junk they put in them or the five cups of burnt coffee I'd sucked down?

I pulled into my garage and sat in the car. It was 10:45 p.m. Cathy would want to know what happened. I took a couple of breaths, reminding myself to keep as much emotion out of it as possible and went inside.

WEINSTEIN SAID Mark's arraignment would begin around at 10:00 a.m. He said he had a call to make and wanted to discuss something after the hearing. I pulled open a huge wooden door, hesitating before entering the courtroom.

I sat in stunned silence between a woman with more tattoos than I'd ever seen and a man with so many piercings he looked like he'd fallen into a tackle box.

I listened to two domestic violence cases and a disorderly conduct one before Mark was brought into the courtroom. Bile splashed the back of my throat as he shuffled in. He searched the room and I stood up, waving.

"Help me, Billy."

Weinstein rushed to his side as the guard removed his cuffs. I banged into knees getting out of the row. Weinstein said something to the bailiff and waved me off.

"Don't worry, Mark. I'm here for you."

"I wanna go home."

The gavel sounded and the judge's voice boomed, "Order! Order!"

I slid into a row, and a woman with more sorrow on her face than Mother Mary scooted over.

The case was called, and Mark entered a plea of not guilty.

Weinstein asked for release without bail, and two minutes later an agreement on a hundred-thousand-dollar amount was made. I was stunned something so important took minutes to complete.

I EXHALED as Mark turned the corner. He was escorted by a policeman. "Hey, buddy."

"Billy. I can go, right?"

"Yep. Come on."

As soon as we stepped into the heat, he said, "We going to get the VR, right? Oh yeah! I can't wait to play with it."

"Stay here. I need to talk to Mr. Weinstein."

"No. Don't leave."

"Come on, sit in the car."

Mark climbed in, and I put the air on. "It'll only take a minute."

I wasn't sure whether the serious look on Weinstein's face was from the sun or if there was a new problem.

"That went faster than expected."

"Fairly routine."

"What did you want to talk about?"

"They compiled data on Mark's browsing history."

I stiffened. "What kind?"

"Mainly things he's searched and places visited."

"Everybody Googles everything."

"True, but a couple of his searches are potential problems."

"Like what?"

"Information on body decomposition and an inquiry on the temperature of a fire needed to incinerate bones."

Trying to process what I'd heard, I said, "That doesn't

mean anything. Who doesn't look up crazy stuff? I know I do."

"You're not accused of murder."

"This doesn't make any sense, and it doesn't prove anything."

"It supports the narrative. They'll claim Mark was looking for a way to get rid of Kate Swift's body."

"That's ridiculous."

"Possibly, but my concern is a jury may consider it bolsters the case. Don't forget the remains were found on your property. It's plausible an attempt was made to hasten decomposition."

"How damaging is something like this?"

"On its own, not much, but it supports the narrative."

The horn honked. I turned toward my car, and Mark was waving like he was at the Indy 500 finish line.

58

LUCA

Clara Kerber had steely-gray hair and either a good plastic surgeon or fantastic genes. She was fit and looked ten years younger than the sixty-two the DMV said she was.

"Please come in, Detective."

Her home was understated and comfortable. We sat in a kitchen dominated by a lazy fan.

"Thank you for reaching out, but can you clarify why you never came forward before?"

"Frankly, I didn't want to get involved. The old neighbors were, uh, bad people."

"How do you know that?"

She motioned to the side of her backyard bordering the Tarases' home. "My roses require a lot of attention. It's not easy growing them in Southwest Florida. You need the right spot to get enough morning sun but not the afternoon sun, it's too hot. Where they're planted between the house and the hedge, they're shaded in the afternoon."

It was an interesting horticultural lesson but I was inpatient. "Everybody loves roses. So, what does the location have to do with the neighbors?"

"Like I said, I'm out there often and I overheard that man—"

"Caesar?"

She nodded. "Yes, I heard him on two occasions, talking about an illegal shipment coming."

"What made you believe it was illegal?"

She put her hands on her hips. "I may be in my sixties, Detective, but that doesn't mean I'm not tuned in. They were engaged in drug transactions, and it's why I kept my distance."

"I understand. Please tell me what you saw."

"I was fertilizing the roses that morning because we were going away, and I saw a woman through the hedge."

"Did you recognize her?"

"No."

"Where was she?"

"She was walking very slowly. In hindsight, it made sense."

"What time was this?"

"It was just after ten."

"Are you sure about the time?"

"Yes. I take a walk every morning at eight sharp. Then I shower and have fruit for breakfast. I'm always done around nine forty-five. I went to the garage for the fertilizer and my trusty spade and gloves and went out back."

"How good a look did you get of this woman?"

"Pretty good one. I've had twenty-twenty vision my whole life and still do."

"Had you ever seen this woman before?"

"I don't think so, but you never know."

I wanted to ask her about the vision she just bragged

about. "Do you believe you can describe her to a sketch artist?"

Her face lit up. "Like they do in the movies?"

Almost nothing about police work was properly portrayed by Hollywood. "It's a process. The lady who sketches for the department is very good. You'll go back and forth with her."

"I'll do my best."

"Thanks. Let me organize it, and I'll get back to you."

Walking down the long driveway, my phone rang. "Hey, Longo. How's it going?"

"It's going, bro. It's going. Look, I got some news for you."

"Shoot."

"Guess who we have sitting in the county jail?"

Working with Derrick, I realized people liked to use the guessing game as a tactic to delay the passing of information. Having knowledge of something another person would want to know gave you a sense of power. Once you conveyed the info, the power was gone.

"The tooth fairy?"

"Always the wiseass, ain't ya?"

"What, me change? Who you got locked up?"

"Juan Banda. He's second-in-command of Frisco's rival gang. If anybody was gunning for Caldera, it's them."

"He talking?"

"No, but we have him on CCTV going into a Haitian social club where two people were shot dead."

"He did it?"

"Didn't get ballistics back, but I'm not sure it matters. Him and two others entered the place with guns drawn."

"He's going away for a long time."

"No doubt. But I thought we might dangle a deal, see what he knows about the murder you're working."

"You think he'll sing?"

"Banda's got a rap sheet that doubles as a table runner. He doesn't play ball, he'll be behind bars until the first colony on Mars is built."

"You guys on board with offering a deal?"

"I talked to the lead prosecutor. It was informal, but he thought they'd go for it as long as Banda gets ten years minimum."

"That's a long time. You think Banda will grab it?"

"These guys make a big deal about loyalty and don't usually squawk, but these days, it's every man for himself."

"I hear you. Look, I really appreciate you thinking of me."

"Anytime, bro. Anytime. I'll give it a whirl, and let's see what shakes out."

I had two leads working, but they were going in separate directions. The chances of Remin letting me back on the Swift case were slim until I figured this one out. The traffic was backed up on Route 41. I put a call into the sketch artist and punched another number in my cell.

"Hey, Frank. What's up?"

I filled Derrick in on the Taras case. He said, "Something will break. It's good you have your buddy in Miami."

"Longo might be a character but he's a damn good cop."

"That would be sick if the poor woman was killed by mistake."

"It doesn't get sadder. But I'm not sold it's gang related. Things aren't adding up with the husband."

"The odds are it's him."

"I know."

"Anything new on the Swift case?"

I told him what the cyber unit discovered about Mark Miller's browsing. He said, "Nobody understands the trails they're leaving."

"And don't tell them; it'll make our jobs tougher."

He laughed. "No doubt."

"How's it going up there?"

"Good. We're moving her in tomorrow, and then we're hitting the road. Be back before you know it."

"Good. I can use the help."

"Believe me. I'm itching to get back."

Crawling toward Pine Ridge Road, I hoped we'd have a drawing of the woman in question. It usually took a couple of hours. Once we had it, we'd get it to the media outlets and see what the public could do for us.

I crossed Pine Ridge and turned onto the service road by Allison Craig Furnishings. Moving along behind a handful of cars also taking advantage, I slowed for a stop sign. The cross street was Center Street. The Miller house was just a few blocks away.

59

LUCA

Mary Ann was sleeping on a chaise in the shade. The book she'd been reading was ready to fall off her lap. I reached for it and she stirred. "Hey, how you feeling?"

"I was reading and dozed off."

"That's good."

"What are you doing home?"

"Going to work remotely."

"What?"

I dug in my pocket and pulled out the thumb drive. "Going to review an interview Remin conducted."

"Oh."

"Go back to sleep." I picked up her water glass. "I'll get you some ice."

She fell back asleep. I put the glass down and retreated to the den. Popping the drive in, I hit play and leaned toward the screen as it came to life.

I was struck by the time stamp. The sheriff hadn't resumed immediately. It made sense. He probably reviewed what I'd conducted before being pulled out of the room. Still, it wouldn't have taken as long as the recess had been.

Remin's interview style reminded me of my partner JJ. Rather than rely on someone else to play the good or bad cop, the sheriff was playing both parts. It was a Dr. Jekyll and Mr. Hyde approach that kept the interviewee off-balance and wanting to please.

He came into the room like Santa Claus. He laid two candy bars and a soda in front of Mark, eliciting a wide grin. As Mark tore off the wrapper, Remin launched into the questioning, starting by asking similar questions to those I had. Mark said nothing too differently, but Remin challenged him over what Kate was wearing, inferring that she had something provocative on.

Mark shook his head, and Weinstein reminded Remin that there was no evidence Kate was wearing anything inappropriate.

The sheriff pressed Mark on where they had stopped, asking if it was an area of the lake where visibility was limited. My stomach clenched. I knew where he was heading.

I cringed when Remin asked where Mark had touched Katie. Mark held his head in his hands but didn't answer. Remin softened his voice: "It's okay. When I was a teenager, me and my girlfriends used to go on a boat in the Everglades, when we wanted, you know, to explore a little. It's natural."

"I didn't do nothing wrong."

"I didn't say it was wrong. It's natural. You know, we have these things called hormones that make us do things. God created us to have strong desires for the opposite sex."

Weinstein said, "Is there a question in there somewhere?"

"Did you touch Kate Swift?"

"Touch her?"

Remin slammed a palm on the table. "You know what I mean, damn it."

Mark turned to Weinstein, who whispered to his client. Mark said, "I'm taking the Fifth with me."

Weinstein patted his client's arm and Mark smiled.

Was Remin onto something? No one had explored the possibility Mark had made an advance, been rebuffed and got angry.

Remin said, "If you're hiding something, we'll find out, and I promise you, you'll regret it."

"Are you threatening my client?"

"It's not a threat. If your client comes clean, we'll recommend as much leniency as the law allows. It's a risk you should consider."

"My client has professed his innocence since the onset. Do you have any other questions?"

"We're far from done, Mr. Weinstein. Remin smiled, softening his voice: "Mark, your brother Billy is older than you, right?"

"Yeah, I forget how many years, but Greg, he's in the middle of us."

"Older brothers are great. My brother always looked out for me. Does Billy look after you?"

"Oh yeah, he does a lot for me. He got me a new boat."

"A new boat? Wow. That's an expensive present. What did you do to get that?"

"He said, I had to be quiet, not say anything, and I'd get a new boat. You have to see it. You want to come for a ride? We can go around the whole lake and go fast."

Weinstein's Adam's apple bobbed. He leaned over, whispering in Mark's ear.

"Billy didn't want you talking about what happened to Katie, did he?"

Mark shrugged, his voice a murmur: "He gets mad."

. "I promise not to tell Billy. Tell me what happened to Katie."

Mark picked at a fingernail and rocked in his chair.

"I'm a policeman. You can trust me. Billy will never know what you tell me."

He sighed like a sixteen-year-old.

"What happened to Katie?"

He whispered, "She died." He started sobbing. "I miss her."

Weinstein stood. "We're going to have to end this conversation."

"Wait a minute. Tell me how she died. We have a witness who saw you fighting with Kate. Stop crying and tell me what happened."

Weinstein put his hand under his client's armpit. "Come on, Mark."

"Sit down, you're not going anywhere."

"Excuse me, Sheriff? My client is traumatized by the loss of a life-long friend."

"Let's take a break. He'll steady himself."

"We're leaving. If you want to talk to him, call my office."

Remin's face was cherry red. "We're going to get to the truth, Counselor. Whether you stonewall or not. I suggest you cooperate."

I sat back trying to understand if the sheriff had pushed the kid to the brink of cracking or if Mark had retreated out of confusion. It was difficult to assess, especially with the revelation his brother had bought him a boat to keep him quiet.

The thought of arresting Mark Miller made me uneasy. No doubt he was a suspect, but his injury made him vulnerable. It made me think of Barrow. He was just a kid who never should have been jailed.

I stood, as an image of Barrow, hanging from a prison-cell pipe, flooded my head. Not standing up to my partner at the time had kept my regret bucket filled for a decade.

Both cases involved the murder of a young woman and a lack of physical evidence. Had the sheriff made a mistake arresting Mark, or had the Barrow case clouded my judgment?

60

MILLER

Cathy bought me a new pair of golf shoes. It was a nice thought, but I always wore G/FORE and she picked up a pair of FootJoys. Putting my foot in a shoe, the doorbell rang. I kicked it off and headed to the door, wondering why Benny was twenty minutes early.

It was Detective Luca. He looked at my sock feet. "Sorry to disturb you."

"I don't have time; we're teeing off soon."

"I'll be quick. May I come in?"

I stepped to the side and closed the door. "You need to go through Weinstein's office."

"Look, I know you're leery, but I'm trying to get this case right."

I didn't understand where he was going.

"And I wasn't on board with arresting your brother."

"That didn't stop it from happening, did it?"

Luca shook his head. "No, the sheriff made the call, and I'm not sure it was the right one."

"But you think Mark did it, right?"

"No. There's not enough to go on."

"And you're here to get more."

"No, I just want the truth. Some of the things said don't line up. If I could ask him a couple of questions."

Who did he think he was, Columbo? "Not without our attorney."

"It'll be off the record."

"You expect me to believe that?"

"I know you feel a responsibility to protect your brother, and I admire that. But I'm afraid he's going to get this pinned on him whether he did it or not."

"You believe he's being framed?"

Luca shrugged. "Not exactly. Things are moving too quickly and only centered on him."

"It's a nightmare, for him and the family."

"I understand. If I can have a quick word with him."

"I can't allow that."

"I'm going to be frank: from day one, you've tried to control the fallout. You've stonewalled and lied—"

"Hold on—"

Luca put his hand up. "You know exactly what I'm talking about, and the fact is, what did it get you?"

He was right, but could I trust him or was he playing me? I didn't know what to say.

"I get it. Family is the only thing that matters. Why did you think I left in the middle of the interview? My wife was rushed to the hospital."

"I'm sorry. Is she all right?"

"Yes. It was food poisoning."

"Thank God she's okay."

He nodded. "Look, I'm not condoning your failure to cooperate, but I understand trying to protect your brother."

He was a policeman and I couldn't trust him, but he was

better to deal with than the sheriff. This detective was still going to nail Mark if he could but appeared to understand my predicament.

"I have a lot of respect for the police and always supported them. If I did anything that came across as uncooperative, it wasn't, you know, intentional."

"I like to talk straight. What you did was intentional. Shielding Mark and creating that sighting with your other brother, to start with, are clearly obstructive."

I couldn't keep denying. It would inflame Luca. "Am I going to have a problem?"

"That depends. If you cooperate now, I'd make sure the charge wouldn't be prosecuted."

The clench in my stomach released. Then came right back. "But the sheriff, he makes the decisions, right?"

"To a degree, but if he pushed, I'd tell the prosecutors I'd testify on your behalf. They'd drop it right there."

"What do you want?"

"To talk to Mark."

"Without our lawyer?"

"It'll be off the record."

I didn't believe that for a second. "I don't know, things have a way of slipping out."

"You're right about that, but anything he tells me wouldn't be admissible in court."

"Really?"

"Yes. Since he invoked his right to an attorney, he'd have to initiate the contact. I really think it's in his best interest to chat. Why not tell him to call me?"

To start with, I was worried Luca was setting a trap. "Let me think about it."

"I wouldn't wait. Once a case gets momentum, it's hard to stop it. Plus, you'll eliminate your obstruction problem."

The way he said it made me believe they were going to come after me. Before I could respond, the doorbell rang. I opened the door. It was Benny.

"Can you hang on a second? I'm finishing up with—"

Detective Luca said, "It's okay. I'm leaving. Thanks for your time."

I stepped aside, and Benny almost bumped into Luca. Benny said, "Sorry."

Luca nodded. "Mr. Alston. Have a good game, fellas."

Watching the detective walk away, Benny said, "What's going on?"

"Nothing. Go in the kitchen. I'm going to get my things together."

Mind racing, I headed into the bedroom, closing the door behind me. Before I could even think of cooperating with Luca, I had to know if it could backfire on Mark or me. I couldn't call Weinstein. He'd shut this down, ending a chance to get me off the hook for trying to help Mark.

I needed to ask someone who knew the law. Scooping up my golf shoes, Charles Berwick popped into my head. He'd handled the family's estate plans for decades. Scrolling through my phone, I found his name and hit dial.

"Charlie. It's Bill Miller."

"Bill, how are you?"

"Pretty good. But Mark is unfairly being targeted in the Kate Swift case."

"I don't handle criminal law."

"I know, but hear me out a second."

"Okay."

"What they have is flimsy, and the detectives don't believe Mark had anything to do with it."

"I see. That's promising."

"If I tell you something, will it be confidential? Protected by attorney-client privilege."

He hesitated for five seconds. "Yes, you're a client, but I don't think we should be mixing—"

"It's nothing. I just want to know if Mark speaks to the detective, unofficially, could anything he says be used against him?"

"He's represented by Weinstein, isn't he?"

"Yes."

"Then he shouldn't be talking to anyone without him present."

"I realize that, but this would be off the record. The detective is trying to help us."

"Still, it's a terrible idea. Don't do it."

"I'm not saying he's going to, but can it come back to haunt him?"

"It's improper contact. No judge will allow it to make it to court, and the detective could be reprimanded."

61

LUCA

I came in through the garage. As I stepped into the family room, the washing machine chimed. Mary Ann was in my recliner. I pecked her cheek. "Hey, how you feeling?"

"Good. I'm not feeling as tired."

"Great. Did you call the doctor?"

She nodded. "He said to wait for two weeks before getting another shot."

"He's playing it safe, like he should."

"How was your day?"

"Busy. I'm going to get changed."

"Busy? That's it? It'd be nice to hear what's going on in the real world."

I turned around. "Went to see a witness in the Park Shore case. She's coming in tomorrow to work with the sketch artist. And I stopped by the Millers'—"

"You're back on Swift?"

"Not officially."

"You'd better be careful; you don't want to cross Remin."

"I know. Derrick's due back, and we'll be on it soon enough."

"Be careful."

The washing machine sounded again, and Mary Ann started to get up. "Stay there. I'll get it, but not for nothing. Does Jessie ever unload anything?"

"She helps."

I knew she didn't. It was a problem we created by doing everything for her. I was going to talk to her. The timing was right; her mother was sick, and she couldn't refuse to pitch in. Who knew, maybe it would become a habit.

Moving the wet clothes into the dryer, I considered Mary Ann's warning. Remin was new and running for full term as sheriff. He was using the Swift case to show he was hands on.

Getting into a pissing match with his lead homicide detective didn't seem likely. It'd prove he'd run a tight ship, but besides alienating a lot of the people he needed, he'd have to explain why a seasoned veteran was in the doghouse.

I wondered if Remin knew the real reason I took a leave from the force was because Chester hadn't backed me up. The old sheriff let internal affairs run all over me, and between that and Derrick getting shot, I lost my mojo for the job.

I'd kept it fairly quiet, but anyone should have been able to read between the lines. Health insurance was important, but I'd made a go of it as a private investigator, and Remin had to be mindful of that.

My preference was to keep hunting killers. I reminded myself to curb my confidence and shifted to the Millers. Bill Miller wasn't going to change from the protective brother and family head he was.

He seemed to bite on eliminating the threat of obstruction prosecution. He wouldn't come entirely clean, but it was my best shot at trying to understand if Mark Miller was involved in the murder of Kate Swift.

———

I WASN'T A HUGGER, but when I came into the office, Derrick got up and embraced me. "Good to see you, Frank."

"Same here. Everything go all right?"

"It's all good. How about Mary Ann and Jessica?"

"Everyone is fine."

I picked up the cup of coffee Derrick brought for me. "Thanks."

"No problem. That lady working with Lee Ann?"

"Yeah, Kerber was here at eight. I'm hoping for a sketch soon."

"Be nice to get a hit."

"Amen."

"What are the chances it could be a woman hit man sent by the Miami gang?"

It was an interesting angle. "A woman hit man? Is that the way you say it?"

"Guess it's hit person these days."

I got up and closed the office door. "Doesn't sound as threatening."

Derrick raised his eyebrows, and I whispered, "I swung by the Millers yesterday."

He pointed to the ceiling. "He know?"

I shook my head. "I just want to talk to the kid, see if I can get to where Remin is on him."

"What did you get?"

"Nothing yet. Waiting to see if Bill Miller will let his brother talk."

"I don't see how he would."

"I dangled dropping obstruction on him."

"They're going after him for obstruction?"

"No, but he doesn't know that."

He smiled. "Cute. You think he believes it?"

"Absolutely. Miller knows he didn't play this straight. He just doesn't know obstruction isn't prosecuted often."

"It should be; make our jobs easier."

My desk phone rang. I answered and hung up. "The sketch is ready."

Derrick was out of his chair. "I'll get it."

As I tapped out a reply to an email, Derrick came back in. "Guess who it is?"

I frowned and he said, "Okay, okay. Here."

He handed me the sketch. "I can't believe it. Cecilia Newly."

"I never thought it was Taras's girlfriend, did you?"

"We don't know for sure, but Taras said she was an obsessed lover who wouldn't let go."

"How do you want to play this?"

"At this point, we have her at the house just before the murder. We also have clear motive; she wanted the wife out of the way so she could have her husband."

"We should bring her in."

"I don't want to get her guard up. If she didn't get rid of the gun, she would if we alarm her. Let's go for a search warrant."

"We have enough?"

My cell began ringing. "We have strong motive, and she was at the scene. I think we do." I answered the call, "Frank Luca."

"It's Mark."

"Mark Miller?"

"Yeah. I'm at work. Come now."

"Sure, that's perfect. I'll head over immediately."

I stuffed my phone away. "I've got to go; it was Mark Miller. He's going to talk."

"Go, go, go. I'll get the warrant prepared and send it upstairs. Good luck."

62

MILLER

Before Mark hung up, a bad feeling swept over me. This was a mistake. A bad one. What was I thinking?

"He said he's coming."

"When?"

"Now."

"Right now?"

"Yeah, you said to do it now."

"Okay, that's good."

"You said he was going to help us, right?"

"Yes, but we have to be careful; he's a policeman."

"Careful about what?"

"About what you did to Kate?"

"I don't understand. What did I do?"

"Did you hurt her?"

"No."

"Tell me the truth."

"I am! Nobody believes me! Why?"

"Take it easy. I believe you. It's okay if you did something. Everybody makes mistakes."

"No! I didn't! I didn't!"

"Okay."

"I can't go back to jail."

63

LUCA

After reminding myself not to push Mark, I tossed my sunglasses on the dash and headed into Miller's store. A man with a potbelly and huge smile welcomed me into the store. I didn't get why retailers needed greeters. They should save the money and lower prices instead.

As I walked up to the customer service counter, a man in a suit got there first. He said to the representative, "You see Benny?"

"No."

"If you do, tell him I want to see him. Now. None of his excuses."

As the woman nodded, he took off. I stepped up. "He's not a happy camper."

She smiled.

"He's the boss?"

"No. Ken is the HR manager."

"Wouldn't want to be Benny."

She screwed up her face.

"He's that bad?"

She nodded. "How can I help you?"

"My name's Frank. I'm here to see Bill and Mark Miller."

"Let me call upstairs."

Bill Miller met me in the reception area that overlooked the shopping floor. We shook hands. "Come in my office."

I followed him, hoping they hadn't had a change of heart. "How's business?"

"Good. I'm concerned about prices. Everyday we get notices of increases. We can't keep absorbing them, and if we pass them on to the customers, they may pull back."

"The government likes to say there is no inflation; they need to go the supermarket."

Back to us, Mark was in a chair in front of Bill's desk.

"Mark, you remember Detective Luca, don't you?"

Mark was quickly turning sections of a Rubik's Cube. "Uh-huh."

I extended my hand.

Mark kept playing with the cube. "Mark, the detective wants to shake."

He looked up and put his fist forward. I clenched and bumped it.

"How are you doing today?"

"All right."

"I wanted to have a little chat. Nothing to worry about. It's informal."

He looked at Bill, who said, "Just like I told you. Frank is here to help."

"That's right. Our little talk is going to be private. Just you and me."

Bill said, "And me. I'll be right here."

I didn't want him in the room. Mark was under his influence. "We'll start in a second. I'd like to talk to Bill first."

He worked the Rubik's Cube. "Okay."

We retreated to a corner. "It's better if we talk alone."

He shook his head. "No way."

"You're too close to him. He'll never open up."

"I can't allow it."

"He'll craft his answers to please you."

"Look, I shouldn't even be doing this."

"But—"

"I'm sorry, but take what you can get or forget it."

It was less than ideal. "Okay, let's get this going. But please, don't interfere."

I pulled a chair closer to Mark. Not in front but to the side. Bill sat behind his desk and said, "Mark, put down the Rubik's Cube."

I said, "No, it's all right. I'm amazed you can do it. I tried a bunch of times but gave up."

"I can show you."

"That would be cool. I have to pick up my daughter later; can you show me tomorrow?"

"Okay, okay. It's easy peasy."

"I'm sorry you had to go the police station."

"I had to sleep there. It was loud and the bed was, like, so hard."

"You know, I stayed a whole week in there a few years ago."

"You did? Why?"

"It's a long story, but let's make sure you and me never have to stay there again."

"Billy says I don't have to go back there."

"That's why I'm here. Let's see if we can put an end to all this, okay?"

He twisted the cube, one side was almost all red. "Uh-huh."

"The last time you saw Kate, you said you went for a boat ride."

"We did. We always went on the lake."

Remembering how Dr. Bruno handled talking about emotional subjects, I avoided asking about him being mad because she didn't want to drive the boat. "Who was at the house that day?"

"Me, Kate and Billy and Benny and Aunt Cathy. And Grandpa too."

Out of the corner of my eye, I saw Bill shake his head. As Mark twisted the cube, I looked at Bill and put a finger to my lips. "Are you sure they were all there the day Katie went missing?"

"Yeah. Kate, Billy, Aunt Cathy and Gramps and Benny. They were there."

"What was everybody doing?"

"You know, hanging out."

"Your Aunt Cathy, was she talking with Billy and Benny?"

He shrugged. "I think she was cooking."

"Your grandfather... was he outside?"

"No, he didn't feel good and was lying down."

"And Benny? Was he with your uncle?"

He shook his head. "He came after. He and Billy golf Sundays. I go with them sometimes."

"So, Benny came after golfing?"

"No, after we got off the boat."

"Was he hanging out with your brother?"

"No, he was fishing."

"Did he catch anything?"

"There's a lot of fish in the lake. One time I caught a big, red one. Remember, Billy?"

"Of course, it was an eight pounder."

"Wow."

Mark raised the Rubik's Cube over his head. "Finished!"

"I hope you can teach me do it that fast."

"I will, I will." He grabbed it with two hands. "First, you have to move the middle one."

"Remember, I have to get my daughter, so, tomorrow, you can teach me."

He frowned.

"I like to look stuff up on the internet. Find answers to things I want to know. Do you do that?"

"Uh-huh, and I like to watch videos on YouTube and TikTok too."

"Me too, but my favorite is to just find information on something I'm interested in, like how far away a place is. Or, one time my dog died and I wanted to bury him in the back-yard, so I looked up how deep I had to dig the hole, so animals couldn't get to him."

"I do that sometimes."

"You lost a dog?"

"No." He looked at Bill. Was he going to shut it down?

The most subtle thing I could come up with was, "What did you bury?"

64

MILLER

Detective Luca gave a big smile to Mark. "I want to thank you for speaking with me. I really appreciate it."

"You want me to show you how to do this?" He held up the Rubik's Cube.

Luca stood. "I do, but I gotta run. My daughter is waiting for me."

"Tomorrow?"

"That should work."

The detective looked at me. "Can we have a quick word?"

"Mark, why don't you go to your office. I'm going to walk Mr. Luca out."

"Okay, bye."

I closed the door. "That had to help. Now you know the web searching was harmless."

"It seems that way."

"Seems? He told you he wanted to bury the squirrels he was killing. He was fixated on them and leaving them around. My wife went ballistic."

"Speaking of your wife. You said she wasn't home that day."

"That's right. Cathy was visiting her family."

"I'll have to confirm that."

"Be my guest. And before you ask, my father was dead when Katie disappeared."

"What about Benny Alston? Was he there the day Kate Swift went missing?"

"No, not that I know of. He doesn't live far and could've come over, but I would have seen him."

"You were outside the entire time?"

I had fallen asleep in a chaise lounge and gone in and out of the house. "Just about."

"I wonder why he said your father was there."

"It's not intentional. Sometimes Mark gets confused over certain things."

"Was he always like that?"

"No. It was the accident. The doctor said the injury created gaps in his memory and that Mark fills in what's missing."

Luca slowly nodded. He was distracted.

"Nobody knows what happened, but you could see how much he loved Katie. He'd never hurt her."

"What do you think happened to her?"

"I don't know."

"You have to have an idea."

"I just think she had to meet someone after she left. Maybe some lunatic was able to lure her into a car and that was it."

"How did she end up buried on your property?"

"Whoever it was wanted to make it look like Mark did it. They knew he suffered a brain injury. It's the perfect cover."

65

LUCA

Stepping into the sunshine, I tried to process the interview. Odd was an understatement. Could anything Mark said be trusted? The excuse for browsing sites for information on decomposition and incinerating bones was plausible. But it could have been concocted. If it was, I'd bet Bill Miller had come up with it.

I started the car and made a call.

"Hey, Doc, you got a minute?"

"Just sitting around, sipping a Côte-Rôtie, waiting for Frank to call."

"Ha ha. Côte-Rôtie? What's that, a Côtes du Rhône?"

"No. Côte-Rôtie is from the Northern Rhône valley. They're mostly syrah with a splash of viognier. In my opinion, they're elegant."

"Cheap like Côtes du Rhône?"

"No, they're expensive. The vineyards are on steep hillsides facing the river. Côte-Rôtie roughly translates to roasted slopes because of all the sunshine they get."

"Interesting. Maybe I'll pick up a bottle when we have something to celebrate."

"You'll love them. What's on your mind?"

"The Swift case. You mentioned a phenomenon called confabulation where someone confuses reality with made-up stuff."

"Someone with the condition fills in the gaps in his memory by creating recollections, making a somewhat cohesive story they believe is what happened."

"Is it possible for someone to say they saw someone who was dead?"

"They're aware this person died?"

"Yes, Mark Miller claims his grandfather was there the day the girl disappeared."

"That was ten years ago. He could have a memory gap regarding the time frame."

"The house was the grandfather's."

"That could support the misunderstanding. He associates the grandfather with the home. But I'm not a psychotherapist."

Another call came in. "Sorry, Doc, gotta run. It's Derrick. Thanks."

"Hey, Derrick."

"We got the warrant."

"That was fast."

"I know. Where are you?"

"Just finished up with the Millers."

"How did it go?"

I filled him in on what Mark said about burying squirrels and who he claimed was at the house the day Swift disappeared.

"Man, that's weird."

"Yeah, I even called Bilotti. He said it's definitely possible, but I'm thinking of calling Dr. Bruno; see what she can tell me."

"She's the one you went to, right?"

It felt good not hiding the fact I'd gone to see a therapist. "Yes, she was a lifesaver. I'm heading in. Get Santiago to arrange a team for the search."

WE LED the procession into Grey Oaks. The guard at the gatehouse looked at my badge and the cars lined up behind. "She's not home."

"It doesn't matter. We have a warrant."

His jaw dropped. "A warrant? I have to let somebody know."

"Call who you want but lift the gate."

I waved to the others, and we proceeded to Newly's house. Getting out of the car, my phone vibrated. I pulled it out. It was John Trane from forensics. I swiped the call away and headed up the driveway.

"She's not home; no need to bust in. Use the lock kit. Put gloves and booties on."

We filed into the house. "I'll take the master bedroom; Derrick's got the kitchen. Divide up the rest."

I hesitated before stepping into the master. Though I had the right, I wouldn't want anyone invading my private space. Seven pillows were on the bed. Only two the sleeping kind.

Pulling on a cord, the ceiling-to-floor drapes opened. I opened the only nightstand. A bottle of melatonin stood beside a checkbook. I thumbed through the ledger; it was empty. Maybe with Taras funding her, she didn't have to worry about balancing her account.

A book titled, *Inner Peace* and a bracelet with a broken

clasp were the only other things. The table on the other side of the bed was filled with pictures of Newly as a young child and teenager. There were no family pictures. Its slim drawer had the second set of car keys and the business card of a nail salon. I moved on to the closets.

One master closet held more women's clothing than most Fifth Avenue boutiques. Shoes filled the racks. The shelf was crammed with shoeboxes. I checked each one. All shoes, no guns.

The other closet had a couple of pairs of men's slacks along with a handful of dress shirts. Next to a large firebox, sat a pair of casual shoes. I was betting they fit Paul Taras.

I knelt down and opened the document box. Thumbing through, I examined Ms. Newly's birth certificate, baptismal papers, and a high school diploma. Three folders remained. One was marked Prudential. It was a life insurance policy on her. The beneficiary was her mother, and the face value was just seventy-five thousand.

My eyes widened when I opened the next file. It was a receipt from Naples Guns and Ammo. She had purchased a Smith & Wesson .38 Special and a box of bullets. Gun ownership among women was around 20 percent, so it wasn't unusual. But it was a red flag.

I took the papers and left the bedroom. "Derrick!"

He was emptying the pantry and turned, holding two boxes of macaroni. "What's up?"

I held the receipt up. "She owns a gun."

"A thirty-eight?"

"Yep, and she bought it just six weeks before the murder."

"We need to locate that gun."

"I hope she didn't toss it in there."

Derrick looked at the lake. "Let's hope not."

Back in the bedroom, I rifled through toiletries under both

sinks. Nothing there or the linen closet. Back in the sleeping area, I got on my knees: nothing under the bed or dresser.

I lifted the bottom corner of the mattress and ran my hand along the side. Under the pillow area, my hand hit something. I put my hand around it and yanked it out. It was a black leather holster. It was empty. I stuck it back and, lifting the mattress, took a picture with my phone.

After bagging it, I finished searching the bedroom and joined the others. No one had found anything. Derrick and I went onto the lanai. We checked the cabinets in the outdoor kitchen and under all the seat cushions but struck out.

"Let's walk by the lake; we might get lucky."

"We're going to need a dive team."

"There's a storm coming tomorrow night."

I never paid much attention to the weather; it was as inaccurate as a politician. "You sure it's going to hit?"

"That's what they say."

They. Another useless pronoun. "O'Leary is going to use it as an excuse not to send a dive team in."

"It's supposed to a be quick-moving storm."

The glare was killing my eyes. I strained to see anything unusual around the lake's perimeter but persisted. My cell rang. It was the sheriff.

"Hello, sir."

"Where are you?"

"Just finishing up the Newly search."

"Get in here as fast as you can."

"What's going on?"

"We have a disaster on our hands. The Swift case just took a frigging turn."

66

Parked in front of the Swift home, I cursed the sheriff. He'd taken the case away from me, and now he wanted me to be the one to deliver bad news. Remin was backpedaling faster than a Ferrari.

Smiling at the thought his plan to use the case for political purposes had blown up in his face, I got out of the car.

Mr. Swift opened the door before I rang the bell. I regretted not telling him when I called about visiting.

"Mr. Swift. Is your wife home?"

"She is. What is this about? You found who did it?"

"No. May I come in?"

I followed him into the family room. It was dark. Mrs. Swift was reading a book with a bare-chested man on its cover. She slowly set it aside. "Hello, Detective. Do you have news for us?"

"No, ma'am. What I have to inform you about is a bit of a setback."

She closed her eyes and shook her head.

Her husband said, "Well, spit it out, then."

"The remains found on the Miller property was not your daughter."

"What? You said the dental records matched."

And you said it was her because they were found where she was last seen. "Not exactly."

Mrs. Swift leaned forward. "You told us it was Kate."

"Yes, at the time we thought it was, but the DNA you gave was compared to the DNA taken from the remains' teeth, and it's definitely not your daughter."

"Well, who the hell is it?"

"I can't reveal that yet. Her family has not been located."

"I don't get it. Are you guys incompetent?"

It served no purpose explaining that the original identification was based on the suspected age and that their daughter had perfect teeth with no unique markings. And that it took an average of two months to process DNA. "I realize how this appears. It doesn't make us look good, but the lab was understaffed and took longer than usual."

She put her hands to her head and started sobbing. "We buried somebody else's little girl."

Mr. Swift said, "This is a fucking disaster. What are we supposed to do now?"

His wife rose, pointing her finger at me. "Get out. Get out of my house!"

"I'm sorry, ma'am."

I TRUDGED INTO THE OFFICE. "How'd it go?"

"Like broccoli at a five-year-old's birthday party."

"That's funny."

"It's a mess is what it is."

"I can't believe it."

"How the hell did a kid from Orlando end up being buried in the Millers' yard?"

"They have to know her."

"I updated Weinstein, told him to check with the Millers, see if they know Monica Diskit."

"They have to."

"Were back to square one. What a frigging waste of time."

"At least we have a ton of background on the Millers."

"I hope like hell it helps. Did the file from Orlando come in?"

"Yeah, I forwarded it to you."

I collapsed into my chair and clicked open the file the Orlando detective had sent.

"She looks like the Swift kid."

"I know. Same hair, eyes, could be sisters."

Monica Diskit was the same age and had a similar build to Kate. Both girls would have easily been overpowered by a male. What was this girl doing four hours away from her home?

Her smile reminded me of Jessie. Blood began pounding in my ears. Who the hell was responsible? "We need to cross-check the state database on missing girls, fourteen to eighteen with blonde hair. We have to know if we have a serial killer on our hands."

"Already made the request."

"Good. Did you check with the DMV? Did she have a car?"

"Nothing in her name."

"We need to find out if she had family down here."

"The report didn't mention her taking a trip; she vanished, walking home."

Just like Swift had. I picked up the phone. "Forensics. This is Trane."

"Hey, it's Luca."

"Man, that was a shocker, huh?"

I wanted to scream at him for taking so long, but the bottom line was the lab was overworked and understaffed. The demand for forensic analysis had outstripped the nation's laboratories' ability to process them. Though processing time had shrunk from eight months, it took too long. "You got that right. We're starting from scratch now. I need you to upload the Swift DNA and her stats to the Doe Network."

"It was never done when she went missing?"

"No record of it. It was almost ten years ago, so I doubt it."

"We'll get it to them."

As I hung up, Derrick said, "Maybe we'll get a hit from the Doe Network."

"She's got to be dead, right?"

I wanted to say no but found myself saying, "Unfortunately. Right now, we need to either clear, or focus on, the Millers."

"Newly is coming in with her lawyer."

"Shit, I forgot. Can you handle it? I've got to take Jessie for a test."

"What's going on? You didn't say anything."

"It's nothing, or at least I hope it isn't. She's getting some genetic testing. You know, with my cancer and Mary Ann with MS, they recommended we find out if she has any mutations."

"Oh man. I mean, it's a good thing but it's nerve wracking."

"Thanks for reminding me."

"Sorry."

"It's okay. You got the Newly interview?"

"No problem. I'm looking forward to hearing what she has to say."

JESSIE and I came into the family room. Mary Ann was reading in my recliner. It was mine in name only. She said, "I was getting worried. What took so long?"

I said, "The woman who does the testing was hung up at Gulf Coast College. They said she'd be back in a couple of minutes, but it was island time."

"What did they do?"

"It was nothing, Mom. They took some blood and swabbed my cheeks."

"How soon will they know the results?"

"Around two months to run the full spectrum of tests."

"Thanks for taking her. I just didn't have the energy today."

"No problem."

"How was your day?"

Jessie headed to the fridge, and I said, "Pick up the pieces kind of day."

"I can't believe Remin made you tell the parents."

"Believe it. He's a piece of work."

"I wonder where the poor girl is."

"You and me both. At least with her DNA, we can upload it to the Doe Network."

Jessie came in holding a bottle of the fruit-flavored water she was addicted to. "What's the Doe Network?"

"A volunteer organization focused on missing persons. They have a database of unidentified remains and work with law enforcement to try and ID the people missing."

"Wow. Sounds so interesting."

Interesting? No, it was morbid but important work. "When I was up in Jersey, they helped identify a corpse on a case I had."

"That's so cool." She headed to her room. "Maybe I'll volunteer with them."

I gave Mary Ann an eye roll a sixteen-year-old would be proud of. She laughed, and I went to get a bottle of wine. It was the only thing keeping me from driving over to the Miller house.

67

LUCA

I was in earlier than Derrick, a rarity these days. As my desktop came to life, my partner strolled in with two cups of coffee.

"Morning." He set the java on my desk.

"Thanks. Give me more details on the interview."

"Like I said last night, she was cagey. I think she did it. She couldn't tell me where the gun was. Played it dumb." He raised the pitch of his voice: "'Are you sure it's not there?' kind of bullshit. Said someone must have stolen it."

"We need to find it; otherwise, we got nothing but an empty holster and a receipt."

"And she was seen there."

"I know, but still circumstantial. She could say she was meeting her lover, and that's how she got in the house, through the back."

"That's a stretch."

"Yeah, but you only need reasonable doubt. Our job is to remove that possibility."

"I really think we have enough. You want me to run it by the prosecutors?"

"No. When we turn over a case, I want to be a thousand percent certain we got the right person."

"I bet she tossed it in the lake."

"That's what I'm thinking."

"We have to wait for the divers. The storm is veering off, but they're still waiting until the day after tomorrow or the next day."

"I'd love to get back in her house."

"We'd need another warrant. Besides, if she didn't dump it before, she had to have by now."

"Not necessarily, Newly knows we're watching her. She may be afraid to toss it. We could have missed a hiding place."

"Let's wait and see what the divers come up with."

"We need to check her office space. Why don't you go to Hertz, take a look at what kind of work space she has. They probably won't let you search, but if it looks like she has some private space, I'm sure Johnson will sign off based on what we know."

"Sounds like a plan. You still didn't hear from Weinstein?"

"No. I left another message, but I'm going to swing by the store."

"You are?"

I smiled. "I need a new screwdriver."

THE PARKING LOT of Miller's Building Supply was jammed. Maneuvering around a man pushing a cart loaded with plywood, I found a space at the end of a row. This guy's business was a lot better than I thought.

I circled the store, picking up LED light bulbs and a bottle of a barbecue cleaner. Waiting to check out, I kept my eyes on the plate-glass window overlooking the store. I was hoping for a chance encounter, but after paying, I went to the customer service department and asked to see Bill Miller.

He met me at the top of the stairs. "Good to see you, Detective."

I held up my bag. "Was picking up a couple of things and figured I'd say hello."

"Thanks for shopping with us."

"Boy, this place is hopping."

He lowered his voice. "Thank God for the weathermen. They play up these storms, and it keeps us busy."

"Good for you. At least somebody is benefiting from the hysteria."

Miller smiled. "Us and the TV stations."

"Can I have a minute of your time?"

"Sure. Come in my office."

Miller's guard was down but he raised it a tad. He closed the door. "Pretty stunning turn of events."

"That's putting it mildly."

"I don't want to revel in someone's misery, but we're relieved it wasn't Katie."

"I understand. Do you know a Monica Diskit?"

He wagged his head. "No. When Weinstein called me, I told him we had no idea who she was."

"Did you ask your brothers?"

"Yes. No one knows who the poor girl is or how she ended up on my property."

"Do you have any stores or business interests in Orlando?"

"No."

"Any family or friends in the Orlando area?"

"None at all. She was from Orlando?"

"Just outside, a little town called Alafaya."

"I know it. Benny's sister lives there."

"She ever come down this way?"

"No, she's not been well for years. Been living in a nursing home since the brain aneurysm."

"Sorry to hear."

"It's sad." He shook his head. "Some people have very tough lives."

"We have to be grateful for what we have."

Driving to Grey Oaks, I considered Bill Miller. He was a successful businessman but an enigma. He'd obstructed my investigation, but his intentions were to protect his brother. With human remains being found on his property, there was no way we could exclude him as a suspect.

That said, his genuine empathy for Benny's sister showed he had a good heart. He had tremendous financial success but having lost a mother in an accident, his father to suicide, and a brother with a brain injury, if anyone had a tough life, it was him.

The guard's shoulders dropped when he saw my badge. He opened the gate, and I took my time going to Newly's house. Golf carts spotted the course. A large lake lay just beyond the tee box. It was too far from the road for Newly to toss the gun in.

A stretch of preserve before her street was a possibility. It was close enough. I made a mental note to get a couple of uniforms to do a search. I pulled up in front of Newly's house, wondering if Taras had pressured her to vacate. It'd be a huge step down to move into a rental complex; it seemed like a different kind of pride as a motivator, more like that of a jilted lover.

Stepping into the bright sunshine, I smiled. The forecast had gone from a direct-hit tropical storm to a multicell thunderstorm. Whatever that was, it was to pass during the night.

No one answered the door. It didn't appear Newly was home. I stepped around the side of the house. The lake looked different from here. I pawed at the bushes along the house, stopping where the air-conditioning compressor sat. I looked under the unit, but nothing was hidden.

Heading toward the lanai, I noticed more of the lake's banks were above water. In anticipation of the storm, they had lowered the lakes to accommodate the expected runoff. I quickened my pace.

It looked like two feet of water had been drained. I crept along the edge and moved to the right. What was that that black thing? I bent over. It was a piece of PVC piping. I stretched my back and continued until thinking I was too far away from the house.

Eyes glued to the water, I backtracked, passing my starting point. I took a half step back; it looked like a snake sticking its head up. It wasn't moving. I got closer. What was it? Squinting, it looked like the barrel of a gun.

I took my shoes and socks off and rolled up my pants leg. The water was warm. Mud squished between my toes. Crouching, I took my phone out and took several pictures. Squeezing the object with my forefinger and thumb, I lifted it.

Water dripped off the revolver. It was a thirty-eight. Was it the murder weapon?

68

LUCA

I weaved around cars like a seventeen-year-old going to the Jersey Shore on a Friday to meet my buddies. Stopped at a light on Livingston, I pulled on my socks and called Derrick.

The words just spilled out. I sounded like Derrick. "You're not going to believe it."

"What happened?"

"They lowered the lakes for the non-storm, and I saw the nub of the barrel sticking above the surface."

"Oh my God. That's amazing."

"We were due for a break. I'm going straight to the lab. I think fingerprints survive underwater for about two weeks."

"We should be golden."

"If her prints are on it and the ballistics match—"

"They will."

I wanted to remind him the remains we thought were Swift's turned out not to be. "We'll find out soon enough. I'm going to call Remin; let him know what we got; have him prioritize this. I'm not waiting long to find out."

"Good idea. I guess you don't need to know about Hertz."

"This isn't over yet."

"Newly has a cubicle she works out of. It's all the way in the back, and there's a storeroom a couple of feet away. I saw inside; it's big, holding a bunch of signs and stuff."

"Could be a place to hide a weapon."

"No doubt."

"All right. I'll see you at the office."

At the next light, shoving a foot into a shoe, my cell rang. It was the sheriff.

"Sir, was just going to call you. I have good news."

"I can use it."

Instead of saying he deserved it, I said, "What's going on?"

"Tell me what you have."

I explained finding the gun and he said, "Good work, Frank. I'll call them and get this processed immediately."

"I think we need eyes on Newly. We don't want her taking off."

"I'll arrange it."

"Thank you, sir. What did you have for me?"

"Just wanted an update. The press is all over me about the misidentification of Swift. It's unfair. They think DNA gets processed like it does on *CSI*. And the kid was missing for a decade. Now we're starting all over."

"We'll get it done, sir."

———

THE AIR SMELLED like a combination of mildew and bleach. I took the last step and headed for the ballistics room. I couldn't waste a minute finding out whether we had a looming solve in the Park Shore murder.

The tech had an earmuffs set around his neck. "Hey, Frank. How's it going?"

"Not bad. I'm hoping you're going to make it better."

"Me? I only shoot 'em. Put some protection on, and let's get this over with."

I grabbed a set of safety muffs off the wall and covered my ears.

The water in the long tank was clear. He gave me a thumbs-up and I nodded. The tech put the lake gun into a sleeve whose other side rested in the water. He squeezed off a shot. The stream reminded me of submarine torpedoes in World War II movies.

It was over in a second. We removed our earmuffs, and he scooped out the bullet with a net. It was silly but I wanted to look at it. "Let me see."

"Your eyes ain't that good, buddy."

"I know. Just like to see for myself."

Light glinted off the brass. Something that small could be deadly. It was the speed and ricocheting that did so much damage.

"I'll take it up for you."

"No can do, Frank. We have protocol."

"All right, just run it up, now. Okay?"

Taking the steps two at a time, I burst through the door to the forensic lab. I donned a gown, head bonnet, and gloves, and was buzzed in. "Trane is in the media room."

I knocked on the open door. "You again?"

"Trust me, I wish we didn't have so much going on." The reality was the lab was becoming the driving force in most cases.

"Well, you have good timing, Frank." Trane pointed to a screen. "Those are the prints we took off the firearm. I'm about to load what we captured off the coffee cup Ms. Newly used when she was being interviewed."

Derrick had used his head. I was proud of him but hated to think how I would have reacted if we had to waste time getting her prints.

"All right, here we go." The monitor's screen went into split mode. "The revolver prints are to the left."

My stomach went queasy. "They don't look close."

"Hold on. Let me overlay a couple and we'll see."

Trane moved an image over another, and the screen split into thirds. It looked like one big smudge. I exhaled heavily.

"Give me a minute, Frank. It looks like the thumbprints may be our best shot."

He moved two larger prints and adjusted them. "This swirl lines up, even though it's a partial. See this arch?"

I took a step. "Yeah, it looks like a match."

"It's a hundred percenter."

We had two points. "We need ten more."

The standard required a minimum of twelve matches to declare both sets were the same person.

"I liked the forefinger as soon as I dusted the pistol. It's a partial but the trigger pressure made it clear."

He maneuvered it into an overlay and declared, "This loop, arch and swirl match. And look at these ridges; they're perfect. She must not have long nails."

"Just a couple more and we got her."

"We'll get there."

Derrick texted me. "I have to get back upstairs. Do you need me?"

"You're leaving? How am I going to do my job without you looking over my shoulder?"

"You're lucky I like you. Let me know, and don't forget, we need the ballistics report."

"It's coming."

I bounded up the stairs, grabbed two cups of coffee, and went into my office. Derrick was staring at his monitor. "How'd it go?"

I set a java on his desk. "Trane is finishing the fingerprints. He's got about ten, so we're almost there."

"Great. What about the ballistics?"

"I'm expecting results in a few minutes."

I took a sip of coffee. It was burnt. "You got the case file from Orlando?"

"Yeah, it's depressing. Seems like a real good kid. Excellent grades, played on the soccer and tennis teams. Was a youth leader at church and even volunteered with the elderly."

"What about suspects?"

"Just getting to the interviews. But the summary mentioned a vagabond and an older kid who was interested in her, but she rebuffed him."

"What's the connection with Naples?"

"Doesn't seem to be one. Looks like it was just a good spot to get rid of a body."

"Could be. Pine Ridge Estates was a helluva lot quieter ten years ago. Big plots of land, not many houses."

My desk phone rang. I answered and fist pumped. "We got a ballistics match."

"We going to wait on the fingerprints?"

"No, we'll get them. Let's get an arrest warrant."

"I'm on it."

"Send me the file on Monica Diskit first."

69

Luca

I stared at the zip file. Alafaya didn't have its own force and was policed by Orlando. I clicked it open, and a picture of Monica Diskit appeared. The resemblance to Kate Swift made me think of the Swift parents.

How unfair it'd been on them. Your daughter disappears and you wonder what happened for nine years. You're told they found her; you hold a memorial service, and it turns out to be someone else.

Thinking they needed justice and a sense of closure, I noticed the file contained a hundred and eighty-nine pages. Should I get into this now or try to shake trees on the Swift case? We could take a double pass over the persons of interest we originally developed.

Maybe the teachers needed more scrutiny. Or take another look at Bill Miller. And his brother Greg. They'd conspired and fabricated a fake sighting. I had to paw over every interview and detail we had. And we never found out who Mr. Linen was. We needed to talk to him.

Getting distracted with the details of another case wasn't

something I wanted. They could be related, but I needed to focus on one thing at a time. An email pinged. It was from the sheriff. The argument I'd made with him over handling more than one case at a time flooded into my mind. If I said I could work more than a case at a time, I better deliver on it.

The sheriff was wasting no time in righting his image. Reading between the lines, he wanted to set up a press conference on the Newly arrest. I suspected he was asking for my report as cover. Half of me wanted Newly to run. The sheriff needed to twist in the wind a little longer, but the reality was, the Park Shore case was going to be in the hands of the prosecutors in a matter of hours.

Halfway through the report, Trane called. He had eighteen matching points. Though not the optimum twenty, it was more than good enough. I put the details into the document and emailed it to Remin.

As if calling me, the cursor landed on the task bar after sending the report to the sheriff. Up popped a little window for the Orlando file. Maximizing it, I began reading the summary.

Her parents had filed a missing person report on May 12, 2010 when she didn't come home the previous evening. It had been twelve years since Monica Diskit disappeared.

She had been walking home from volunteering at Heritage Nursing Home. There were two persons of interest Orlando police identified: Chuck Cutowski and Peter Shelly.

Cutowski had a long record, comprised of offenses like public intoxication, loitering, and living in public spaces. He didn't appear to be violent, but he was seen badgering Diskit for money.

Peter Shelly attended the same high school as Diskit and, by all accounts, was obsessed with her. Shelly had asked her out several times and was rejected. One encounter, where

Diskit told him no in front of a group of students, put Shelly on the radar. After the embarrassing episode, he'd mouthed off, telling two classmates that he was going to make her pay for showing him up.

Neither was charged, but they weren't cleared either. Interestingly, both didn't have plausible alibis. Cutowski claimed to have been drunk and slept the day away under an overpass. Shelly said he went home after school and stayed there. His parents, visiting family in New York, were unable to corroborate, and there was no one else to back his claim.

I flipped to the profile section developed on each of the suspects. Cutowski had a scruffy beard and eyes that were too close together. He was thin and had a scar on his forehead. Was it from a fight or a drunken fall?

Shelly had a round, doughy face and sandy hair. Dark, almost black eyes and a small mouth. He had rounded shoulders. If you showed him a ball, he'd ask what it was.

I popped Cutowski into the system. The drifter had been booked for three violations since Diskit went missing. One was for squatting in a home whose owners were snowbirds. But the other two were for assault, one incident involving a stabbing and the other, a beating with a piece of pipe.

This guy had a violent streak after all. Though both offenses were committed against males, Diskit could have somehow set the unstable vagabond off. He was someone we'd have to track down.

In the twelve years since Diskit vanished, Peter Shelly had also proven himself a worthy suspect. There was a fraud charge, for passing a bad check, but what caught my attention were two domestic violence charges. Both led to restraining orders. I didn't get it; two different women had appealed for help and were granted orders for Shelly to stay at least five hundred feet away. Why wasn't there a law to put people like him away?

The complaints were filed four years apart. I wondered if there were more women too scared to file charges. Or had there been and Shelly killed them?

First order of business was to locate both pieces of scum. Let's see if they could weasel their way around me. Opening up the DMV portal, Derrick burst into the office. "Newly's lawyer is here. They want to talk."

"Talk? They're hoping for a deal?"

"Guess so."

I scoffed, "This is first-degree murder. It's either life in prison without parole or the death sentence, but that's rare."

"Maybe she's looking for a possibility of parole."

"Probably. It's not our call, but I wouldn't entertain a plea bargain unless she serves twenty-five."

"Let's see what they have to say."

I got up. "I hope this isn't a long dance; we have to get back to the Diskit case. I looked into the two suspects; both have been in serious trouble since the kid went missing."

"Like what?"

I told him what I'd found, and he said, "And no one in Orlando followed up?"

"I didn't see any evidence of it."

70

LUCA

As soon as we got back in the office, I said, "I would've pushed for twenty-five."

"She'll be in her sixties by the time she sits in front of the parole board."

"And Mrs. Taras will be dead twenty-five years."

"Yeah. I didn't think of it that way."

"There's just no way to make it right. Even the death penalty doesn't even things out when you lose a loved one."

"It sucks. I can't imagine. Do you think Paul Taras knew she had it in her to kill?"

I slid behind my desk. "I think he saw signs she wasn't for him but not a murderer. Bottom line—you never really know somebody."

"Yeah, remember that case where the guy told his wife he was on one flight but came in on an earlier one?"

"Tough to forget that one. But what we have on our hands now is climbing the ranks. Let's get to work and dig into the mutts in the Diskit case. You get a handle on where Cutowski is, and I'll find out where Shelly lives."

DMV records had Shelly's address as 1111 Gulf Shore Boulevard. He was living in Naples? It was a tony address. Many of the most expensive properties in Naples lined the Gulf side of the street. Popping it into Google Earth, I zoomed in. It was a tower overlooking the Gulf of Mexico.

How had this coward got his money? Wondering if he married it, I pulled up his driver's license photo. A hint of gray and a slight jowl were the only differences. He had a smirk on. Was he laughing at me?

"Hey, Frank. Guess where Cutowski is?"

Here we go. "The penthouse at the Ritz?"

"Nope. Lake Stafford Cemetery."

Collier County buried those without means in a place near the Immokalee casino. That meant Cutowski had also moved to Naples. "He's dead?"

"Died about four years ago."

"Damn it. I hope we're not chasing a dead man."

"Talk about tough."

"I don't know. What are the odds that both Cutowski and Shelly ended up down here?"

"I'm not going to say coincidence because I know your response."

He was right; I didn't believe in them. "We can check if anybody remembers seeing his car down here. Be kind of hard to miss a green Gremlin."

"They stopped making them before I could drive."

"Don't rub it in. You're not that much younger than me."

"Wasn't—"

I threw up a hand. "Just kidding."

"I think I should start with the Millers. Is that all right?"

"Sure. The guy next door seemed to have good recall. See what he says."

"I got it. You have a beat on Shelly?"

"Looks like he's doing pretty good, living in a high-rise on Gulf Shore Drive. I'm going to see what he says."

I made a left onto Park Shore Drive and wound my way west to the water. The causeway rose over water. Venetian Village, a colorful enclave of shops and restaurants on the bay, on both sides of the street. Every time I was in the area, the ice cream shop we'd taken Jessie to scores of times, came to mind.

Making a right on Gulf Shore Boulevard, I proceeded past a couple of towers before pulling into a modern-looking structure's driveway. From what I could recall, and the fact it had water views, I couldn't see a unit being under two million. As I got out, I was hit with salt-infused air.

The circular lobby was bathed in white-and-gray marble. A curved stairway led to a mezzanine level I figured was laden with amenities. I approached the reception desk, and the young lady manning it put her phone down. As she rang Shelly, I wondered if the place had a spa. I needed to get Mary Ann a gift certificate; massages were good for her MS.

Shelly lived on the sixth floor. The elevator opened directly into his apartment. I'd seen this type of thing before, but it was still cool.

A male voice said he was coming. I stepped to the left: a magnificent view of the Gulf. I wondered if it were possible to take the sight of shimmering water for granted, but I knew it was.

It looked to be a two-bedroom apartment. High-end furniture. And what was hanging on the walls didn't come from Home Goods.

"Mr. Luca? You're from the engineering firm?"

Since the collapse of a condo building on the East Coast, no one challenged impromptu visits from building engineers.

I showed him my badge. "With the Collier County Sheriff's Office."

"The sheriff? Did someone in the building do something?"

He was genuinely surprised. Or a good actor. "No. I'd like to talk to you about Monica Diskit."

"Who?"

His face and question didn't line up. "Think again. Monica Diskit. The girl you were infatuated with who went missing a dozen years ago."

"Oh, oh. Yeah, I saw something in the paper about they found her."

"When did you move to Naples?"

"Oh, about five, maybe six years ago."

"Good move. I came down from Jersey about ten years ago."

"Wish I would've come sooner."

"You have family down here?"

"Oh yeah. Most of my family has been here for years. Orlando started changing, and one by one, they left."

"This is some place you have here."

"Thanks. I wasn't sure I'd like it in a high-rise, but it's great."

"What business you in?"

"Got lucky with a video game. I had an idea, and one of my college buddies was a programmer and it hit pretty big."

"Wow. What game?"

"*Combat Island.*"

Sounded violent. "Good for you."

"Thanks. I've been trying other ideas but no interest at this point."

"It'll come. Say, since they found Monica's remains down

here, I've got to put in a little work before kicking it back to Orlando."

"Okay."

"I'm hoping you can help me with some background."

"Sure, whatever I can do."

"You knew her from school."

"Yes, we went to University High."

"You were romantically interested in her."

"No. That's not true."

"Everyone says you were obsessed with her."

"It was a kid's thing, that's all."

"You threatened to get her when she declined to date you."

"Hey, what's all this? I had nothing to do with what happened to her. Way back, the police asked questions and looked into it, but it was all bullshit. They cleared me."

"They never cleared you."

"Look, I had nothing to do with it."

"You like to hit women, don't you?"

"Those charges were bullshit."

"Everything's bullshit to you."

"I want you to leave. I'm not saying anything without a lawyer."

71

LUCA

As soon as I stepped out of the elevator, Derrick called, "Frank, the neighbor is pretty sure he remembers seeing the Gremlin. He even said it looked like a lime. I couldn't believe it."

"He's good. He remembered seeing Amanda Pearson. Must be the experience he got serving in Iraq."

"Probably. You misread something there and you're history."

"Amen. So, what did the Millers say?"

"They weren't living there at the time. The father was."

How the hell did I miss that? Was it chemo brain? "I know. It was worth a shot they could have seen something when visiting."

"What now?"

I wish I knew. "We need to see if we can put Cutowski and Diskit together. The day she went missing. Try and track down his movements that day."

"All right. How'd it go with Shelly?"

"He denied everything, even the domestic violence charges filed against him. He asked for a lawyer."

"What do you think?"

"I don't like him one bit, but I need more. I'm going to dig in."

Getting in my car, I hoped it was Shelly. He was a danger to women.

———

IT WAS good to see Mary Ann standing by the stove. I pecked her cheek, "Feeling good?"

"Pretty good. I couldn't keep laying around all day."

"What are you making?"

"Collard greens."

Not exactly appetizing. "Does it go with pasta?"

She frowned. "I took turkey burgers out of the freezer."

I wondered if I could slip out to McDonald's. "Where's Jessie?"

"On the way home."

I held up a little cannister. "I want Jessie to keep this with her. All the time."

"Pepper spray?"

"Yeah. She needs to be able to fend off a jerk, if she has to."

"What happened today?"

Were there captions running across my forehead? "Nothing."

"Frank?"

"There are cowards out there getting their rocks off pushing women around. Anybody gets physical with her, she gives them a zap of this."

She raised her eyebrows.

"Come on, Mary Ann; you know what I'm talking about."

"I'm not disagreeing with you. I don't want you to scare her."

"She's going to college soon. A campus is not as safe as people think it is."

"Jessica knows how to take care of herself."

"It's not her I'm worried about."

"If it makes you happy."

"Me? I'm trying to protect our daughter."

"I know that, but every time you get a case with a twist, you make it personal."

"I can't help it. Jessie is everything."

She wrapped her arms around me and kissed me. "She knows that. We'll both talk to her tonight, okay?"

"Thanks."

"Sure. Now, put the grill on. I'm hungry."

I put a pod in the dishwasher and closed the door. Jessie and Mary Ann were taking showers, and I retreated to the lanai with my laptop.

The sky was bright orange. A tropical breeze rustled the palm trees. I opened the file Orlando had sent to us, went straight to what they had on Shelly, and began reading.

They'd conducted two interviews with Shelly. Why hadn't they interrogated him more times? Recalling that the domestic violence charges came well after Diskit disappeared, I dialed down my anger.

The investigator, a Detective Daly, cautiously questioned Shelly about his relationship with the victim. He never asked him if he was obsessed with Diskit despite what people had said.

He may have been gentle because Shelly was a minor and

his mother and an attorney were present. When I finished reading the transcript of the initial interview, the only thing Daly obtained was Shelly lived in the same subdivision as Diskit.

The second exchange was conducted a week later. Daly covered the main points of the first exchange, always a good idea, to see if the story changed. Shelly maintained he hadn't seen Diskit that day.

Daly was ready, mentioning two students who said Shelly and Diskit were talking in the parking lot when school let out. Shelly denied it, claiming they must have had their dates mixed up. Daly pressed, but the lawyer stated his client had denied it and asked to move on.

The detective circled back to the relationship. He asked Shelly if he'd been disappointed that Diskit wouldn't date him. Shelly said it didn't bother him. Then Daly asked about the threat he'd made to get revenge on her for embarrassing him.

Though only seventeen, Shelly was arrogant, claiming he never said such a thing and said anyone who said he did was lying. Daly countered with a signed statement from a witness. Shelly demanded to know who said it and continued to say it was false.

The interview devolved, and it ended shortly afterward. I sat back and thought it over. Everything they had was circumstantial. Contradictory and incriminating but still circumstantial.

Shelly was someone who needed to be squeezed. Why hadn't they continued to apply pressure? The kid was lying. Why let him off the hook?

As I stared at the screen, Jessie began blow-drying her hair. How did a kid just disappear? I scrolled down to the interviews with her parents. I'd avoided reading to spare myself the misery.

I began reading the notes taken by an Officer Johns who went to the house after the parents reported her missing. The mother recounted the morning before Monica left for school. When I read where she volunteered, I felt a tingle at the base of my skull.

72

LUCA

I read it again. Monica Diskit had been volunteering at the Alafaya Nursing Rehabilitation Center. Paging through the interviews, I found two conducted with employees of the nursing home.

Glenn Fitch was the administrator. He stated that Monica was one of four girls who came in twice a week. Monica worked alongside Carol Freeland, the director of activities. Fitch said Monica was well liked by staff and residents. He mentioned seeing her when she arrived at the facility and offered the CCTV footage.

I scrolled to the evidence log. The DVD had been logged in with tag number A73. In the notes section, Detective Daly stated Diskit was seen on camera leaving the facility at 6:04 p.m. She left through the main entrance, walking off-screen in the parking lot.

I had to see the film. I read the interview with the woman in charge of activities. Freeman said Monica was a favorite with the residents and got along with the staff. She didn't have any idea what happened to her and offered no clues to possible suspects. Daly pressed her if anyone working there had expressed an interest in her or had a conflict with her.

It was a mistake that no other employee of the nursing home was interviewed. It was the last place she had an interaction with anyone.

I began to think of the possibilities. It seemed probable that Diskit had been swept off the street, either willingly or forced into a vehicle. Where she might have been brought was unknown, as well as whether she had been killed in the Orlando area and driven to Naples, or met her maker in Collier County.

We knew she was volunteering until 6:00 p.m. I wondered what was around the facility and pulled up Google Earth. I was sure it looked different a dozen years ago, but there was a church, St. Joseph's Catholic Church, across the street. Based on the look, it was built before Diskit had been born.

A question popped into my head, and I did a search. St. Joseph's had a soup kitchen. Did Cutowski frequent it? I also wondered whether we could connect Shelly to the area. Did he have friends there? Or any reason to be in the area?

I scanned the Cutowski and Shelly interviews. Not one question concerning the location of the nursing home. It felt like a huge miss. I picked up the phone.

―――――

THE TRAFFIC on I-75 was light approaching Tampa. The speedometer read ninety. I was pushing it. Wasting time was one of life's biggest irritants. I'd get my fill when I hit Route 4 to Orlando.

I slowed to eighty and called Mary Ann. "How you feeling?"

"Good. Where are you?"

"About to get on Four."

"I don't know why you couldn't put a request in to have it sent to you."

"It would take a week, minimum."

"The case is twelve years old."

"You know I don't like to criticize a fellow officer, but based on what's in the case file, they didn't drop the ball, they threw it away."

"You said the detective who handled it passed away?"

"Yeah, heart attack five years ago."

"He wasn't homicide, was he?"

"No. It was a missing person case that went cold."

"That explains it."

"Not to the parents."

"They still around?"

"Yeah. I was thinking of talking to them. They might know more about Shelly, but let's see what the footage shows."

"You should stay overnight. That's too much driving for you."

"I'm okay; it's not that bad."

"You're not a kid, Frank."

I didn't need the reminder. My ass was killing me already, and no matter how I adjusted the seat, my back was beginning to bark. "Hey, you said you liked mature men."

She chuckled. "There's only one for me. I just want to make sure you don't come home so tired, you can't, you know..."

"I don't know. Tell me."

"Bye, Frank. Keep your eyes on the road, and call me when you get there."

The building housing the Orlando Police Department was all glass. It was modern, with shutters extended off the roofline. The area was as busy as it gets. The Citrus Bowl complex was just south and the Explora Soccer Stadium two blocks north.

Waiting for Detective Ryder, I couldn't envision working in a metro area with three million people. After five minutes, I heard, "Detective Luca."

I looked up, a woman in a blue pantsuit was beckoning. How did she know it was me?

"Detective Ryder?"

She held out her hand. "Call me Mary."

"Nice to meet you. How did you know it was me?"

We walked down a long hallway. "I have friend, she works in your courthouse, Penny Velasquez. She said you looked like George Clooney, but I'm not sure about that."

I hadn't heard the Clooney reference in a while. Was it another sign of aging? "I don't know her."

"She's a stenographer. Anyway, I'm pressed for time. We're in here."

The building was new, but the equipment lining the small room was from the Woodstock days. She gave me documents to sign and handed me an envelope. She turned on a monitor and pointed below it. "That's the DVD player."

"Okay, I got it."

"Knock yourself out. You need anything, my extension is four-one-nine."

"Thanks." I slipped the DVD out and inserted it. It was amazing how quickly we'd moved from actual film to DVDs, and now everything was digital. I fast-forwarded to 5:45 p.m.

The video was clear but herky-jerky. The driveway was wet. Raindrops were splashing into a puddle. It was raining. Why hadn't the record reflected that?

At ten minutes before six, an older couple came into view. The man held the door and followed his companion in. They looked to be visitors. It was quiet for six minutes until a large woman left the building. I watched her walk off-screen as a man, with a cane, ambled out. A car swung up and he got in. They drove off, and there was someone walking out.

It was unmistakable. There she was. Monica Diskit. She had a bounce to her step and was smiling. She pulled her white jacket over her head and walked off-screen.

Bemoaning how quickly life had changed for her, I saw a man exit the building. I froze as he slipped to the right and disappeared. Rewinding it, I zoomed in. It had to be him.

73

LUCA

As soon as I got on the highway, I hit my strobe lights and stepped on the gas. Was there a way it could be a coincidence? Benny Alston's mother was a resident in the nursing home that Diskit volunteered in. That was possible.

But being there the day Diskit disappeared and leaving the facility within minutes of Diskit leaving? The odds were deep into the apparition zone. Had I missed something?

As the miles ticked down, my stomach twisted. What I had was circumstantial and a dozen years old. The Orlando police had only spoken to two employees of the nursing home. There was no record they interviewed visitors or residents.

If it were Alston, he'd not only gotten away with it, but he also avoided suspicion. My phone rang. It was Derrick.

"Sorry, Frank, just got out of court. Where are you?"

"About an hour away. Look, Benny Alston left the nursing home right after Diskit did."

"Alston? The Millers' friend?"

"I know it's weird, but his mother lives there."

"And he lives near where her body was found."

I shifted to take the pressure off my hip. "Bingo. It can't be a coincidence."

"You think he's got something to do with Swift as well?"

"Could be. Who knows, he could have dumped the poor kid up in Orlando somewhere."

"I don't get why he tried to incriminate Mark Miller if he knew it wasn't Swift."

"At the time, we thought it was Swift. The bastard was probably laughing at us."

"We don't have much. Should we bring him in?"

"I don't know. These cases are old. Any evidence is deteriorating by the hour. We haul him in, he'll make sure to get rid of anything that might tie to either girl."

"Alston doesn't seem like a serial killer."

"We don't know enough about this guy. But it doesn't matter; you never really know someone."

"A hundred percent. You want me to dig deeper into his background?"

"Absolutely. You never know what we might find."

"I'm on it."

***

"Where are you going?"

"To the office, I can't sleep."

"It's five thirty."

"I know. I've got to find a way to get a warrant on Alston. We don't have enough."

"Don't wake up Jessica."

"Go back to bed. I'll call you later."

After dressing, I tiptoed to the garage, bypassing a needed coffee. I crawled into the car, put my shoes on, and headed into the dark. Sometimes I was able to sort out an issue by driving or walking the beach. My hope was misplaced but lying in bed wasn't cutting it.

The drive-through lane at Dunkin' was empty. I rejected the first cup; the zombie manning the window put too much milk in it. The coffee hit the spot, and I eased onto Route 41. I slowed for a red light at Pine Ridge and pulled into the turning lanes.

Driving along East Road into Pine Ridge Estates, I reminded myself to avoid stopping. It would draw attention, and if Alston was walking a dog or putzing around, I didn't want him noticing me.

Slowing as I approached the Miller property, I thought of Mark. My heart tugged. He had almost been tagged with a murder. A picture of him solving the Rubik's Cube put a smile on my face. Thinking it would be cool to learn how to do it, it hit me. "Holy shit!"

What Mark said about Benny being at the Miller property the day Swift went missing could be the link to a warrant. I made a U-turn and drove straight to the office.

"MORNING."

Derrick handed me a cup of java. I took a sip without lifting the lid. "I needed this. I've been here since six."

"Whoa."

"Just walked the warrant request upstairs."

"You said we didn't have enough."

"We have Alston on tape, minutes after Diskit is last seen. Her body ends up a short walk from his house and on the property of a lifelong friend. Alston is the common denominator for Diskit and Swift."

"And he lied about seeing Swift the morning she vanished."

"Yes, but the key is, I remembered Mark Miller saying Benny was there the afternoon when Swift went missing."

"Yeah, but he's, uh, you know, got the brain injury."

"He's an eyewitness." I lowered my voice: "And I may have confused the Miller brothers' names in the warrant." I smiled. "A little bit of embellishing never hurt anybody. If we're wrong, we're wrong."

"But if it's him, we stop him from preying on another kid."

"Exactly."

"The key is trying to find something that links him to either girl."

"Serial types like to keep mementos."

My stomach dropped. "They're sick bastards. I hate to say it, but we have to hope he filmed them or kept a lock of hair or something to tie him to them."

I picked up my ringing desk phone. It was the sheriff. He wanted to see me.

After waving me to a chair, Remin ran a hand through his hair. "Judge Richardson is going to sign off on the warrant."

"Good to hear, sir."

"I want this kept as quiet as possible. If Alston's clean, we'll look incompetent or worse."

"If the press wants justification, I'd be happy to explain why he was of interest."

"The team has to be kept to a minimum. How small can it be to be effective?"

"The home is three thousand square feet under air. A two-car garage and a shed. With two forensic techs, Derrick and I can handle it."

Remin inhaled deeply. "Okay. Take a uniform to guard the entrance."

"Thank you, sir."

"I hope you're right about this."

"He deserves the scrutiny."

"We'll see."

Walking down the stairs, I mulled over his last comment, and my confidence dropped.

74

Luca

Alston's home wasn't directly on the lake. It was one house away. Heavy landscaping and a small preserve area shielded the home from others. It was a short walk to the Millers' home.

Set back from the street, the beige house was shaped like an upside-down U. A two-car garage was built off the right side, matching the left, which I suspected was the master suite.

I eyed the shed, pointing to it. In the far corner of the lot, it was shaded by a pair of oak trees. That was a likely hiding spot. Derrick said, "You want to start there?"

"I don't know. All the courses I ever took said these wackos like to keep their mementos close."

He shook his head. "Using them to relive what they did."

"Okay, everyone, let's put booties and gloves on."

I turned to the techs. "All right. Let's gain entry."

They picked the double lock within two minutes.

I said, "Take your time. You see anything female, or kid related, let me know. You come across a box or tin with buttons, hair, or clothing, anything, I want to know about it. And remember, any evidence is bound to be old, so be careful and keep your eyes open."

I stepped inside. The house was neat for a bachelor. "Derrick, search the kitchen. One of you check the shed and the other go through the family room."

The master bedroom was in the wing, I'd surmised. Alston made the bed with less wrinkles than Mary Ann did. A large TV was hung opposite the bed, over a low table. I pulled open the drawers and fished around. Underwear and socks. I pulled both drawers out, flipping them over. Nothing attached to the bottoms. Before putting them back, I took a peek inside the cavity. Zippo.

Two sets of bifold doors covered the closets. Dress clothes were to the right and his casual wear to the left. I paged through, squeezing pockets as I did. My eyes settled on four shoeboxes sitting above the hanging garments.

Taking one down, it felt heavier than shoes should be. I opened the lid; it was filled with rubber-banded batches of baseball cards. The next one had a pair of expensive navy suede shoes, and the third, the same pair of shoes but in dark brown.

The last box was light. I took the top off. It was filled with newspaper clippings. I flipped through them. Every one involved the Miller family. There were several on the accident and suicide. The balance was about store openings. A strange sadness rolled over me.

I shook off the weird feeling and checked under the bed and mattress. I pulled open the nightstand drawer. A Glock 17 dominated the drawer. I bagged the pistol. The drawer had a jar of Vicks, a dental retainer, and a ring of keys. I picked up a bottle of prescription medicine. The little blue pills were Viagra.

There was a panel providing access to the attic in the hallway leading to the master bath. Someone else would have to climb into the heat.

Checking under the bathroom vanity, all I found were cleaning supplies. The shower doors were streak-less. I looked inside; a squeegee leaned against a bottle of Dove shampoo.

The linen closet was neat; the only item of note were three bottles of Just for Men. My gray had crowded out the black. Would using it make it too obvious?

I surveyed the room before leaving. "We find anything?"

Derrick said, "No, but this guy's a neat freak."

I held up the Glock. "Bagged this, just in case."

The tech who'd been checking the shed came in. "Nothing but a lawn mower and gardening supplies out there."

"Do me a favor and check the lanai and outdoor kitchen."

He pulled open a slider and went out. "Derrick, comb over the other bedroom and have him check the attic spaces."

I circled the house looking for hiding spaces. Sometimes people put their secrets right under your nose. I spied a tall, blue vase sitting to the left of the TV. An assortment of sticks was protruding out of it.

Grabbing a handful, I lifted them out of the vessel. The bottom was filled with glass pebbles. I tipped the vase over. Nothing was hidden under them.

I scanned the kitchen, pulling open the stove and freezer. Nothing. My neck muscles tightened. Was this going to be embarrassing? Opening a door leading to the garage, I was hit with heat.

The floor was one of those speckled, epoxy ones. They looked nice, but I couldn't spend that kind of money on a garage floor. Tools lined two walls, and a table saw sat in one of the garage bays. Alston probably painted the floor himself.

I headed straight for two short stacks of metal boxes lined up on a workbench. My heartbeat ramped up as I reached for the top one. I lifted the lid. It was filled with electrical fittings.

I opened the next. Nothing but large bolts. The bottom one was filled with screws. Going through the last one, I slammed in on the table. It was loaded with Velcro strips.

Surveying the space, something felt off. I studied the area but couldn't put my finger on it. I wiped a stream of sweat off my temple and headed back inside. Hand on the knob, I froze. The water heater was on the right, on the same wall as the door.

But to the left, there was a return wall. The garage was about six feet narrower. I checked the ceiling and floor lines. They looked normal. The water heater was in a good niche, next to the garage door, in case of a leak. I stepped into the house and went in the room abutting the garage.

75

LUCA

Alston used the room as an office. There was a bifold door on the wall separating the garage. I pulled it open. What was a full-length mirror doing in a closet?

I leaned it away from the wall and froze. Behind the mirror was a door. My field of vision shrank. There was a deadbolt. And a brace with a padlock. Plus, a heavy-duty floor lock. I took off.

I fished the keys out of the nightstand in the master bedroom and ran out. "Derrick! Get everyone to the bedroom by the garage! Now!"

Running down the hallway, Derrick called after me, "Frank! What's going on?"

In front of the fake closet, I spread the keys in my hand, trying to match one to deadbolt. The second key worked. "Got it."

Looking for one to open the padlock, Derrick was on his knees messing with the floor lock. "There's a pin. I got it."

I slid a key into the padlock. Click. I removed it and swung the latch away. Backs to the wall, I finger counted to three. Turning the knob, I pushed the door in. We waited two beats.

I stuck my head past the doorframe. It took a second for my eyes to adjust to the darkness. My jaw dropped. "Oh my God."

Sitting on a mattress, legs pulled to her chin, a blonde-haired woman was chewing a thumbnail. Windowless, the only light in the carpeted room came from a small lamp. My tongue thickened when my eyes hit on a toilet in the far corner.

Partially shielding it was a rack with clothes and a laundry basket. At the foot of the bed, an old TV, with a tube. It sat on a DVD player.

I took a step in. Her eyes widening, she pressed herself into a corner.

I fumbled for my badge. "I'm a police officer. We're here to help."

Derrick and the others piled in. She shielded her face with her hands and moaned. I said, "Back up, back up, and call an ambulance."

As they retreated, I said, "Is there anyone else here?"

She shook her head.

My voice cracked, "My name's Frank. What's yours?"

She peekabooed through her hands but said nothing. I guessed her age to be around twenty.

"It's okay. I have a daughter. Her name's Jessie. She's a couple of years younger than you."

I took a small step forward and she whispered, "No, please, no."

Stepping back, I said, "It's okay. I'm here to help you."

A tear rolled down her cheek. My voice faltered, "There's nothing to be afraid of."

She wiped her face with the back of her hand.

"You hungry? Thirsty?"

She shook her head.

"We're going to get you out of here."

"No, don't, please."

"It's okay. Tell me your name."

"I can't."

"You can tell me. I'm a police officer; nobody is going to hurt you anymore."

"No. Please. No."

"It's okay. You don't have to say anything. Help is coming."

I stuck my head out. "Derrick, get some uniformed officers here as soon as possible and make sure one's a woman."

"Okay."

"Ask them to get any patrolman in the area over here."

"I'm on it."

"And get forensics down here. I want this entire room processed."

She was as scared as anyone I'd ever seen. It was weird being the source of someone's fear. Someone who wasn't a criminal. I stood in the doorframe wondering who she was.

I tried to envision what Kate Swift would look like after ten years. After a decade in captivity. I swallowed a mouthful of bile.

Who this poor girl was was crowded out by my anger. I wanted to empty my revolver into the bastard. "Derrick!"

"What?"

"We've got to get Alston."

"Let's roll."

"I don't want to leave her; she's scared out of her mind."

"I'll grab the bastard."

I hesitated. "No. I need to do it."

"He's going to get tipped off and run."

He was right. A neighbor wondering what was going on would call him if they hadn't already.

I heard a woman's voice. Looking over Derrick's shoulder, I saw Mary Rourke, a relatively new hire. I approached her. "We got a young lady who's been held against her will. The kid is scared, scared of me, maybe because I'm a man."

"I understand. I'll do what I can to reassure her."

A distant siren drew closer. "Give her space. She might have been held for around ten years."

"Oh my God."

"You up to this?"

"Yes, sir."

Derrick and I stepped outside as an ambulance and marked car pulled up. I briefed them quickly and we got into my car. Derrick switched on the strobes, and I jammed the pedal to the floor.

Shoppers scattered as I screeched to a stop in front of Miller's Building Supply. Shutting off the car, Derrick said, "There he is!"

Benny Alston was running out the entrance. He made a left. I jumped out of the car and took off after him. Alston cut diagonally across the parking lot, and I followed. I heard tires squeal. Derrick had never regained his ability to run after he'd been shot. He was making a U-turn to cut off Alston.

This guy was older than me. I'd get him. "Police! Stop! Put your hands up!"

I was closing in on him. Alston cut through parked cars, and I fell back a step. A car door opened in his path. Alston slowed. I leapt at him. My hand grabbed the back of his shirt.

I hit the pavement. Alston toppled on top of me. I slammed an elbow into his temple. Alston moaned, and I pushed his face into the asphalt. Knees on his back, I pulled his arm back and slapped a cuff on. Grabbing his other hand,

I snapped his forefinger. Alston screamed as I cuffed his wrists together.

Derrick pulled me off Alston and lifted him to his feet. I got in his face: "You bastard! Who is she?"

Alston dropped his head but said nothing.

I jammed my forearm under his neck. "Tell me who the girl is."

Derrick got in between us. "Take it easy, Frank. This piece of shit is going away for a long time."

I smashed the heel of my shoe into Alston's instep. "You sick bastard." As he yelped, I stepped back. A crowd had formed. I wanted to tell them what Alston had done and get immediate justice but said, "Stand back, please."

A patrol car pulled up, and we stuffed Alston into the back seat. We headed back to our car. Derrick pointed to my torn pants. "Your knee feel okay?"

It hurt, but not as bad as my heart.

76

LUCA

The media room was standing room only. I followed Sheriff Remin in. The department's spokesperson pleaded with the reporters to settle down and the room quieted. Remin approached the podium, and I scanned the attendees. Mainstream media was out in full force, occupying the first two rows normally filled with locals.

"Thank you for coming today. It's a bittersweet day for all of us, including the hardworking people of the Collier County Sheriff's Office. After nine long years, Kate Swift is where she belongs, at home with her family."

The room burst into applause. Remin bathed in it a little too long before raising his hand. "This department never gives up, and in particular, I'd like to acknowledge Detective Frank Luca, who tirelessly led the effort to rescue Kate Swift."

The entire room stood and clapped. I nodded, mouthing a thank-you. Sheriff Remin continued, "Benny Alston, the man who held Ms. Swift captive, has admitted to killing Orlando resident, Monica Diskit, burying her in Pine Ridge Estates."

Remin conveniently left out arresting Mark Miller for it.

"We believe Mr. Alston is responsible for at least one other homicide and will make a further statement after we confirm all details. I'll take a question or two."

Hands flew up. Remin pointed to a reporter from *WINK News*.

"Thank you, Sheriff Remin. You stated that Mr. Alston committed at least one other murder. It sounds like he's killed many more women."

"I can't say more at this time; however, we're working with the Orlando police and law enforcement agencies across the state to determine the extent of Mr. Alston's criminal activity."

"But you expect there to be more?"

"I can't answer with any certainty. But profilers believe the likelihood he kidnapped or killed another girl after abducting Ms. Swift is low. If he was involved in another disappearance, it's likely before snatching Kate Swift." Remin pointed to a *Naples Daily News* Reporter.

"Mr. Alston held Ms. Swift captive for nine years. How was he able to avoid getting caught?"

"He was extremely careful."

"How specifically did he evade capture?"

"I don't want to release any details that would tip off anyone with similar ideas."

The word careful was an understatement. The space where Alston kept Swift was actually a room within a room. It was the same soundproofing techniques music studios used. Alston never let Swift venture out of the room, even installing a composting toilet for her to use.

Alston had thought of everything, even buying a Shower Toga, a product I'd seen pitched on *Shark Tank*. Alston wasn't a loner but kept a low profile. I wondered if being a friend of the Millers had given him legitimacy.

A reporter from ABC was chosen next. "I believe people would like to hear from Detective Luca. May I ask him a question?"

Remin's face slackened, but he waved me over. "Sure."

Reluctantly, I stepped up to the podium. The reporter said, "Thank you for taking Benny Alston off the streets."

Over the applause, I said, "It's my job, ma'am."

"How did you feel when you first saw Kate Swift? What was going through your mind when you found her?"

"As you can imagine, a mix of emotions. I was happy to find her alive, though I wasn't sure who she was when I entered the room. But I was also disgusted and angry that anyone could do something like this."

"Before, you said it was your job, but it sounds like you took this personally."

"We should all take incidents like this personally. It's our collective duty to protect children and the young from predators."

"Do you think Mr. Alston should get the death penalty?"

"I have faith in our justice system. Benny Alston will get what he has coming to him. Who I worry about is Kate Swift. She's gone through the wringer. I hope you and the rest of the press will give her the time and space she needs to recover."

Remin sidled up. "Thank you for coming."

The reporters jumped to their feet, shouting questions as we left the room. "Thanks for attending, Frank."

"No problem, sir. But next time, it'd be good to have Detective Dickson there."

"We can't let these things get unwieldy."

"We're a two-man department."

I expected a rebuttal that we didn't work in a vacuum, but Remin said, "Remind me the next time around."

"Thank you, sir."

"Take the rest of the day off; you deserve it."

He was right about needing the time off. Uncomfortable with the deserving part of it, I was as tired as I'd ever been. Maybe it was the stress or Father Time, but I was run down.

I'd need more than a couple of hours, but I looked forward to napping on the lanai. On the way to the parking lot, I made a quick call to Mary Ann to tell her I was on my way home.

Driving home, I decided to clear the air on something that had been bothering me and made a detour.

77

LUCA

Mary Ann met me in the garage hallway. "You had me worried. You said you were on your way home."

"I made a stop to see Bill Miller."

"Why?"

"I just had to be sure he wasn't involved somehow."

"You thought Bill Miller was in on the kidnapping?"

"No, but there was a chance he may have been covering for his friend."

"I can't see that. What did he say?"

"That he had no idea and was as shocked as anyone. I could tell he was telling the truth; he was really unsettled by the entire thing."

"They were friends forever."

"You know what I say: You never really know somebody."

"Are you keeping secrets from your wife?"

"Guilty. I had a Big Mac yesterday."

"Oh my God. You scoundrel."

"And I hate collard greens."

"I'm calling my lawyer."

I wrapped my arms around her. "What time does Jessie get home?"

"Not for a couple of hours."

I ground my hips into her.

"You said you wanted to take a nap."

I led her to the bedroom. "I'll sleep much better afterward."

"DAD! It's for you. The guy said he's from *WINK News*."

She handed me the phone. "This is Frank Luca."

"Detective Luca, my name is Sandra Tomaso. I'm WINK's programming director. I'd love to do a segment with you on the Swift case."

"I don't do much media, ma'am."

"I understand, but this is a powerful story that has high interest in the community. Kate's story had unsettled everyone in Southwest Florida. We have an obligation to cover it."

"She needs time to recover, not be on TV."

"We respect her need for privacy and wouldn't expect her to make an appearance. The family may make a statement, but we believe having you on would reassure the community."

"You should contact the PR people in the department. They'll send someone."

"This case is too personal. The public doesn't want a spokesperson; they want to hear from you."

"I don't know; it's depressing what happened to her."

"It's sad and cautionary, but there's hope as well. Look at how it ended."

Hope? You couldn't do my job with a truckload of hope. You needed training, determination, and instincts. "Does WINK do community grants?"

"Excuse me?"

"I'll do it, if you can raise funds to pay for teaching the children of Southwest Florida about predators and providing self-defense training."

"I'm uncertain what Fort Myers Broadcasting does in the donor area, but this is an idea we can get behind. If there's an issue, I have a number of contacts that would step up for an effort like this."

The next book in this series is, The Preserve Killer. Find it in eBook & Paperback.

I hope you enjoyed reading this book as much as I enjoyed writing it. If you did, I'd appreciate it if you would write a quick review on Amazon or your favorite book site. Reviews are an author's best friend and even a quick line or two is helpful. Thanks, Dan

OTHER BOOKS BY DAN

THE LUCA MYSTERY SERIES

Am I the Killer

Vanished

The Serenity Murder

Third Chances

A Cold, Hard Case

Cop or Killer?

Silencing Salter

A Killer Missteps

Uncertain Stakes

The Grandpa Killer

Dangerous Revenge

Where Are They

Buried at the Lake

The Preserve Killer

No One is Safe

SUSPENSEFUL SECRETS

Cory's Dilemma

Cory's Flight

Cory's Shift

OTHER WORKS BY DAN PETROSINI

The Final Enemy

Complicit Witness

Push Back

Ambition Cliff

You can keep abreast of my writing and have access to books that are free of discounting by joining my newsletter. It normally is out once a month and also contains notes on self- esteem, motivational pieces and wine articles.

It's free. See bottom of my website: www.danpetrosini.com

ABOUT THE AUTHOR

Dan is a USA Today and Amazon best-selling author who wrote his first story at the age of ten and enjoys telling a story or joke.

Dan gets his story ideas by exploring the question; What if?

In almost every situation he finds himself in, Dan explores what if this or that happened? What if this person died or did something unusual or illegal?

Dan's non-stop mind spin provides him with plenty of material to weave into interesting stories.

A fan of books and films that have twists and are difficult to predict, Dan crafts his stories to prevent readers from guessing correctly. He writes every day, forcing the words out when necessary and has written over twenty-five novels to date.

It's not a matter of wanting to write, Dan simply has to.

Dan passionately believes people can realize their dreams if they focus and act, and he encourages just that.

His favorite saying is – "The price of discipline is always less than the cost of regret"

Dan reminds people to get the negativity out of their lives. He believes it is contagious and advises people to steer clear of negative people. He knows having a true, positive mind set makes it feel like life is rigged in your favor. When he gets off base, he tells himself, 'You can't have a good day with a bad attitude.'

Married with two daughters and a needy Maltese, Dan lives in Southwest Florida. A New York native, Dan has taught at local colleges, writes novels, and plays tenor saxophone in several jazz bands. He also drinks way too much wine and never, ever takes himself too seriously.

He puts out a twice-a-month newsletter featuring articles, his writing and special deals and steals.

Sign up at www.danpetrosini.com

Made in United States
North Haven, CT
17 March 2023

34210183R00232